Lafayette Place

LAFAYETTE PLACE

JEFFERSON FLANDERS

Cover design by Mick Wieland Design

ISBN-13: 978-1-7354805-2-7
eBook ISBN: 978-1-7354805-4-1

Munroe Hill Press
Lexington, Massachusetts

DEDICATION

For the next generation: James, Avery, Penelope, and Evelyn

AUTHOR'S NOTE

This novel tells the story of a family as it faces the complications and glories of life before and after the turn of the century. It's a distinctly American family, one perhaps like yours or mine, or perhaps not.

In fashioning *Lafayette Place*, I relied on equal parts of experience, observation, and invention.

The characters, places, and events in the pages that follow are a product of my imagination, a free-wheeling flight of my fancy. Nonetheless, I believe that a fair measure of authenticity, and some lasting home truths, can be found in my tale—but, in the end, readers will decide for themselves if that is so.

Jefferson

April 2022

PART ONE

ONE

JAMES

Princeton, April 2008

My father's house stood before us, dark and deserted.

As we walked up the front steps, the wind came sweeping up Lafayette Place, stirring the leaves in the nearby trees and ruffling Julia's hair.

When I first tried the key in the front door lock, it didn't turn, frozen in place for a moment. I cursed a few times, causing Julia to giggle, and then gripped the key tightly, and turned it with more force. The bolt opened with a clicking sound, and the heavy door creaked and groaned as I pushed it in with my shoulder, letting us into the house.

"It's an old door, an ancient lock," I said. "And you know, we always went in the back door and through the mudroom."

"Let's have a locksmith come and fix it before Veronica starts showing the place," she said.

I nodded, and Julia wrote a note down on the clipboard she had brought with her. She had organized our walk-through my father's house. We were to make a list of personal items—family photographs, jewelry, antiques, furniture—that Beau or Hanna or I might want to claim. We would have to ship whatever they wanted to California. It would have been easier if we had divvied things up when they were in Princeton for the funeral, but they were in a hurry to get back to the West Coast, and it would have been ghoulish to inventory the house so soon after my father's death.

We stood in the foyer for a moment before I switched on the lights. It was an overcast day with little sun, and the interior of the house was dark and quiet. Next to me, Julia sighed. It had been two weeks since my father's funeral service at Trinity Episcopal Church.

"Once we've removed the family stuff, Veronica wants to have an interior decorator look over the house," Julia said. "She'll decide what needs to be done to stage it properly for the showings."

"Is that necessary?"

"We want it to sell for the highest price, don't we?" Julia had always been the practical one in our marriage.

"We do."

"Then let's get to work," she said. "We should start in the living room."

There are only five houses on Lafayette Place. It's a quiet haven of sorts, a tree-lined side street hard to find if you don't know the town well, yet within easy walking distance of Nassau Street and the University. For more than three decades, my family occupied a brick colonial mansion at 4 Lafayette Place, an imposing structure built in 1921 by a wealthy railroad executive and purchased by my father, Alexander Tarkington Kincaid, after his book *Status* landed on the bestseller lists and remained there for a year.

My father once told me that everything about the house appealed to him: its handsome brick exterior, wrought iron fence, and circular driveway, the private tennis court, the manicured acre with its flower gardens, the stone walls marking the property boundaries. The interior of the house was no less impressive: high ceilings, a spacious dining room, numerous bedrooms for his large family, a wood-paneled library with a fireplace where he could write, and a large kitchen with updated appliances.

Lafayette Place had been named in honor of the Revolutionary War hero, Marquis de Lafayette, who had stopped by the Princeton battlefield during his farewell tour of 1824. There was considerable old money in the neighborhood; most of the homes were owned by families that had been in Princeton for generations. We were newcomers; my father, even though a tenured professor, only had the financial means to afford the house because of his literary success.

My father felt he deserved his good fortune. If anyone was going to occupy 4 Lafayette Place, why not him? He was an unapologetic elitist, albeit a believer in the meritocratic elite. It was quite natural, in his view, that some would rise to the top and, as a neo-Darwinist, how could he believe otherwise? He enjoyed the convergence of thought and deed embodied in his house purchase—he had acquired his mansion because of the royalties from a book suggesting that evolutionary forces drove the human quest for status.

"I know I made myself a target by acquiring this house," he conceded once to me. "It has provoked envy. My fellow members of the Academy ask 'Who does he think he is?' They're aware of the price of real estate in this neighborhood, the considerable cost of a Lafayette Place house. But there's more to it. My ideas threaten them. They hated my book, first because it was popular, and secondly because it presented a thesis that challenged their fashionably leftist beliefs."

"Comparing the politics of the faculty lounge to the social interactions of mountain gorillas in the Congo might have something to do with it," I replied.

He gave me a grin. "That was a provocation, I'll admit, but it was done with humor, was it not?"

"Which is why it stung your colleagues even more. You mocked them. That's not easily forgiven."

He shrugged. "It's not my fault that they ape their betters." He smirked at his choice of verb. "They blame me for pointing it out."

It didn't help that every year on the Sunday after Thanksgiving my father invited his fellow academics to an annual holiday cocktail party, offering them a chance to see the validation of his success up close: the slim and attractive wife, handsome children, elegant house. He would don his best suit with his dark red tie, a glass of Scotch malt whiskey in hand, and hold court.

He had to recognize that many of his colleagues attending the party resented him for his advantages, earned or not.

"And yet they show up, year after year," he said. "They're hypocrites. There's no place more obsessed with status than institutions of so-called higher education. Consider their medieval ranks—provost, chancellor, department chair, tenured professor, assistant professor, lecturer, teaching fellow. They mouth egalitarian platitudes, but they care deeply about rank and position. Prestige. Power. They say they despise it, but secretly worship it. Don't be fooled by what they say; watch what they do."

I'm aware that this description of my father doesn't portray him in the most flattering light. It doesn't do him full justice. There was his other side, best characterized with adjectives like charismatic, engaging, and funny. Yes, funny. He had a sly, subversive sense of humor. It stemmed, in part, from his study of primates and the behavior he observed in the wild and how, despite our human pretensions that we were a special species, we acted much like our near relations. He appreciated the comic side of humanity, perhaps because he found much of primate behavior amusing—chimpanzees and monkeys laughing as they played, copying the expressions of their playmates, making faces, yawning, vying for attention. He loved Pierre Boulle's novel *Planet of the Apes* for its recognition of the absurdity of seeing humans as anything more than another branch on the primate tree.

My brother Desmond had a similar sense of humor. He shared my father's sense of the absurdity of life, and they both had the gift of making people laugh. Beau liked slapstick, and I enjoyed puns and plays on words. Hanna, a Monte Python fan, gravitated to the silly. My mother would laugh with us—she got the humor—but it wasn't in her nature to join in with her own funny stories or jokes.

Julia's list grew longer as the day went on and we wandered through the house. It was a strange experience, the flood of memories that our inventory naturally sparked. I remember being trapped inside the house for a few days after Christmas during the nor'easter of December 1969, the wind rattling the windows, the snow piling up outside, blocking the doors.

Every room had a connection to the past. My bedroom upstairs, where Julia and I had made love for the first time as teenagers when the house was otherwise deserted; the living room where we held the farewell party for Beau when he left for flight school; the kitchen floor where my mother had collapsed during her final stroke.

Julia knew that I would want to spend a fair amount of time in my father's library in the north wing of the house. It was a magical place for me. Built-in bookshelves lined the walls. They were crammed with volumes on biology, zoology, botany, and the natural sciences, but also a complete set of Shakespeare's works and a long row of small red and green books—the Greek and Latin authors of the Loeb Classics. There were a few I wanted to keep, but the rest of my father's collection would be donated either to Firestone Library or the Bryn Mawr-Wellesley book sale, which was held in Princeton and was said to be the largest annual used-book-selling venture on the East Coast.

I can remember finding my father at work at his massive oak desk, composing in longhand on yellow legal pads. My mother would convert those pages of script into a typewritten manuscript, which in turn he would revise with a red pen, and she would retype the corrected manuscript pages.

He had left my mother's workspace, her studio, undisturbed all these years, the brushes, tubes of paint, and palette where she had left them. Dust had settled over the uncovered surfaces. When Julia and I entered the studio, there were several blank canvases stacked in one corner and an unfinished painting in dark tones of heroic figures from *The Saga of the Sworn-Brothers*.

"Your mother loved this place," my father told me a few years after her death. "The privacy. Having a space for her painting, her studio. Karin loved the light in the mornings, coming through those big bay windows, how it illuminated the room." He shook his head. "There were some sad times for her in this house. For me, as well. But pleasant ones, and on the whole, it became our sanctuary."

My mother didn't take to Princeton at first. She had lived with my father in Cambridge when he was finishing his doctorate, and sleepy Nassau Street with its few shops paled in comparison with Harvard Square's urban energy. But she loved Princeton's trees—they reminded her of home, of Täby, north of Stockholm, especially the oaks, elms, and pine trees. I have distinct childhood memories of her pointing out the various species—the native elms, maples, and oaks—when we went on walks around town and campus. The massive tulip poplar on the Prospect House lawn. The huge ginkgo near McCosh Hall. Her favorite was the Washington Road elm allée, the tree canopy reaching over the long roadway to town that provided a dramatic entrance to the University.

She welcomed the move to Lafayette Place house. I remember how she was happiest there during the holiday season, how she so enjoyed the Swedish Christmas traditions, the lighting of the four candles, the glögg she insisted visitors imbibe, the huge smorgasbord feast on Christmas Eve—when we opened half of our gifts, saving the other half for the next morning. She would make thin, delicate Swedish pancakes in her cast-iron Plett pan. Beau and I would compete to see who could eat more of the delicious golden-colored pancakes sprinkled with sugar and melted butter and strawberries or ligonberries before she would make us stop.

I have vivid memories: the wonderful smells emanating from the kitchen—pepparkakor, gingerbread biscuits, hot from the oven—the radiator hissing, the lights on the Christmas tree in the living room, the fireplace warming us.

After her stroke, Lafayette Place became a refuge for my mother. When she came back from the hospital, she retreated to her studio. She would sit for hours with her brushes and paints, rarely touching the canvas, frustrated that she couldn't translate the images in her mind into brushstrokes on the surface before her. She was different, a changed woman, struggling with her hand-eye coordination and with her memory.

Her relationship with my father changed. Before, they had rarely, if ever, disagreed in front of us. After the stroke, she didn't hide her anger and resentment. I found the loosening of her characteristic emotional reserve a bit jarring. We had been told that brain injuries could lower inhibitions, but we were unprepared for her changed personality.

Her emotional swings weren't all dark. She became softer, too. There was a sudden, and previously muted, sweet focus on her grandchildren. She spent more time with King, and with Hanna's daughter Rose, and she talked about the importance of family to Beau when he returned from California for a visit. I was there when she questioned him directly about his romantic prospects.

"What about children?" she asked Beau. "Why don't you marry and have children? You're still a handsome man. You're not too old."

Beau shook his head. "It doesn't work like that," he said with a wry smile. "Haven't found the right woman, yet. Considering how it ended the last time I got married, you could see why I want to be careful."

"Don't wait," she said.

"It's not something you can hurry," Beau replied.

"Ju äldre bocken är, dess hårdare blir hornen."

"You know none of us speak Swedish, Mother."

"Your grandmother used to say it: 'The older the buck gets, the harder his horns get.' You're very stubborn, Wilson."

"That I am. Where do I get that from, do you think?"

My mother smiled, satisfied that she had made her point.

She didn't live to see Beau remarried or to hug his twins, Philip and Marco, and I know that my older brother has regrets about that.

As we went through the house, room-by-room, I experienced Lafayette Place now through different eyes, adult eyes. I was struck by how grand and stately its architectural plan was: an expansive living room, high ceilings, long hallways, wide windows and French doors to let the light in, and more fireplaces than a domicile equipped with central heating ever needed. In short, a residence of the wealthy.

After years of living in cramped apartments and shabby hotel rooms, I savored the sheer size of the house. It was palatial. As a teenager, I realized that our house was larger, that not every family had a tennis court in the backyard or several working fireplaces, but my mother had impressed upon all of us the virtues of modesty. We were never to brag, not about our accomplishments, nor about our possessions.

We were lucky to live there—winners in the lottery of life, I suppose—but I didn't feel any guilt about it. Still don't. Someone fortunate was going to reside at 4 Lafayette Place, was going to occupy the house, and we'd had our turn. Ownership would pass from the hands of this generation of Kincaids.

It took us most of the afternoon for Julia to feel her list was complete. As we worked, we talked quietly about the past, of the times we had spent in the house, about the occasional visitors and overnight guests who had passed through its front door, all of the things that had happened within its four walls. Some of the memories were bittersweet.

The hush in the empty house was eerie. Its rooms and corridors had echoed with the sounds of our family, a talkative family. Now it was silent.

Today the idea of a patriarch isn't in favor, certainly not in the liberal Northeast and the Amtrak corridor from Boston to Washington, D.C. My father was unashamedly one. He saw himself as the head of the Kincaid family—since our roots were originally Scottish, he sometimes talked about the Kincaid clan with a slight smile—and he took a keen interest in his children and their upbringing.

My father was a study in contradictions. He wasn't political in a partisan sense, but he was a fierce patriot, convinced that the best of Enlightenment thinking had produced the institutions that made up the United States. No monarchy, no aristocracy, a system of checks-and-balances, an openness to new ideas and new people. A free press. He loved the promise of mobility in American life, that immigrants—Carnegie, Pulitzer, Levi Strauss—could rise. He had little interest in politics, and while he voted on Election Day—his civic duty—he never donated a penny to a candidate, Republican or Democrat.

Another contradiction: he didn't believe in a supernatural God, but he made his way every Sunday to a pew in Trinity Episcopal Church on Mercer Street, a short walk from our house on

Lafayette Place. He insisted that we attend Sunday School there until we became teenagers. Why? I asked him once, years later.

"I wanted to give all of you a grounding," he said. "An exposure to the spiritual. The world around you is a product of Protestantism, one way or the other, and you should have a passing knowledge of its theological underpinnings. I figured you would make your own mind up about believing."

I shook my head. "But why do you go?"

"I find it calming," he said. "The ritual. The Eucharist, the sharing of a meal. 'This is my body.' There's a community in that, stretching back thousands of years."

"But you reject the idea of God."

"And you haven't. That is where we part company. There is no Other, no Supreme Being. It's the name we've given to those feelings of spirituality that we feel when we confront the beauty of nature. Have you ever seen the waterfall dance of the chimpanzees, our primate cousins? It is religious in nature. They're awed by the sound and power of the waterfall, just as we are moved by the wonder of the music in our cathedrals, the majesty of a high mass."

"I can't preclude the idea that there's something more there," I replied. "A force. Something more than randomness. It's not all in our heads. We seek transcendence, and we seek the sacred. God calls to us."

"You take a more mystical view," my father said. "That's your right, James. I must say that your hero Teilhard had some very intriguing ideas about our spiritual evolution. A brilliant spin on Darwin. What we really want is grace. We want understanding, we want to be surrounded by beauty, and we want to be surprised constantly by discoveries of something unlike ourselves. But there is no Other."

"Too materialistic for my taste," I said "We agree on the search for the spiritual, but I can't reject the possibility of the divine. Is it more likely we invented God or God invented us? I'm sure of one thing. If He's there, your disbelief can't abolish Him."

In his will and last testament, my father urged us to keep Lafayette Place in the family, as well as the beach house in Boca Grande. There was never any question about the Florida place—it had been placed in a family trust and the taxes were low. All of us loved spending time there: the memories there were golden—we were freer there, far from judgment. Or so it felt.

But the Princeton residence was a white elephant—too large, too expensive to maintain with shockingly high property taxes. None of us planned to live in Princeton: Beau had no intention of leaving San Diego; Hanna was happy in Sebastopol; and Julia and I were content with our condo on the Upper West Side, blocks from Columbia.

We could use the money from a sale of the house. Our inheritance from my father was smaller than any of us had anticipated. Alexander had lived to eighty-five, and his accounts and investments had been drawn down over the years. Further, none of us had chosen lucrative careers. Beau had his military pension and his law practice, but he had a young family to support. Hanna's landscape architecture firm had its financial ups and downs. And while I had found a job at a publisher of travel guides after years of freelancing, I hadn't saved enough for retirement.

And so we agreed to sell 4 Lafayette Place. As my father's executor, I contacted a local real estate agent, Veronica Estrada, a friend of Julia's, who was properly enthusiastic about "representing this marque property" and pocketing her ample listing commission. I assumed it would be purchased by someone enriched by the financial and technology bubble of the past several years. A hedge fund operator, or the CEO of a software company with a corporate lawyer spouse. They and their one child would rattle around in all that space. The large families of my childhood were long gone, as obsolete as the wood-paneled station wagons of the early 1960s. I find that somewhat sad, although we had only King, our son, and I'm the one to blame for not having more.

As a journalist, I learned that very few in the public eye handle fame particularly well: they begin to believe their press clippings; they grow arrogant; they see themselves as more deserving than others. My father was the exception that proved the rule. He was amused by the sudden attention paid to him after *Status* joined the bestseller lists—he joked that the best thing about writing the book was that it had raised *his* status.

He was unprepared for what came next.

The trouble began with his second trade book, *Hierarchy*, where he argued that humans had inherited their zeal for egalitarianism from our hunter-gatherer ancestors. My father maintained that such principles wouldn't work in the more complex tribal societies that emerged after farming replaced the hunt. He singled out Marxism as a terribly flawed attempt to establish equality and noted that—as George Orwell had depicted in *Animal Farm*—when Communists gained control they established their own rigid hierarchy, with Party members and leaders at the top. A chapter on the evolutionary differences between men and women which suggested that young women were drawn to Alpha Males (today's "bad boys") caused additional outrage, but it was two paragraphs in a chapter entitled "Success" that provoked the most criticism. He argued that Japanese and Chinese Americans had achieved success because of their stable families, reverence for education, and possibly, some genetic advantages when it came to Spearman's g, a measure of intelligence and cognitive performance. That was apparently beyond the pale—his critics claimed that my father was a reactionary, a eugenicist, and a closet racist. (In short order they dropped the adjective "closet").

The first newspaper reviews of *Hierarchy* were mixed. Then, in the fall of 1983, a group of leftist academics published what they called an "Open Letter on Alexander Kincaid." It claimed my father had twisted data in his eagerness to advance his theories and that he and Harvard sociobiologist E.O. Wilson were promoting ideas that represented a "threat to human dignity." The Open Letter called on Princeton's Biology Department to disavow Alexander's book, and for Princeton University to publicly censure him. While there was no danger of that happening, my father was wounded, nonetheless, because four junior members of the Princeton faculty had signed the letter.

The Open Letter provided the news hook for newspaper and magazine stories about this suddenly controversial Princeton professor. Conflict makes for good headlines, and there were plenty of left-of-center academics ready to opine on the wickedness of Alexander Kincaid. For reporters and editors educated during the late 1960s, my father made the perfect villain: patrician in bearing, an elitist, a proponent of research that was thoroughly loathed by academics on the Left. It was easy to apply the adjectives "divisive" and "problematic" to his views.

My father was slow to recognize how badly his enemies had

damaged his reputation, but he eventually conceded their public attacks had been effective.

"They've done a marvelous job of labeling me," he said to me once during a long walk across campus. "Labels that stick. Now I wonder what the students think of me when I lecture. Does Professor Kincaid believe African-Americans are intellectually inferior? Is he a racist? A misogynist?"

"But you're not any of those things."

"I think it's Mark Twain who claimed a lie can travel around the world and back again while the truth is lacing up its boots. It's something I'm going to have to live with, but it angers me nonetheless."

The personal nature of the criticism stung. He had often quoted the maxim about academic disputes that "the smaller the stakes, the nastier the politics" but I don't think he ever reconciled himself to the vitriol directed his way.

In the years that followed the Open Letter, he changed. My father spent less and less time on campus; he taught his undergraduate course and weekly seminar and then retreated to Lafayette Place. His book-lined study became his safe harbor, where he could think and write, shielded from outside distractions.

I doubt he ever fully accepted what happened, his sudden and public fall from grace. He was puzzled, at first, by the distortion of his views, and the attacks on his character. He proved to be surprisingly naive about how our culture of celebrity worked.

Later, I came to appreciate his courage. At the time, I had wondered whether he should have taken a more conciliatory tone. He saw more clearly than I did that there really wasn't any middle ground, any compromise. My father and other like-minded biologists were arguing for a fundamental shift in the way we understood social behavior. He believed that ignoring the truth about human nature doomed most attempts at social engineering—however well-meaning they might be—and that progress depending on a realistic appreciation of the role of heritable traits.

Did our tour of the house stir up painful memories for Julia? Regrets? Had she imagined earlier in our marriage that one day we would inherit the house and fill it with children and grandchildren? I don't know whether that fantasy appealed to her, but we had paused after King. I didn't want the challenge of supporting more children while I pursued my career goals. Was that selfish? In retrospect, it was a mistake. When the time came to try again, Julia couldn't conceive. It was one of the issues that contributed to the rockiness of our marriage, part of the resentments and slights that built up over time.

And then there was the other crisis in our marriage, triggered by my restlessness. During our separation, my father sided with Julia, blaming me for the breakup. He was right in one sense, and wrong in another: the discontent wasn't completely one-sided. Nonetheless, he judged me severely for my deficiencies as a husband and father. I hadn't experienced the weight of that judgment before—as the first-born son Beau had lived with it since he was ten years old. Even after Julia and I got back together, his disappointment in me was always there, just below the surface.

We stopped our inventory for a supper of ham and cheese

sandwiches, potato chips, and beer in the kitchen. Outside, it was beginning to grow dark as the afternoon sun began to wane. I suggested that we make a final pass through the second floor. We found a few extra items to add to Julia's list, one of Karin's small paintings stashed in a closet, and a pair of my father's silver cufflinks that I thought Beau might like.

We were moving through the hallway by the far guest bedroom when we heard tapping noises coming from the first floor. They grew louder, and there was another sound mixed in I couldn't immediately place.

"Do you think there are ghosts in this house?" Julia asked. "Des always thought there were. He heard strange sounds at night, people whispering. Did he ever tell you about it?"

"He did not."

"It didn't frighten him. He didn't think they were hostile."

"And who would these ghosts be?"

"Spirits of the people who lived and died here. The original owners. And I guess now you would have to add your parents and Des."

"No, Jules, I don't think my parents, or Des, are haunting Lafayette Place. Or anyone else. It's just the wind." As I finished talking, there was another tapping sound, and then a different one which I couldn't place at first, and then I realized it was wind chimes.

"Chimes," I said. "The ones Mom hung at the back of the house. After we lost Des."

"I've been having dreams about the old days," Julia said. "I know you're the one with all the dreams, but I've been having them, too. You and me and Des, and sometimes Beau, turn up in them."

"That's natural. We all have the past on our minds now."

I took Julia's hand in mine, and we went downstairs together, drawn by the sound of the chimes. We moved through the kitchen and stepped outside to the patio that flanked Karin's rose garden. It was a balmy April evening and the stars in the now clear night sky glittered above a line of elms. A light breeze swept through the trees, ringing the chimes.

I paused. "I can take the chimes down."

"No," she said. "Leave them. They should stay here. They belong to the house."

I didn't say out loud what I thought—the new owners would most likely discard them. Julia knew me too well.

"Who knows?" she asked. "Maybe whoever buys the house will keep them."

"That would be nice."

"It's lovely here, isn't it?" Julia asked. "But it's a shame. It will never be the same, will it?

"No, it won't, Jules," I said.

She glanced up at the sky.

"Look at them," she said and stretched her arms out above her head. "The stars. They're so beautiful, Jimmy. I wish we could stay here. Lose track of time."

I looked over at my wife and was surprised to see tears on her cheeks. I took her into my arms and told her everything would be fine as she wept, quietly, and clung to me as if it was our last embrace.

TWO

The first Kincaid came to the New World in chains.

In mid-December 1650, Jonathan Kincaid arrived in the Massachusetts Bay Colony aboard the merchant ship *Unity*. He was one of more than 100 Scottish soldiers, now prisoners held below deck, who had been captured at the Battle of Dunbar, the losers in an ill-fated and brutal encounter with Oliver Cromwell's Model New Army. Sentenced to indentured servitude as a consequence, they had been transported across the Atlantic—forced cheap labor for the Godly Puritan worthies who ran the colony.

Jonathan had been a captain in Sir David Leslie's Covenanter army, the force gathered to defend Scotland against the English after the Scots made the fateful mistake of supporting the claim of Charles the Second to the Scottish throne. Jonathan hadn't joined the Covenanter ranks out of any deep religious or political conviction—he was a Presbyterian in name only, and he was no Royalist. Jonathan was skeptical about the cause, aware of the shifting and confusing politics of the past decade where allies became enemies and then allies again. In truth, he didn't particularly care who sat on the throne of Scotland. He considered himself a practical man, a soldier of fortune, having already fought in Sweden for Gustavus Aldolphus. He had returned to his homeland along with several fellow Scottish officers, largely because of the generous pay offered by General Leslie.

Jonathan knew how quickly the fortunes of war could change, and they turned against the Scots that cold and rainy September morning at Dunbar. General Leslie had positioned his army on Doon Hill, pinning Cromwell's forces against the sea. All Leslie had to do was wait for Cromwell, outnumbered and short of supplies, to try to storm their position. Jonathan had watched in disgust as a flock of black-suited ministers convinced the general that it was his righteous duty to immediately confront the invaders. These same dour clerics had purged the army of many of its experienced officers on the grounds that they held "unsound" religious beliefs, a move that weakened the command structure and contributed to the sorry collapse in discipline that morning.

Leslie ordered his forces to advance to the foot of the hill and its lower slopes. At dawn, however, Cromwell's seasoned Roundheads assaulted the right flank of the Scottish army. The Covenanter cavalry broke under the assault, and quickly thereafter, Leslie's raw infantry recruits panicked and broke ranks. Jonathan tried to rally his fleeing men, but found that an impossible task. He did what any veteran soldier would do under the circumstances—he dropped his sword and ran. Later, he learned, the English had called their pursuit of the panicked Scots the Race of Dunbar.

Jonathan found temporary refuge in a cottage two miles from the battlefield, but later that day was captured by patrolling English dragoons. He was one of the 5,000 prisoners who were marched south more than 100 miles to Durham. Exposed to the cold, given scant food and water, many died on the journey. By the time they reached the Durham Cathedral, nearly a third had perished. There, by order of the Council of State sitting in London, they learned their fate. Major Samuel Clarke told the

Dunbar prisoners that they could volunteer to fight for the Model New Army in Ireland or be transported to Virginia or Massachusetts where they would toil as indentured servants for seven years.

Jonathan remained silent after Clarke's invitation. "We're professional soldiers, are we not?" his friend and fellow officer Donald Drummond asked. He had served with Jonathan in Sweden. "Why not ply our trade in Ireland?"

"I'm done with war," Jonathan replied. "Had a belly-full of killing. Better to begin anew."

"Are ye daft? Take yer chances with the heathen savages in Virginia? Not for me."

"What's the difference between the heathen savages there, and the Christian ones here, pray tell? Could they be any crueler than what we experienced on the march here? Little food and water. The sick and weak who couldn't keep up slaughtered by the side of the road. And the hundreds who have died in this cathedral, their bodies dragged away. Did ye see any Christian mercy on display?"

"I'm for Ireland," Drummond said, shaking his head. "It's a lang road that's no got a turnin', and I'm a patient man."

"Good luck to ye, then," Jonathan replied. "I'm for a different road."

And so it was that Jonathan heard his name called aloud by a clerk from the list of those sentenced for transport to New England. In Southampton, he was herded aboard the *Unity* and joined his fellow prisoners below deck, crowded into a dark, cramped space, fettered to forestall any threat of mutiny. They set sail on November 11th, the captain, one Augustine Walker, risking a late autumn crossing of the Atlantic. Two weeks into their voyage, they encountered rough weather, with strong winds and high seas. The *Unity* rolled violently with the waves, and cold seawater washed over the deck and poured into the hold. Jonathan would have prayed to God if he had any faith left—he had faith only in his own determination to survive. Five of his fellow Scots died during the voyage, their bodies dropped over the side into the sea after a perfunctory prayer. Jonathan told himself that he could persist and survive, that he was strong enough to make it through the voyage. After five long weeks, the *Unity*'s lookout spotted land and a cheer went up from seasick, hungry, and cold Scottish prisoners at the news.

Jonathan was twenty-eight years old when he set foot on a Boston wharf, stumbling onto dry land, blinking in the weak December sunlight. The wind came whipping off the harbor, piercing his ragged clothes and chilling him to the bone. If he survived his seven years of servitude—never a sure thing—he would be young enough to begin a new life. At least, that's what he told himself.

During his first days in Massachusetts, Jonathan finally encountered a bit of good luck—he was indentured to a kindly and fair man, William Macy, who farmed five acres in the coastal settlement of Salisbury, north of Boston. Macy and his wife, Frances, needed help, as their two young daughters couldn't contribute to the hard work of farming in the rocky soil found near the Merrimack River.

When he entered William Macy's house for the first time, Jonathan found a young Indian serving girl there, who the Macys called Hannah. She was twelve years old, with long dark hair, smooth unblemished skin, and warm brown eyes. He stopped, struck by her beauty, and was surprised and secretly pleased that she stared back at him. Only later did he learn her Indian name, one he found hard to pronounce, which translated meant "Snow Child," as she had been born during a blizzard. Her parents had died of the flux, and she had been baptized by missionaries and placed with the Macys.

Jonathan worked for William Macy for the full seven years of his indenture, a term that included both lean and prosperous times. At Jonathan's urging, they planted apple and cherry trees and added a milk cow. Jonathan proved to be canny in matters of commerce, advising William on negotiations and on drawing up contracts.

On a warm summer day in 1657, the day after he became a free man, Jonathan made a down payment on ten mostly uncleared acres from a nearby landowner, Josiah Wentworth. It cost him most of the silver William had given him as a parting gift. He spent a month framing a small saltbox house, and when it was habitable, he put down his tools and washed his hands and face in a bucket of water and donned his best shirt.

It was nearing dusk when he arrived at the Macys' front door. He softly called out Hannah's name, and she left the kitchen where she was helping Frances prepare dinner. Hannah returned to the kitchen to tell the Macys that she was leaving with Jonathan.

William Macy knew better than to object. While Jonathan had always behaved properly around Hannah, his attraction to her had been obvious. But William also knew his neighbors and how they would not countenance a couple living in sin.

He took Jonathan aside. "Ye must ask Pastor Winslow to post the banns," he said. "Marry Hannah before the magistrate as swiftly as ye can."

Jonathan frowned. "I've waited years for this day," he said. "We've waited. We don't need any man mumbling over us to start our life together."

"Hannah's a good Christian girl. Make her a respectable woman."

"She's coming with me, William."

"I know. There would be those eager to judge ye and punish ye. For Hannah's sake, do as I suggest. I'll stand with ye when ye make your vows in front of God and the magistrate."

Jonathan nodded. "For Hannah, I will."

They were married by a magistrate from Boston and held a party afterward at the Macys, where the ale flowed freely. Hannah didn't stray from Jonathan's side, regarding the guests warily. She knew that for some in Salisbury her presence was unwelcome.

The early years of their married life had their share of challenges. The winter of 1663 was a particularly hard one, with a deep snow cover from New Year's Day to March. That summer, blight attacked their wheat and much of their crops were not worth the reaping. Jonathan told himself that if he could survive the death march to Durham and seven years of servitude, he could survive a bad season in his fields.

His love for Hannah deepened during that year. She never complained, and she spent hours picking fruit and vegetables and salting meat, preparing food for the winter.

She bore him seven children: four sons and three daughters. One son was still-born. Two of the girls died before they reached the age of five. Their boys were tall and rangy, with dark hair and tawny skin. Mary, their daughter, inherited her father's height and her mother's good looks.

For several decades, Jonathan and Hannah and their children eked out a living from the rocky New England soil, toiling from dawn to dusk. Hannah nursed her babies, cooked the meals, and made sure the family attended church on the Sabbath.

The Kincaids tilled the land, gathered their crops, and kept to themselves, for the most part. At times, Hannah faced hostility from others in town, and once, she was brought before the magistrate because of a dispute with Ruth Brown. Hannah had caught Ruth stealing apples from the Kincaid orchard; when Ruth had called her a "dirty squaw," Hannah had boxed her ears. In court, Ruth had brazenly lied, claiming Hannah had attacked her like a "wild heathen savage" over a simple misunderstanding. The magistrate rebuked them both for quarreling and fined Hannah ten shillings, ignoring Ruth's theft the apples. Jonathan paid the fine and hustled Hannah out of court before she could object. It was better to accept the unfair judgment, he thought, and avoid further trouble with any of his neighbors.

For nearly twenty years, Jonathan and his family lived in peace in Salisbury. That changed in 1675 when conflict between the colonists and the Wampanoags in Plymouth Colony erupted and spread to the rest of New England. Early that year John Sassamon, a Christian native, had warned of an attack led by the chief Metacom, who the English called King Philip. When Sassamon was found murdered, the colonists arrested three Wampanoag, tried them, and executed them at Plymouth Plantation. Jonathan was not surprised when the hangings sparked an uprising, nor when Metacom recruited warriors from the Nipmuck, Pocumtuck, and Narragansett tribes in an attempt to drive out the English, nor when the colonists fashioned an alliance with the Mohegans and the Mohawks. As a young man, he had seen the same spiraling violence, the same alliances of convenience, in Scotland, England, and on the Continent.

He had no appetite for the carnage he knew was coming. Jonathan understood Metacom's anger—the loss of tribal land, the decline in the fur trade, the humiliating need to submit to English authority. His sympathy for the natives only went so far. Jonathan was a realist. He knew neutrality would not be an option. He had seen too much of the cold, wide world to believe that he and his family would be left alone.

"What will ye do?" his neighbor Isaack Fletcher asked.

Jonathan shrugged. "We will fight." He knew that his older sons—half-breeds in the eyes of their neighbors—had to fight for the English, or their loyalty would be questioned. He couldn't risk that happening, for he had seen in Scotland what choosing the wrong side could mean, and he was determined not to repeat his past mistakes. So he outfitted Charles, who was seventeen, and Jacob, who was fifteen, with muskets and hatchets, and they joined the local militia. Jonathan's knowledge of military tactics and his fighting experience made him the logical choice as their captain.

It was hard for him to hold his tongue when he heard his minister cite Deuteronomy in his sermon, exhorting the men of Salisbury to "smite every male thereof with the edge of the sword." He had heard that scriptural justification before during the Civil War in Scotland when Christian was encouraged to kill fellow Christian. He knew the harsh cruelty of war and there was nothing Godly about it.

In this Indian war, there was no quarter given. There were atrocities on both sides—torture, summary executions, rape, mutilations. It sickened him. Jonathan tried to keep his men in check—but it was hard to reason with a man whose wife and children had been burned alive in their farmhouse by raiding Indians, to keep him from retaliating in kind.

In the end, Metacom and a small group of his warriors were

discovered by Captain Benjamin Church and his company of soldiers. It was ironic that the fatal musket shot that killed Metacom was fired by John Alderman, an Indian soldier, who sold the rebel leader's severed head to the authorities for thirty shillings, the going rate for Wampanoag heads. Metacom's head was mounted on a pike in Plymouth where it remained for decades.

After months of taking part in raids and skirmishes, Jonathan and his sons were happy to return to Hannah and his farm. He vowed never to take up arms again. The Kincaid men's service against Metacom's warriors cemented their standing in the community. Jonathan's sons married local women and followed the Biblical proscription to be fruitful and multiply, and he became a grandfather several times over.

Jonathan Kincaid died in December of 1699, one month shy of the new century. He had caught a cold that he couldn't shake, and he took to his bed and never rose again. His family gathered around him on the night he died. "You are Kincaids," he told them. "Never forget that. You are Kincaids."

In the decades and decades that followed, most of Jonathan Kincaid's descendants stayed in New England, not venturing far from Salisbury. Most farmed, others found work in the small towns of Massachusetts or New Hampshire as mill workers or carpenters. One of Jonathan's great-grandsons served in George Washington's Continental Army. Ezekiel Kincaid rose to the rank of captain. He saw action at Long Island, Trenton, Princeton, and was there at Yorktown when Lord Cornwallis surrendered, ending the war.

Unlike many of their neighbors who were lured to the West

by the promise of more fertile land, the Kincaids stayed in Massachusetts and New Hampshire during the nineteenth century.

One branch of the paternal Jonathan Kincaid bloodline nearly ended in the final decades of the century. Nathan Kincaid, an only son who plied his trade as a shoemaker in Plaistow, New Hampshire (only a few miles northwest of Salisbury), married late in life, at the age of forty. His much younger wife, Mariam Adams, miscarried twice before producing an heir, a boy born in 1892 in their downstairs bedroom. They named him Wilson. At a very young age, Wilson displayed a quick intelligence coupled with a near-photographic memory. His parents were pleased, but slightly unsettled by their precocious and strong-willed son. Once in school, Wilson took to Greek and Latin and read the classics. He gravitated to the Stoics, and found their philosophy more appealing than the sermons preached by the Reverend Carlisle in their local Presbyterian church.

"You're a bright one," his father told him. "You can rise. Make something of yourself."

They somehow found the money to place Wilson at Phillips Andover Academy, where he felt out of place with the sons of lawyers and doctors, but quickly impressed his classmates with his prowess in the classroom.

Wilson's teachers there encouraged him to apply to Harvard College, and he became only the second Kincaid to attend college. After graduation, Wilson entered Harvard Law School and continued to impress his instructors and fellow students with his keen intellect. And there was his ambition—a drive to succeed that he had learned to hide. Strivers weren't gentlemen. Wilson understood the hypocrisy in that formulation, but he smiled and kept his own counsel. He clerked for a federal judge and then joined a prosperous Boston law firm. In 1917, he continued the Kincaid martial tradition, serving during the First World War—although never leaving the United States.

Wilson married a pretty young woman, Constance Tarkington, who came from an old New England family that had seen better times. Their first child, Priscilla Jane, arrived in 1920. Alexander Tarkington Kincaid followed three years later. Alexander was a precocious child, speaking full sentences at the age of two, and beginning to read at age three. He was very curious, asking his older sister question after question. He loved exploring and was particularly drawn to the natural world.

Wilson saw his son's gifts, and he hoped that Alexander would follow in his footsteps: a Harvard education, the partnership at a white-shoe law firm, memberships in the Athenaeum and the Somerset Club, lunches at Locke-Ober, a comfortable townhouse on Beacon Hill and a summer place in Edgartown. Boston was the Athens of America, and Wilson believed Alexander could cement the Kincaids' standing as a leading family in the city. What more could a man ask?

"You could go far staying here," he told a fifteen-year-old Alexander.

"That's a contradiction in terms. To go far, you need to go."

"Give it some time. I'm sure that you'll see that this is the best path for you."

As it turned out, Alexander had other ideas about his future, and they didn't center on a quiet life spent among the fading Brahmin families of Boston. The conventional held no appeal for him and in that, he was much like the first Kincaid to set foot in the New World.

THREE

During his childhood, Alexander Tarkington Kincaid was first exposed to the wonders of the natural world in two places, two islands—Martha's Vineyard and Gasparilla Island. His father, Wilson, had a summer home in Edgartown, and during the winter the Kincaid family stayed at Uncle Blake's beachfront residence in Boca Grande, an airy and spacious house which was situated on the Gulf Coast side of Gasparilla Island.

In the summers, Alexander, his sister Priscilla, and their mother would spend almost three months in the family house in Edgartown. His father would join them on long weekends and for two uninterrupted weeks in August—the demands of his thriving law practice would otherwise keep him in Boston.

Living on Martha's Vineyard introduced Alexander to the natural beauty of the island, its tidal flats, sandy beaches, and saltwater marshes, its freshwater ponds and meadows, its back roads leading to small farms. He was fascinated by the birds of the island. Alexander learned to identify them: American oystercatchers, night herons, least terns, common eiders, herring gulls, Baltimore orioles, and mute swans. He loved the sound of the cicadas at dusk, the lights of the fireflies in a nearby field, and the stars in the night sky. For a child fascinated by nature, it was nothing short of heaven.

In January, the Kincaids would escape to Florida by train, making the final leg of their journey on the Seaboard Railway special from Arcadia to Boca Grande. Alexander would eagerly peer through the window as they neared the island, sitting on the right-hand side of the train so he could be the first to spy the green-blue waters of the Gulf. He felt as if he was coming home when they crossed the bridge to the island, and the train slowed as it neared the terminus.

Boca Grande presented new delights. He loved the velvet softness of the air, the warmth of the Gulf waters, and the lazy Southern air of the place. He filled notebooks with sketches of the Port Boca Grande Lighthouse, drawing contrasts to its northern counterpart in Edgartown.

When he was older, he took the skiff on expeditions to the islands near Gasparilla—Cayo Costa, Punta Blanca, and Mondongo. He was fascinated by the wildlife, the fish, birds, and small creatures that populated these islands.

It was at the summer house of Cameron Muir, an eccentric friend of his Uncle Blake, that he first encountered Muir's pet monkey, Babe. Alexander was struck by Babe's ability to learn new things. The animal was mischievous and seemed to enjoy playing with guests. Alexander was fascinated by his obvious intelligence. It was the beginning of his lifelong fascination with primates and simians.

When he was fourteen years old, he read Darwin's *On the Origin of Species* from cover to cover. It was a turning point in his intellectual development. Alexander would never see things the same way again; Darwin's insights convinced him that evolution explained most of the mysteries of the natural order.

"Do you think we're cousins to the apes?" Priscilla asked him. "That doesn't seem quite right."

"If I have to choose between evolution and Jehovah creating Adam out of mud, I'll take evolution," he replied.

"But we're civilized!"

"Our brains have evolved. That's the reason for our progress."

Priscilla shook her head. "What about this Missing Link? An animal between us and the monkeys?"

"If there was such a creature, someone would have found their bones. Fossils." Alexander smiled. "I think you might be a little vain, Pri. Don't worry. You're much prettier than any chimp I've met."

"And you're impossible."

God could only be found, he decided, in the design of the world. There were hints of that insight in many of the world's religions, he discovered, in the Shinto belief that spiritual energy existed in all things, trees and rocks and humans (although he wasn't sure about rocks…), and in the Baha'i notion that nature was a reflection of the divine.

Alexander proved to be a keen observer of all around him. A curious child, his mother decided, and she wasn't quite sure what to make of her son. Priscilla, her daughter, two years older than Alexander, accepted things as they were. She tried to fit in, to get along. (That was to change when Priscilla reached her age of majority and rejected the traditional in favor of a quite different life). Alexander didn't worry about what people thought. He was always probing, always asking another question.

A dogged reader, Alexander plowed through book after book,

reading at a frantic pace. It annoyed Priscilla, a slow reader, that Alexander retained what he read so quickly—she had challenged him once about a bulky textbook he had finished in record time and she was surprised, and dismayed, at how much he had retained.

Alexander's father never forgot that he was the son of a shoemaker, a common cobbler, and that he owed his elevated social standing and his comfortable balance at the Bank of Boston to having applied his intelligence and drive to the practice of the law. He tried to impress upon Alexander the lessons he had learned and he counseled him to follow the same path.

He encouraged Alexander to learn Latin and Greek, and with an eye on what Winston Churchill later called the gathering storm in Europe, French and German.

When it was time for college, Alexander was drawn to Princeton by the chance to learn from a noted biology professor, Alfred Stein, who studied chimpanzees and the great apes of Africa. Stein, a brilliant scholar, although somewhat idiosyncratic, took a shine to Alexander, encouraging him to pursue an academic career—a path Alexander hadn't previously considered. His father hoped that his son might return to Cambridge for law school. He did enroll at Harvard, after Alexander returned from his service in the Army, but it was to seek a doctorate in biology.

The war hardened Alexander, as it did for many men of his generation. He left Princeton for officer candidate school in 1944, and because of his fluent German, he was attached to General Patton's Third Army staff in the final months of the war. He was called upon to translate captured Wehrmacht documents and to participate in interrogations of captured soldiers, many of whom were older men and teenagers in ill-fitting uniforms, the conscripted final line of defense for the Third Reich.

As the Third Army moved deeper into Germany, Alexander confronted the depravity of the Nazi regime firsthand. After the 4th Armored Division liberated the slave labor camp known as Ohrdruf-Nord Stalag III, near the quaint town of Ohrdruf, a town where Johann Sebastian Bach had composed music at the Church of Saint Michael, Alexander was shocked at the condition of the emaciated prisoners. Later, he saw the depravities of Buchenwald, scenes of horror he never forgot.

Not long after seeing the camps, he questioned one detained German captain, a distinguished-looking man in his mid-forties, who had been a professor of chemistry at Heidelberg University before the war. Captain Hans Mueller had lost an arm in Crete, but had been serving on headquarters staff. When Alexander asked about the camps, Mueller looked down at his scuffed shoes.

"The German Jews," Alexander began. "The concentration camps. Did people know about them? What was transpiring in them?"

"We knew that they were being treated harshly," Mueller said. "Many of them had left Germany. There was talk of atrocities on the Eastern Front. I served in North Africa and Greece. No Jews or gypsies to speak of there." He glanced at his empty sleeve. "Fate works in strange ways. The Tommy sniper who shot me saved my life. Had I not been crippled, I would have most likely died outside Stalingrad or defending the Fatherland at the Rhine."

"What did you know?" Alexander pressed him.

"I never joined the Party," Mueller said. "I kept my distance from the political types. As to the camps and the Jews? It would have been suicidal to ask questions about this subject, to draw the attention of the Gestapo." He sighed. "It is a stain on our honor. As a German, I am thoroughly ashamed. We elevated a failed house painter, a corporal of no distinction, to a position of absolute power. We let his chosen degenerates and thugs rule over us. Why did we? We Germans love rank, you see. The pecking order. Like birds."

"Or apes."

"Apes wearing uniforms and shiny boots." Mueller shook his head. "It has brought us to ruin."

Alexander never forgot the conversation. He loathed the Nazi perversion of science and the bizarre fusion of eugenics, racism, and pagan superstition Hitler and his henchmen used to justify their actions. He saw clear parallels between the patterns of submission, cruelty, and violence found in great ape populations and those adopted by the German leaders. Except the apes didn't have V-2 rockets or gas chambers.

His time in Germany convinced Alexander to pursue a career in science. He believed that in unlocking the mysteries of primate behavior, he could contribute to understanding how an advanced society could descend into such barbarism and help guard against it happening again. At the same time, he knew enough of the academic world to realize that he needed to first establish his *bona fides* as a scientist and scholar before he theorized about the human condition. Alexander recognized that he would have to produce a scholarly dissertation of some specificity, and he decided to explore the social interactions of larger primates—gibbons, chimpanzees, apes, and gorillas. At Harvard, he found a thesis advisor, Francis Collamore, who had been trained by Alexander's Princeton professor, Alfred Stein.

During the years that followed, as he observed primates in their natural habitat, he continued to see striking parallels to human behavior. He kept a journal, jotting down his thoughts, and those impressions became the foundation for his later, more controversial, work. He never imagined that one day he would stand accused of the very false science he so detested.

FOUR

They first met at a dinner party at Professor Harald Lindstrom's house in Stockholm. Karin had been invited at the last moment, and she realized when she arrived that she had been invited to balance out the table—there were four couples, her, and the guest of honor, a promising young American academic from Harvard.

Earlier that day, the American, Alexander Kincaid, had participated in a seminar with the biology faculty of Uppsala University, contributing an informal talk on his recent field research on primate behavior in Africa.

As Kincaid answered the questions of the guests at the dinner party, Karin found she was both intrigued and attracted by him—she hadn't met very many Americans, and she was surprised to find one so cultured and knowledgeable. He spoke fluent German, enjoyed classical music, and seemed knowledgeable about the world outside, including the current state of Swedish politics.

She could tell by the way he looked at her that he, in turn, found her attractive. Did he desire her? Karin thought that he might. He made a point of sitting by her when they had their desserts—strawberry-rhubarb pie with coffee—in the Lindstroms' sitting room.

"Have you visited Europe often?" she asked him.

"Before the war, with my father and sister, we toured London and Paris and Rome."

"And Germany? You do speak the language."

"Austria. Vienna. I didn't make it to Germany until 1945."

"You fought in the war?" she asked.

"I served in the military, yes," he said. "In Germany at the very end of the war. They needed interpreters and I spoke the language well enough to be of some use."

"You were a soldier, then?" Professor Lindstrom asked. He had been listening intently to their conversation, and Karin found that she resented his interruption. She wanted this handsome young American all to herself, as silly as that might seem.

"I was in General Patton's Third Army." Alexander tilted his head slightly. "I can't say I ever thought of myself as a soldier. I'm a scientist by training and by inclination."

"Nonetheless, you and your Army saved us," Lindstrom said. "In the end, you saved Europe from those gangsters. Saved civilization."

"No thanks to us," Karin said. "Sweden stayed on the sidelines. Hiding behind our neutrality. To our eternal shame."

"What would you have had us do?" Lindstrom asked, annoyed. "We would have been invaded. Like Norway and Denmark. A disaster. Thousands of young men sacrificed."

"But it would have meant Hitler had fewer troops to fight elsewhere. And today, many of us wouldn't be so ashamed."

"You are very young, Miss Johanson." Lindstrom's face had

flushed a light red. "We are fortunate that our government acted prudently. That is nothing to be ashamed of."

Alexander had listened to them, watching the back-and-forth.

Karin turned to him. "What do you think, Professor Kincaid?"

"Please call me Alexander," he said. "I'm a guest here, so I'll tread lightly. It's not my place to judge Sweden's decision to remain neutral. I can only speak as an American. After what I saw, what I experienced, in Germany, I only wish my country had entered the war earlier."

Karin rewarded him with a warm smile. She felt vindicated by his answer—it was clear that he agreed with her.

Professor Lindstrom cleared his throat. "A scholar and a diplomat," he said with a slight smile, turning to Alexander. "You'll go far, young man."

He nodded to them both and to Karin's delight, moved to talk to another couple, leaving them alone.

"Do you take an interest in politics, Miss Johanson?" Alexander asked her.

"Please call me Karin."

He nodded and smiled.

"I read the newspapers, of course, but that's not my main interest," she said quickly. "I'm really not political. I'm an artist."

"Is that so?"

She felt his eyes on her, and she blushed. "I've been drawing since I was a little girl. My aunt would scold me for getting my dresses dirty from my pencils and charcoal."

"What did you draw?"

"Everything I saw around me. People. Buildings. Animals. My parents encouraged me, bought me sketch pads. Then I discovered watercolors, and I experimented with the different colors. I loved it, and soon I tried oil paints. It opened my eyes!"

She explained that she had taken several classes at the Royal Academy of Fine Arts. As part of the curriculum, she had studied the works of Swedish artists like Anders Zorn, Johan Axel Gustaf Törneman, and Eugène Fredrik Jansson. "I do admire Jansson's blue paintings," she said. "His nightscapes." She hesitated and then told him about her latest project, her paintings of scenes from the sagas.

"I find the sagas fascinating," she said. "So much of what we know about the Scandinavian past, our myths, comes from the skalds in Iceland, this tiny island. Not from Denmark or Sweden or Norway."

"What are you painting now?" he asked.

"The story of Saemundr the Learned," she said. "It should appeal to you, as a scholar and diplomat. Saemundr the Learned was a priest and scholar from Iceland in the eleventh century. As it happened, he desperately needed to get from Paris to Iceland, and to do so he made a pact with the Devil. He negotiated a ride home on the back of a seal in exchange for his immortal soul. When Saemundr and the seal neared the shore, he hit the seal on the snout with his book, a thick Bible, stunning it, and then swam to safety before the Devil could respond."

"Quite a legend. I would very much like to see your painting."

"It's not done yet," she said. "Another month and I should be finished."

He smiled and remained silent. Karin was flattered by his curiosity, his interest in her not only as a pretty young woman but also as an artist. Would he pursue her romantically? She found herself hoping so. She realized she had told him a lot about herself.

When it came time for Alexander to leave to return to his hotel, she accompanied him to the front walk. They had a few moments alone and he brought his face close to hers and gave her a soft kiss on the lips, thrilling her. She had kissed a boy or two, but never a man—certainly not one as confident and assured as Alexander.

"I will be back in a month," he told her.

"Another lecture?"

"No," he said. "To see your painting and to court you properly."

She averted her eyes for a moment. "I would like that," she managed to say.

Karin spent the next month in her studio, hard at work on her painting. She portrayed Saemundr as a handsome bearded young man with one hand on the seal's neck and the other holding the Bible aloft. She wanted to capture the moment before he struck the seal. She tried not to think too much about the handsome young American who had kissed her, but it was hard not to. He was unlike anyone she had ever met before, and she knew that was part of his appeal.

Karin wanted to marry some day. She wanted a family. Was this American professor the right man? Could she spend the rest of her life with him? Would Alexander Kincaid be a good husband? She thought he might, but how could she be sure?

When Alexander returned to Stockholm he came directly to the

Johansons' house. Karin took him directly to her studio and boldly took his hand and brought him in front of the painting of Saemundr.

He studied it carefully and then turned to her. "It's marvelous," he said. "It brings the story to life."

"Do you think so?"

"I do. You're very talented. I suspect this is not the first time you've been told that."

That night he took her to dinner at Den Gyldene Freden, the Golden Peace, in Old Town. She wore her favorite light yellow dress and the golden earrings her mother had given her on her eighteenth birthday, knowing that the combination complimented her hair.

He seemed much older than her, even though there wasn't a large age gap—six years or so by her calculation. He had been to war, he had traveled extensively, his family had wealth. Karin was the only daughter of an absent-minded professor of biology, and she had been shielded from much of the unpleasantness of life.

He told her about his upbringing in Boston, and his travels around the country with his father, who was a lawyer for manufacturing interests, and had taken Alexander with him on business trips to New York, Chicago, San Francisco, and Los Angeles. Alexander's scientific interests in college and graduate school had meant field trips to South America and Africa.

"It sounds so exciting," she said. "I envy you. I haven't traveled to many places. Norway and Denmark. Paris. Not very far. Never to your country."

"Would you like to see America?" he asked.

"I would."

"Would you like to see it with me?"

"What are you asking?"

"Marry me. Come with me. We'll see the world together. All those places I talked about and more. You can bring your sketch pad. It will be an adventure for the two of us. Together."

He didn't take his eyes from her face. She wasn't surprised by the suddenness of his proposal. During the war years, many marriages had been carried off at short notice after whirlwind courtships. Karin found his decisiveness exciting and loved that she would not have to abandon her painting if she married. He valued her artistic side. Did she love him? She wasn't sure, but he was very attractive, and he desired her. She wondered what sort of lover he might be, and found herself blushing.

"I don't know you well enough."

"I think you do," he said. "Marry me, Karin. I've fallen for you. I hoped you might feel the same."

She studied his face for a long moment, and then, surprising herself, nodded. "Yes," she said. "I will marry you."

The following morning, Alexander formally asked her father for her hand in marriage. Karin's parents seemed pleased with the match, although they were saddened by the thought of their daughter leaving Täby for life in America.

Karin and her mother spent the early afternoon planning the wedding. Alexander needed to return to the U.S. in three weeks, so they decided on a small ceremony in the local church. After lunch, Karin changed into one of her favorite sundresses and her father drove them to the city and dropped the couple off. At one of the best jewelry stores in Stockholm, they picked out matching gold wedding bands.

She smiled when he suggested they rest in his hotel room before returning to Täby. "Will we rest?" she asked, teasing him.

"That depends on you," he said.

Once they were in his room, he kissed her on the lips and took her hand. "You are very beautiful, Karin Johanson," he said. "I would like to make love to you."

"I would like that, Alexander," she said and kissed him. They undressed each other, and Karin was surprised to find that she wasn't shy around him. They slipped under the sheets, and he began to caress her slowly, touching her breasts and thighs. She pulled him closer, enjoying the strangeness of a male body next to her. She knew what was going to happen next, and she felt herself readying for him. He kissed her again and entered her gently and slowly, and then began to press deeper into her. There was some discomfort and then Karin found herself responding, gasping with unexpected pleasure at the rhythm of his movements. He whispered her name and she felt the sudden warmth of his climax inside her.

Alexander held her in his arms, stroking her hair, and she laid her head on his chest. She was happy—in the space of a day she had become a woman, and would soon be married to a man who she admired and who respected her.

"You're my first," she told him. "I'm glad we didn't wait until the wedding night."

"Why is that?"

"I didn't want to wait, and I didn't want that night to be awkward. Our first time as husband and wife. And now, it won't be."

Karin enjoyed living in Cambridge while Alexander finished his doctorate at Harvard. Alexander rented a spacious house on Williard Street, where she could easily walk to Harvard Square and drink coffee and stop by the Fogg Art Museum and admire its collection of Early American and Impressionist paintings. She was delighted to find works by Paul Cézanne, Edgar Degas, Édouard Manet, and Henri Matisse there, paintings which had been recently donated to the Fogg after the death of a wealthy collector, Maurice Wertheim.

There was a small first-floor room in the house where Karin set up her studio. She spent her mornings wandering around with a sketch pad, looking for scenes to draw. In the afternoon she would paint.

She had stretches of loneliness, far from home. Alexander's older sister, Priscilla, was his only family, and she spent most of the year on Martha's Vineyard. Wilson and Constance Kincaid, Alexander and Priscilla's parents, had been killed in a late-night car accident years before, driving back to Boston from Woods Hole. A drunk driver had crossed lanes and crashed into their car head-on. Karin had asked about the accident, but Alexander had been reluctant to talk about his parents' tragic deaths.

"It must have been terrible," Karin said.

"It was a dark time," he said. "I try not to dwell on it."

"I'm sorry."

Alexander shrugged. "I learned about randomness during the war. No rhyme or reason behind who lived and who died. It just happened. Had my parents taken an earlier ferry back from Vineyard Haven they wouldn't have been on the highway at the same time as that intoxicated idiot. Wrong place, wrong time. As I said, there's no point in dwelling on it."

One consequence of the accident was that the Kincaid children became financially independent—the estate was quite extensive. They sold the Beacon Hill place, and Priscilla moved to the Edgartown house; it was agreed that Alexander would inherit the Boca Grande winter home when Uncle Blake died (he was in a nursing home, in poor health).

Karin wasn't surprised when Alexander accepted a tenure-track faculty position at Princeton. She wondered whether he wanted the change in part because of the memories of his parents inevitably connected to Boston. Princeton was a small town, not a city, and while she couldn't deny its charms, she felt quite isolated immediately after their move.

She made few friends at the start. One of them, Tessa Knight, told Karin that she had experienced the same thing when she arrived in Princeton. Tessa was the wife of one of Alexander's colleagues in the Biology Department.

"You're new and different," Tessa explained. "And there's a fair bit of jealousy."

"Jealousy?"

"You're a dead ringer for Grace Kelly. They see the way their husbands look at you. You want other reasons? You're married to a brilliant man on the rise, and you're an artist. No children tugging at your apron, yet. You have the freedom they don't have. It's more than enough to make them jealous."

"I'm not like that," Karin replied. "I don't want their attention. The men, I mean."

"Enjoy it while you can," Tessa said. She patted her right hip. "Twenty pounds since Betsy. I just can't seem to lose the weight. You'll see, once you start having babies. So enjoy being the sexy Swede."

Karin's first pregnancy, with Wilson, proved a difficult one. She was in labor for ten hours, and she was exhausted and drained by the time they placed her son in her arms. Alexander was delighted, passing around cigars to his colleagues. Two years later James was easier. Her mother came from Stockholm and stayed with them for six months, and she insisted that the Kincaids hire a nanny. Karin wanted a large family, and she welcomed the arrival of her third, Desmond. Hanna was a different matter, a surprise pregnancy, but Karin was pleased to finally have a little daughter.

She grew used to the rhythms of the University's academic calendar: the arrival of students in September; the golden autumn with its faculty teas and tailgate parties and football games; the reading period after the Christmas holidays followed by January's first semester exams; the spring with its own cycle of classes and lectures, and finally the pomp and ceremony of graduation and Reunion, with its P-rade, a procession of alumni down Nassau Street.

"Like salmon returning to the spawning grounds," Alexander said with a smile.

There were some specific times she so looked forward to—spring break in the Boca Grande beach house, the quiet of June after school let out—and ones she dreaded—the holiday cocktail party Alexander insisted that they host, the boring faculty gatherings where the men congregated in a corner drinking and smoking cigars, ignoring their wives (and Alexander was occasionally guilty of abandoning her for that circle, although he was better than most of his colleagues).

She discovered how little time she had for herself. Even with a nanny helping with the children, there was always something—a doctor's or dentist's appointment for one of the boys, a teacher's conference, planning for a dinner party—that demanded her attention. She found herself painting less and less. When she found herself in the studio at the end of her day, she was too exhausted to concentrate and make much progress.

Karin wasn't about to complain to Alexander. He had his own concerns, the obligations of teaching and research and writing, to say nothing of fieldwork. And, she told herself, he wasn't to blame. She hadn't anticipated what being a mother to four children would mean. When she read Virginia Woolf's "A Room of One's Own" she found herself deeply moved. How could she balance her desire to create art and her duties as a mother? It was very hard.

"I imagine that I must wait until the children are older," she told Tessa. "That shouldn't be too long."

"You should tell Alexander that you need time to paint. Hire more nannies. Whatever you need to carve out the time." Tessa frowned. "You have a right to be happy, too."

"It's not that I'm unhappy. It's just that something is missing. I guess I can wait."

Tessa shook her head. Lincoln Knight had abandoned Tessa for a graduate teaching assistant he met at an academic conference in Chicago, leaving her to raise Betsy and Emma by herself. It had been the scandal of the season. "Don't compromise so much that you lose yourself," she said. "I gave up my academic career for Linc, that bastard, to look after the girls, and look at my reward."

Karin didn't respond. She didn't see any similarity between her situation and Tessa's. She didn't worry about Alexander straying—he wasn't the sort of man who would leave his wife and children, and he still desired her as a woman. And she couldn't see asking him to bring on more domestic help; one nanny seemed enough. No, she would wait until all of the children were in school and she had the peace and quiet she needed to paint. It wasn't a great sacrifice to make, or so she told herself.

FIVE

ALEXANDER

July 22, 1960

Dear Pri,

We've been back in Princeton three days and I've finally had a chance to sit down and write you.

Thank you again for hosting Karin, for looking after her during a particularly trying time.

When I picked her up in Edgartown to take her to the ferry, she was rested, happy, full of energy—a far cry from the depressed woman I dropped off five weeks ago. The turn in her mood was nothing short of miraculous, and you deserve the credit.

Karin tells me that you and Dolores took her sailing and that Dolores took her to the tennis courts and gave her lessons. How often does one learn tennis from a player who competed at Forest Hills and Wimbledon?

The sea air and the sunshine and your care and attention have worked wonders.

I'll confess now how deeply worried I was about Karin. Her pregnancy with Hanna was difficult. Her obstetrician, Dr. Chapman, told me that her delivery, which was prolonged, was quite taxing. In the days that followed Hanna's birth, her apparent disinterest in the baby was shocking. I had never seen her like that. She was exhausted. She didn't bounce back the way she had after Wilson and James and Desmond. Was it because her mother didn't come from Stockholm to help out this time, as she did with the other boys? Did that contribute to Karin's negative state of mind? Or were there other factors? A proclivity to sadness and moodiness? I'm not sure what the cause was. Karin seemed bewildered by the change in her emotional state.

Dr. Chapman was reluctant to label her condition postpartum depression, but I'm convinced that was the proper diagnosis. When he strongly advised that she rest in a quiet environment, preferably in a resort setting with fresh air and sun, your offer to host her on the Vineyard was a Godsend.

Karin is never one to complain. I don't think it's like Swedes to gripe or whine. They're Nordic Stoics, a function of their forbidding weather and tight-lipped culture if I had to hazard a guess.

The last two years have been difficult for Karin. We lost a child to a miscarriage last year. When she became pregnant with Hanna, we were both relieved and pleased. Was it too soon after the miscarriage? I do wonder about that, now.

I made a field trip to Africa last year, which meant Karin had to handle the children by herself and our nanny, Helga. Wilson came down with the measles, and then James, and then Desmond. It wasn't easy for Karin. When I returned I could tell she was resentful, but she didn't say anything at first. What's the saying: go into marriage with two eyes open, but once in it, keep one eye shut. She was keeping that eye closed.

While she was with you on the Vineyard, the boys missed their mother, but you know how boys of the age of Wilson and James strive to hide their feelings. Des, on the other hand, was quite vocal in his unhappiness over Karin's absence. By the way, Wilson's friends have nicknamed him "Beau," because he organizes the fun and games, just as the oldest brother in the movie "Beau Geste" does. Beau is the neighborhood knight, and James is the storyteller. Sometimes James' imagination is too active—he is a vivid dreamer and suffers from nightmares now and then.

Children do have a mind of their own. Beau is quite headstrong and I've had to discipline him more often than I would like. He appears to have a very strong spatial intelligence—he's disassembled several vacuum cleaners and a radio or two.

There's an irony that as I struggle with these family issues, my work has never gone better. I've had a long productive stretch since returning from the field, with several journal articles published, and two guest lectures.

I've continued to work on the ideas I mentioned when we had our brief talk on the Vineyard. I'm struck by how often I encounter the social patterns I've observed in primate populations reflected in human behavior. We are animals, after all, although we're embarrassed by it, like Victorian ladies denying their sexual urges and wearing layer after layer of clothing to disguise the shape of their bodies. We think we've transcended our evolutionary past, but we haven't. We're crafty and adaptable, but the DNA we share with our hominoid cousins can't be denied.

Others have begun to consider some of these questions. At Harvard, there's a brilliant man by the name of E.O. Wilson who studies, of all things, ants. Ants! There's talk he is working on a general theory of biology. One of his colleagues, Stuart Altmann, has written on the social behavior of rhesus macaques, and he is said to be like-minded with Wilson on evolutionary questions. I guess you could say I'm firmly in their camp.

I hope to write about these topics someday, although it will have to wait until I'm more established and can deal from a position of relative academic strength. I'm sure that what I may have to say at the start will be met with resistance. Any fundamental reappraisal is. While all scientific theories are meant to be provisional, they quickly are elevated to conventional wisdom. Reputations are made. Government grants won. There are plenty of people ready to defend the old order and attack the barbarians at the gates who dare to challenge the pieties of the past. (I apologize for the clumsy mixed metaphors.) So I will bide my time. It's not as if I don't have enough occupying me, with my field studies and several papers I've been drafting for submission to the leading journals.

As always, you and Dolores are welcome to join us at Thanksgiving. My best to you both.

Your devoted brother,

Alex

P.S. I do hope young Jack beats Tricky Dick in the fall. I've met him a few times in Cambridge at social events and he's quite bright, although he does have a reputation as being a bit of a playboy. (I'd rather have him chasing skirts than emptying whiskey bottles like half of the pols in Washington). And wouldn't it be grand to have a president who appreciates the life of the mind?

PART TWO

SIX

JULIA

The snapshot has faded, the Kodachrome leached by time and continued exposure to sunlight, the colors no longer vivid, but there we are nonetheless—Beau, Jimmy, and myself—proudly posing in front of the gigantic American beech tree that towered over the backyard of the Kincaid's house on Prospect Avenue. There we are. It's the only photograph I can find of the three of us when we were that young, an impromptu group portrait snapped by Karin Kincaid with her Brownie Starmite camera.

The last time I walked by the tree still stood there commanding the backyard. It had been pruned back somewhat by the new owners, but its branches covered most of the yard, keeping it in shade, except for the north side, where the sun catches a trellis adorned with climbing roses. The tree remains large, as large as in my memory, and that is satisfying in a world where so much seems to shrink with the passage of time.

When I look at the photo, I am struck by how handsome the boys are, squinting in the sun as they smile ("Say 'cheese'!" Karin had commanded us in her accented English). They are tall and lanky, these Kincaid boys, a family trait: Beau, thirteen years old, his dark hair long in the style of the time, on the verge of becoming a man, his intensity visible in his taut features; Jimmy, almost eleven, still in a crew cut, with that same slightly puzzled look on his freckled face that I have always loved. You can see the men they will become in that photo, evidence of the adult persona, there, under that innocent exterior, the steel in Beau, Jimmy's endless curiosity.

And what of me? I am squeezed in between them, a head shorter, my face tilted slightly upward to the right because I had been watching Beau just before Karin clicked the shutter. I was drawn to him, always pulled by his mysterious and magnetic force. My streaked blonde hair is in bangs—I am nine years old, a year younger than Jimmy, not yet old enough to argue for the extravagant fashions of the day, the Haight-Ashbury bell-bottom jeans, the psychedelic tie-dyed t-shirts in garish purples and yellows. Thank God I was too young for that grubby look. In the photo, I wear a simple jumper of light blue corduroy.

When I study the picture, I wonder about that little girl, about what I was thinking then, just before the click of the shutter. Aren't our memories like coats of paint, slapped down one on top of the other, layered and mixed together so that they cannot be separated? What I can remember are impressions from that time—still strong—of how I adored Beau, and how I believed he could do no wrong, and how I thought of Jimmy as my best friend in the world.

Beau owes his nickname to me. He had been christened Wilson and had gone by his full name, or Will, until I began calling him Beau, when I was eight years old, after I first saw the movie *Beau Geste*. The name stuck, for good reason, because Jimmy and the third Kincaid brother, Desmond, followed Beau's lead just like the two younger Gestes followed their older brother in the movie. Back then, we all followed Beau.

We always climbed too high and too fast in that damn beech tree, Beau's favorite tree. But we followed his lead, all of us, and I so desperately wanted Beau to notice me, to know that I was loyal and true. So I went higher than a small, nine-year-old girl should have, desperate to keep up with the Kincaid boys.

I remember the shocking suddenness of the fall, my Keds slipping on the grayish bark of the trunk and then my body weight shifting and my right hand violently tearing away from the branch. My body bounced off limbs and snapped branches on my descent, and the lush July fullness of the tree probably saved my life, painfully slowing my plunge to the ground.

It happened so quickly that all I could think was *I am falling* and then moments later I hit the ground hard, stunned by the abruptness of it all, my left arm pinned under me with a sudden sharp pain I had never experienced before.

Above me, I heard Jimmy calling for his brother, a strange, frantic note in his voice. "It's Julia. She's fallen. Hurry, we have to help her!"

I knew I was hurt, but not how badly. I was scared and dazed by the fall. I stirred cautiously.

"I'm okay," I called out, struggling to catch my breath. That initial shock was starting to wear off and I could feel searing pain in my arm whenever I moved. "I'm okay," I called out, again, only I wasn't, even though I wished desperately that it was true.

It seemed only moments before Jimmy was at my side, and seconds later, Beau joined us. He had descended from the heights of the tree—like Johnny Weissmuller in one of the Tarzan movies, it seemed to me, swinging from branch to branch—and as I looked up at their faces gazing down at me in concern, I was secretly delighted, despite the pain, by the sudden, focused attention of both older Kincaids. I sat up, cradling my left arm in my lap, and felt dizzy from the sudden surge of pain. Unbidden, tears came to my eyes.

"Where does it hurt," Beau asked.

"My arm," I told him in a whisper.

"Anywhere else?"

I bobbed my head no, but that wasn't completely the truth. I ached all over. Still, I could tell that my arm had been badly hurt. I knew tears were streaming down my cheeks, their saltiness already reaching my lips. I gritted my teeth against the throbbing pain in my arm.

"Run to the house," Beau commanded his brother. "Tell Mom that Julia fell from the tree and hurt her arm. She should call for the ambulance and for Mrs. King. Julia has to go to the hospital. I'll stay with her here."

Jimmy disappeared from sight and I heard his footsteps on the wooden steps of the Kincaid house and then the slamming of the back door.

I leaned back against the tree trunk, my left arm limp on my lap. I could see there was blood on my skin and wondered if it was from being scratched by the branches during my fall. Beau was looking intently at my arm, too, and I remembered that he had earned a Boy Scout merit badge in First Aid.

"Don't move," Beau said. "They'll be here soon and will take care of you."

"It hurts," I said. "It really, really hurts."

"I'm sorry."

"It's not your fault," I told him. "I'm the one who fell."

"I should never have let you climb so high. I should have known."

"You couldn't have known, Beau," I said. "I must have slipped."

"You're very brave," Beau said to me, brushing back the bangs from my forehead and then kissing me on the cheek, gently. It was the first time that Beau—the fierce warrior when we battled with snowballs in our neighborhood wars, the leader, the architect and conductor of our play—had shown any tenderness toward me.

With his face so close to me, it was so easy for me to shift slightly and kiss him back, but full on the lips, delighting in the sensation, but paying for it with a sudden jolt of burning pain in my arm. Beau heard me gasp.

"Please don't move," he said.

"I won't."

He didn't say anything about the kiss.

"I am going to stay with you," he said. "I'll come to the hospital. You'll be fine. They will fix your arm and it will be just fine."

In the distance, I could hear the sound of an ambulance siren. It grew louder by the moment as it neared us. I believed Beau when he said I would be fine, despite the pain in my arm and my dread of what I suspected lay ahead, of the doctors and their needles. If Beau was convinced then I was convinced. I saw Beau glance over toward the house and then Jimmy and Mrs. Kincaid—the boy's ravishingly beautiful Swedish mother—appeared.

"Julia," she said. "I have telephoned and your mother is coming. How are you feeling?"

"It hurts," I said. "But it's my fault. No one else."

"It was an accident. No one is at fault."

I don't remember much more from that point on because that was when I fainted. They told me later that Beau was true to his word, staying with me as best he could. While they wouldn't let him ride in the ambulance with me (Beau had a spirited argument with the paramedic), he convinced Karin that he should go along with my mother to the emergency room.

He waited there with my mother for hours, staying through the X-rays and examinations and then my surgery.

I have a few sharply-defined memories of the hospital: the grinding sound of the X-ray machine with its evil-looking dark cone pointed at my arm; the suffocating mask descending over my face as I was anesthetized; waking up with a fresh, dazzling white plaster-of-Paris cast on my arm; and the half-surprise of finding my mother and father (who had reached the hospital then) by my bedside and my mother saying, "Hello, sweetheart." I was surprised at the huskiness in my father's voice and the rush of my mother's tears.

I did not know that Dr. Brewer, the orthopedic surgeon who had set my arm, had informed my parents that the fracture had just missed the growth plate. If the break had been five millimeters closer to the wrist, he told them grimly, I might have ended up with a left arm permanently shorter than my right.

Beau wasn't allowed to see me then—even though I asked for him—but he was there when my parents brought me home the next day. Always the romantic, I hoped that his appearance might signal the beginning of love on Beau's part. Perhaps our kiss would draw him to my side. Years later I realized a more likely explanation for his behavior was simple guilt. It was *his* tree, and he hadn't kept me from falling out of it. When he came over to our house and my father brought him to the living room—where they had me propped on the couch—I insisted that he sign my cast first, and only after he had scrawled his name (*Get Well, Julia – Beau*) would I let Jimmy and Des and my other friends sign.

Beau devoted himself to my recovery, visiting every afternoon for the full three days my parents kept me inside, filling me in on the latest happenings in the neighborhood. I had a miserable summer because the cast had to be removed, and replaced, twice and I was under strict orders not to run or engage in rough play. What was worse was that it was Beau who enforced my sentence—refusing to let me participate in anything remotely strenuous, which meant all the best games, from capture-the-flag to kickball to cannonball splashes in the community pool, were off-limits. But at least it meant Beau was paying attention to me, and I reveled in that.

When they sawed my cast off and removed the stitches I was ashamed of the atrophied wrinkled, pale arm underneath it, and the angry scar where the bone had pierced my skin. It took more than six months before my left arm looked like it belonged to me. Until then I wore unfashionable long-sleeves.

I kept the secret of my after-the-fall kiss that Beau had bestowed upon me, and the kiss on his lips I offered in response. At times I worried that in my pain and fear and confusion that I had imagined it all, but the memory was so vivid that I somehow knew it had happened. I was sure Beau remembered as well. How could he not?

I carried the secret hope that it signified something more. I believed that somehow I was destined for Beau, and he was meant for me. I just had to be patient. Beau would come to love me, I believed, and in the meantime, I would stay true. I found the perfect description of the way I felt when I first read *Great Expectations* at the age of twelve. I told myself I loved Beau the way Pip loved Estella: "against reason, against promise, against peace, against hope, against happiness, against all disappointment that could be."

I guess, in the end, I was wrong. I was in college when I stumbled upon a quote from Anthony Trollope: "There is no happiness in love, except at the end of an English novel." But by then I knew that life wasn't at all like a novel. In the end, Beau wouldn't be the Kincaid brother I would marry.

That backyard photo is incomplete. It doesn't include Des Kincaid, who would have been nearing his eighth birthday, the third of the Kincaid brothers, nor Hanna, their little sister. Hanna is too young, just a toddler, so I'm not surprised by her absence. Des is a different matter. He was a sickly child, always battling his asthma, desperate to follow us, but often confined indoors. I can picture Des in his room, playing by himself with his cherished tin knights and a makeshift castle of wooden blocks, lost in his own private kingdom.

The tree may have been Beau's fortress, his place for testing climbing skills and courage, but for Des it became a place of refuge, his sanctuary from all that troubled him. It's not hard to understand why a child might climb a tree to get away from experiences he or she does not like—think of it, you are separated from others, free and clear from the ugliness on the ground, and you are hidden. If you climb high enough, no adult can reach you, as the tree branches will not support their weight. I think that was part of the tree's appeal for Des.

I don't pretend to know what drove Des to climb that tree more often as he grew older. I know it was common for him to ascend whenever there were arguments between Beau and his father, arguments that became more and more heated as Beau reached his late teens and asserted his independence. Professor Kincaid was not a man used to yielding, least of all to his oldest son, and the war between them raged for most of Beau's high school years, with occasional truces. All of us suffered in one way or the other from that conflict.

The substance of the disputes today seem almost laughable: how long Beau could wear his hair, whether he had to continue his trumpet lessons, and what were the consequences if he broke his curfew. No doubt their arguments mirrored what was going on between fathers and their sons all over the country—perhaps all over the world during that troubled time.

It was almost as if a virus of rebellion had spread from teenager to teenager through the music, the clothing, the politics. In Beau's case, it surfaced in different ways. It was what drove him to attend the University of Virginia against his father's expressed wishes and later to enlist in the Army, of all things, which made no sense unless you understood Beau. He had a first son's self-confidence, an unshakeable faith in his own judgment.

Jimmy, the calm observer, took the conflict between his brother and father in stride. He could see both sides and he often would give me a crisp summary of the latest dispute between Beau and Professor Kincaid. It was different for Des. He shied away from confrontation. He was more likely to retreat, to escape from the situation, than deal with it directly.

One September afternoon I found Jimmy sitting on the back porch, reading a copy of *Stranger in a Strange Land*. He gave me a wan smile when he looked up.

"Beau and the Professor are at it again," he said. "Beau got him yelling, and that doesn't happen too often."

"Where's your mother?"

"She took Hanna with her to the grocery store. Beau's in his room and my father is in the study with Beethoven playing on the stereo." That meant it had been a major upheaval. Professor Kincaid saved Beethoven's Fifth for his darker moods.

"Where's Des?"

"In the tree," Jimmy said, looking over my shoulder. "Where else?"

"A bad day?"

"A bad day."

"What was the argument over?"

"What does it matter?"

I climbed gingerly up about half of the tree. I didn't want to go any higher for I remembered my fall. I had gone back and climbed it again, of course, because I didn't want anyone thinking that I was chicken. I never ventured too high, though.

Fortunately, Des hadn't climbed to the top. I could see his body above me and I called out his name, but not too loudly, even though I can't imagine that we could be heard inside over the majestic strains of Beethoven emanating from the house. (When I married Jimmy I made him promise that he would never play classical music after we had quarreled. He agreed to my conditions and kept his promise. He confessed that Beethoven had been ruined for him—he couldn't hear the music without immediately flashing on Beau and his father yelling at each other.)

Finally, I had climbed high enough that Des could not pretend I wasn't there. I reached up and gently touched his sneaker resting on the juncture of the tree and the branch above me.

"What's going on, Des?" I asked.

"Not much."

"Will you come down with me?"

"I'm happy here," he said. "I don't want to be around them when they fight."

"Why don't you come down and we can go for a walk?"

"Thank you, but no," he said, always the politest of the Kincaid boys. "I'll stay here."

"Are you sure?"

"I'm not like the rest of them, you know," he said suddenly, defensively.

"Who?"

"Beau and Jimmy."

"You're not?"

"I'm not as smart as them."

"That's ridiculous. Of course you are."

I didn't say out loud what I was really thinking—that I wasn't sure that I was smart enough, either, for his family's constant intellectual jousting. Could I ever hope to match wits with Beau and Jimmy, let alone Professor Kincaid or Karin Kincaid? I was the daughter of a grocer, and my father had taken a few classes at Trenton State, not graduating. My mother hadn't gone to college.

Des stared down at me, a challenge in his eyes.

"I'm not sure that I'm as smart as them, either," I whispered to him.

"I'll never be like them. I don't want to argue all the time and prove how smart I am. It doesn't matter, anyway, does it?"

"Why don't we go get Popsicles?" I asked. "I've got enough money for both of us."

"I like you, Julia," he said. "You're always kind to me."

"And why shouldn't I be? You're kind, too, Des. Everyone says that."

"They do?"

"Of course. Now will you come with me to the store for Popsicles?"

Des nodded reluctantly, and we both climbed down the tree. As an only child, with no brothers or sisters, I understood loneliness. I could recognize the telltale signs in Des. He was lonely. I wondered how he could feel that way, surrounded by his brothers and his sister. Des was a loner, by nature. Of course, there was more to it. Only later did his struggle with depression surface.

When I was a month shy of my thirteenth birthday, I persuaded my parents to let me go with the Kincaids to Florida, to Boca Grande, over the winter school break. It had been my idea and I had cleverly maneuvered Jimmy and Des into inviting me. I pointed out to my mother that I would stay with Hanna in her room, so everything would be proper, and I let the brothers convince their mother.

The Kincaids stayed in a beach house owned by Professor Kincaid's uncle, and I did, indeed, room with Hanna, in one of the back bedrooms, but I spent much of my time with Jimmy and Des. I guess that was unusual for a girl at that age, but that's how it was.

I loved the island's narrowness—so little space between the Gasparilla Sound to the east and the Gulf of Mexico to the west—and its shady streets, with their banyan trees and ramshackle ancient cottages which had weathered a hurricane or two. I admired the turn-of-the-century look of the Port Boca Grande Lighthouse at the tip of the island, next to the pass where the tarpon fishing was said to be the finest in the world.

The air was sweet and warm and the sunlight seemed to cascade everywhere, illuminating everything in a clear light. The contrast to Princeton's February dingy gray couldn't have been sharper. When we waded into the Gulf, it was as warm as bathwater.

I would have stayed there for months, never going back to school, if I could.

We spent the week playing tennis and swimming in the Gulf and biking around the island. Beau joined us on occasion, but he kept to himself most of the time, curling up with one of the books he always seemed to be reading (for this vacation it happened to be Ayn Rand's *The Fountainhead*).

I knew why he was moping—he was in love, and he hadn't made any headway with the girl. It made me jealous.

I acted on that jealousy one Thursday when the Professor and Karin took Jimmy, Des, and Hanna for a late lunch at the Boca Grande Club. When I found out that Beau wasn't going, I faked a headache so I could stay in the cottage.

I waited ten minutes before I invaded his bedroom and found

him lying on his back, lost in thought. I sat next to him on the bed and, summoning up my courage, boldly took his hand in mine. "Should I read your fortune?" I asked.

"Do you know how?" He was skeptical but he didn't pull his hand away.

I studied the palm of his hand, searching for the lifeline. I hadn't really thought through what I was going to tell him—it was just a pretext to get him alone.

"So you really want to know your future?" I asked. "Who might be in it?"

"That depends."

"What if I was the girl in it? In your future?"

"I'm not a cradle-robber," he said.

"I'm old enough." I held onto his hand and wriggled closer, a clumsy initial attempt at seduction. My bare leg touched his.

"I don't think so," he said. He moved away from me and rose to his feet, leaving the bed. "I'll give you a rain check, Julia. For when you're eighteen. But by then you'll know better."

"Why do I have to wait?" I asked. I stood up and closed the distance between us. "It can be sooner than that."

Beau shook his head. "You don't really know what you are saying."

So I put my arms around his waist and pulled him to me. Before he could protest, I had kissed him on the lips hard. I pressed my small breasts firmly against his chest and he didn't break away, at first, and I sensed that he was tempted. Then he was pushing me away with both of his hands.

"You're too young," he said. "Trust me."

"No, I'm not."

My words were directed at Beau's back, because he had walked away from me, out of the bedroom, and I had to hurry to catch up to him.

I was strangely happy, for I believed that I now had acquired some sway over Beau. I had made him notice me. He would have to see me in a different light.

I was proved wrong. If anything, my advances that day opened a gap between us that never closed. Beau kept his distance from then on. (Now, I'm glad he did.)

One Kincaid didn't resist me. When we became lovers—and he was my first and I was his—Jimmy told me that he thought we had always been destined to end up together. I smiled and didn't say anything. To this day I believe that we make our own destiny.

I know that I cherish that backyard photo because of how it transports me back in time, evoking all those lazy, seemingly endless days of play. The world may have been in turmoil around us—Martin Luther King, Jr. and Robert Kennedy had been assassinated, murdered, in the months before the photo was snapped, American boys were dying in a war no one believed in, and in Chicago the cops were about to bludgeon the college students chanting "The Whole World is Watching"—but we played on in our leafy Princeton neighborhood, untouched by the violence and discord, oblivious to the thunderclouds and the ugliness that was descending on the country, safe in our privileged haven.

I never wanted that to end, no matter how selfish or self-absorbed that sounds today. You could argue that I got what I wanted, in some ways, connected to the Kincaids as I am. As Julia King Kincaid I became a Kincaid by marriage, although I will never completely be one to the extent that my son, King Teilhard Kincaid, is. (That's some name to give a child, isn't it? I take responsibility only for the first name.) Even though King is my contribution, my bit, my nine months and so much more, for continuing the Kincaid line I will always be slightly outside the circle.

Yet some would say that I am the most inside of insiders. After years of diligent study, I'm an expert on all matters Kincaid. I could be the family historian for the Princeton branch, with a specialty in modern history, say from 1965 on. Sometimes I think I know more about Beau, Jimmy, Des, and Hanna—and the Professor and Karin—than they do themselves, because I was there, fascinated, observing, taking mental notes, missing little, if anything. And I am part of that history, now, intertwined in it to the point where I have lost all objectivity, where my memories aren't completely reliable. Whose memories ever are?

SEVEN

JAMES

Around our long mahogany dining table, we learned how to craft an argument, how to marshal evidence, how to defend our positions against our father's penetrating counterarguments, and how to devise convincing rebuttals. Julia once called it the Kincaid Debating Society and the name stuck.

Beau and I engaged in this ongoing verbal combat with my father from the time we entered middle school until we left Lafayette Place for college.

Des and Hanna watched us go back-and-forth, rarely entering the fray. When Julia joined us for dinner, she remained a silent observer, although she always had interesting takes on the discussion later.

"It's like a competition," she said once to me. "You and Beau trying to score points. And your father the scorekeeper."

"There's nothing wrong with competition."

"What does your Mom think about it?"

I shook my head. I didn't really know what my mother thought of the Kincaid Debating Society. She rarely participated.

I did know that the intellectual cut and thrust in the Kincaid household wasn't typical, that other families talked about the Yankees and the latest episode of *Bonanza* and other quotidian topics. At times, I envied the boys my age who were never challenged at the dinner hour.

The Kincaid brothers debated differently. Beau was more of a logical thinker; I was more intuitive in my approach. Once he had thought through the logic of a position, Beau would doggedly defend his views. My approach was more fluid. I liked to question my way to a sustainable case.

In that, I guess that I took after my father, with his commitment to the scientific method rooted in asking questions. Like father, like son, at least in this.

And Beau inherited his certainty from Alexander Tarkington Kincaid.

Our debates also encouraged us to read broadly, to find ammunition for our arguments, fresh evidence for our positions.

On the few occasions that Des joined in, he offered something witty, a clever play on words, or a quick dissection of the contradictions in our thinking.

Did I enjoy these dinner time sessions? They could be fun at times, as long as they didn't become too heated. I think Beau also welcomed the intellectual combat.

In retrospect, it was solid preparation for our future professions, the law and journalism.

I think my father saw it as preparation for life. In that, he was probably more right than wrong.

While Beau and I often united in debate with our father, we competed in other arenas. The classic sibling rivalry.

It seemed that I spent much of my childhood trying to keep pace with Beau. That competition shaped us both. It was easier for me, because as the second son, the expectations were lower. Beau was expected to lead the way, to come in first.

I looked up to my older brother—there was no hostility involved. When we fought, we fought as brothers, and afterward we were always friends.

And we were different. Beau possessed a self-confidence that I never seemed to be able to match. He was sure of himself. He had the cockiness of a first son.

Beau's certainty that he was in the right made clashes with our father inevitable. Their battles would become more and more pronounced, and more and more difficult over time, two stubborn men unwilling to bend. Their loss, and our loss.

It was during those years that I had the first of a series of vivid dreams. Sometimes they became nightmares. I once asked Beau if he dreamt very much and he laughed at me.

"Nope," he said. "I hardly ever dream."

"Are you sure? They say we all dream."

"Maybe that's so, but I don't remember them. So it's like they never happened."

I couldn't argue with that logic. But I remembered my dreams. They were always set someplace remote, places I had never been.

In one recurring dream, I knew I was lost. I wandered around in a desert trying to find water. In the distance, I could see palm trees—an oasis! As I walked toward the oasis, I could see a veiled woman ahead of me, in white robes, beckoning for me to come closer. But as I moved closer, her image would flicker and fade, and then disappear.

Had my dream been triggered by the romantic tale of the Lady of the Lake that I loved reading in *The Story of King Arthur and His Knights*? It had a striking illustration of the beautiful and mysterious Lady by Howard Pyle, the author and artist. No doubt it influenced me, but the face of the woman in my dream wasn't familiar.

I had darker dreams as well, ones where sirens would wail and there would be a roaring sound and a flash of light. I would cry out and wake up. As a child of the atomic age, it wasn't hard to figure out how those images had been seared into my subconscious.

Beau's political worldview changed after high school.

I would describe it more as an awakening than a transformation. Beau read the newspapers every day, as did I, but neither of us were political or partisan.

My parents were traditional Democrats: my father's heroes included Franklin Roosevelt, Harry Truman, and Jack Kennedy; my mother instinctively sided with the underdog, and she struggled to understand why her adopted country resisted the welfare state that Sweden had established. My father had been saddened by the turmoil on campus triggered by Vietnam, but he understood why students around the country were opposed to the war. Princeton didn't experience the same upheaval that Harvard, Columbia, and Cornell did, but there were a few radicals—and later, more, as the Academy veered leftward.

It was a trip to France during the summer between high school and his first year at the University of Virginia that triggered Beau's political awakening.

He had encountered open anti-Americanism and it had rubbed Beau the wrong way. "I hung around with a few college students," he told me. "My French was better than their English, believe it or not. They were eager to tell me how evil and immoral America was. Vietnam. Imperialism. Hamburgers and Coca Cola."

"How did you respond," I asked.

"I listened, at first. Politely. Didn't say anything much in response. But they wanted me to agree with them. I couldn't do that. I pointed out that Vietnam had been a French colony, and that they had a fought a war to try to hold onto it. For better or worse, we were backing Saigon to prevent a Communist takeover, like we did in Korea."

"How did they react?"

"A bit surprised. I don't think they were used to debating their views. Certainly not when it was a kid challenging them. Most of them just had picked up some half-baked radical slogans. Capitalism is doomed. The United States is racist and the source of evil in the world. I conceded that we have a long way to go to fashion that perfect union, but we're making progress. And I also reminded them without the U.S. Army, they would all be speaking German today. They didn't like that at all."

"Doesn't sound like you made any friends."

"With friends like that, who would need enemies?"

In the years that followed, Beau moved toward the right. (Just as the country did, with American hostages in Iran and Soviet troops invading Afghanistan.) In Charlottesville, where he went to college, radical types among his professors and classmates were few and far between—not like the students and faculty I encountered at Columbia who were fashionably left-of-center in their politics. UVA had been relatively untouched by the anti-war movement, no main buildings occupied, no prolonged student strike with a list of demands to the administration. It was a conservative school with a conservative, largely-male student body—it had only become fully coeducational at the end of the decade.

Beau divided his time between his studies and, beginning in his junior year, flying lessons at Charlottesville–Albemarle Airport, north of the city. He took a course on military history and told me that he had flirted with enlisting in ROTC.

I frustrated Beau with my political moderation. I lacked his certainty on the issues of the day; I always wondered if I had all the facts, whether I was missing something, and I was reluctant to arrive at a final judgment. Where Beau saw black and white, I saw gray. Later, as a journalist, I rarely encountered a story where there wasn't ambiguity or fuzziness and I became wary of the passion of the true believers—William Butler Yeats had it right about how "the best lack all conviction."

I watched with interest, and with some concern, as Beau's views hardened. We are shaped by our experiences, by what we encounter in our journey through life; that Beau's politics turned more hawkish reflected his entry into the warrior culture of the professional military, a path that surprised us at the time, but later seemed almost inevitable.

EIGHT

JULIA

Princeton, 1970

I never expected the romance between Beau and Angela Jackson to last for as long as it did. They were high school students, after all, when brief flings and dramatic breakups were all too common. Then, there was another complication: Angela was black, one of the few African-Americans enrolled at Princeton High School. It's hard enough to handle a relationship at that age let alone the complications of dating someone of a different color during a time when racial tensions were high.

The first time I saw them together, in the hallway of the high school, it was clear how they were drawn to each other. They were talking and laughing and I could tell where things were headed. They had eyes only for each other.

The truth about how I felt? I was jealous at first. Angela had won Beau's heart so quickly and completely and that alone turned me against her. And I envied her physical beauty, her long legs, the curly ringlets of her hair, and her smooth, light-brown skin. She seemed already a woman, when I was still a girl in many ways. What made it even worse was that Angela was much more than a pretty face—she was very smart. She wrote poetry and was president of the French Club and had earned A's in two Advanced Placement classes, English and U.S. History.

I suppose I shouldn't have been so jealous of her. I had begun dating Jimmy, but I guess I still felt possessive about Beau.

After I got to know Angela better, I understood why she so appealed to Beau. She was mature and independent and she thought for herself. That intrigued him. Angela wasn't in awe of Beau. She was willing to stand up to him. When they argued, she won as much as she lost.

"I've never seen Beau like this," my friend Adrienne Harris said. She had long had a crush on Beau, and I think she was also jealous. "Angela Jackson must have hypnotized him. She's got him wrapped around her little finger. It seems like he never leaves her side."

I shook my head, still loyal to Beau and to my image of him as the Alpha male in charge, Beau Geste. "He has the upper hand. I'm sure of that."

"Are you? Felicia Winters says Beau is lucky that Angela agreed to go steady. Angela's last boyfriend was a Rutgers student." Adrienne lowered her voice. "He was one of those black militants. That's what Felicia heard."

"I don't believe rumors," I said. "As far as I'm concerned, *she's* the lucky one."

"Do you think they're, you know, doing it?"

I made a face. "How would I know?" I assumed Beau and Angela were sleeping together, but I wasn't about to share that with Adrienne.

"I think they are," she said. "And if I were in her shoes, I'd be spending as much time alone with Beau as I could."

Angela lived close to Community Park School in the neighborhood occupied by most of Princeton's African-Americans for decades. Her family's rented house stood just three blocks away from the FitzRandolph Gate, the famous entry to the Princeton campus. She lived a quick walk or bike ride from Lafayette Place but the distance between there and the Jackson's modest home might as well have been thousands of miles.

Once, I tried to explain to Angela that I also felt out of place in Princeton. My parents worked for a living in unglamorous jobs, and neither had college degrees. We didn't take winter vacations in sunny places. I wore jeans and a t-shirt to school because I didn't have a closet full of fashionable dresses and blouses. I confessed that I often felt uncomfortable around the Kincaids. "So we have that in common," I said. "But it gets better the longer you know them."

She shook her head. "We don't have that much in common," she said. "It's different for me."

"But my family isn't wealthy," I replied.

"But you're white."

I shut up at that point. I could have continued to argue that we were on the same side of the class divide in Princeton, the invisible but real barrier between *them* and us. But she was right. It was different for her and always would be. Had Princeton ever truly welcomed its black neighbors? Woodrow Wilson, the president of the University before he went to the White House, was a dedicated segregationist, a Southerner with deeply ingrained prejudices. The student body had been drawn from privileged white families for decades.

Many on the Princeton faculty and those wealthy families living in the Borough would have considered themselves enlightened on the question of race, but I doubt any of them really saw people with darker skins as equal. They had their own club and they were choosy about who became members, and while I might someday join through my connection with the Kincaids, I doubted the door would ever be opened for Angela.

One Friday night in late October, I caught a glimpse of the depth of Beau's feelings for Angela. They had been going steady for months by then.

Beau invited Jimmy and me to join him and Angela for dinner at the Princetonian Diner on Route 1. Beau drove with Angela in the passenger seat and I was happy to sit in the backseat with Jimmy and hold hands. The waitress led us to a corner booth and we ordered Cokes and hamburgers and fries.

A beefy, red-faced man occupied a nearby table. He was talking to another man with a crew cut and a bad complexion. The red-faced man looked over at us and made a snorting sound. I was sitting closest to him, and when he began making nasty comments, I could hear what he was saying. It was ugly and racial and aimed at Angela and why Beau was with her.

"I get it," he said loudly. "I'd like some of that brown sugar, myself. Even if I wouldn't be the first to get a taste."

That must have crossed the line for Beau because he scrambled to his feet. Angela stared at the Formica table top. My heart went out to her—she had to be hurt by his vile comment.

Beau walked over to the table where the red-faced man sat with his friend. Jimmy shot me a worried look. We both knew how volcanic Beau's temper could be. There was something scary about him when he was angry, how underneath his cool exterior you could sense barely controlled fury.

He stood in front of the man, his hands clenched in fists.

"I heard what you had to say," Beau said. "So now, you're going to shut your mouth."

"Or what?"

"Or I'll shut it for you."

The man stood up and faced Beau. He was bigger than Beau, but he was out-of-shape, with a beer belly. "You're a kid. You're not telling me to do anything."

"I can bench press 230 pounds," Beau said. "And I've been boxing since I was ten. You want to risk getting your ass kicked by a kid?"

Beau stared at the man, their eyes locked. I think that was when the man began to waver. Beau didn't flinch, and I think the man realized he wasn't going to back down.

"Screw you," the man said. "I'm gonna cut you a break and not take you out to the parking lot. We're finished here anyway."

Beau had kept his voice down, and there were only a few people in the diner who could have heard the conversation. Beau didn't move and the red-faced man and his friend got up and went and paid their bill and left the diner.

Beau returned to our booth and sat down. I could see that his hands were trembling slightly.

"You didn't need to do that," Angela said.

"If he had kept his thoughts to himself, I wouldn't have gone over there," Beau replied. "But I'll be damned if we have to sit here and listen to his racist filth."

"Were you ready to fight him?" she asked. "Really?"

"No need," Beau said. "Like most bullies, he was all mouth."

"Never thought we'd run into that sort of crap here in Princeton," Jimmy said.

"Then you need to wake up," Angela said. "What do you think it's like for someone like me? What people say, or don't say?"

"I don't know what it's like," Jimmy said. "How could I?"

"You scared me," I told Beau. "I was afraid what you might do to him."

"And what would that accomplish?" Angela asked. "Do you think it would teach him a lesson?" She placed her right hand over Beau's. "I'm not looking for a knight to defend me." She smiled, softening her tone. "Certainly not a white knight."

I'm sure that Beau thought long and hard before he invited Angela to dinner at Lafayette Place. He made sure that Jimmy asked me to join them that night. It took me years before I felt completely comfortable at the Kincaid's dining room table. Angela must have been intimidated by her surroundings, but to her credit, she didn't show any noticeable discomfort.

She was so beautiful that night in her sundress, her soft curly hair pinned up, her features so animated when she talked. I could see why Beau had fallen for her, and so could everyone around the table.

"We're happy when Beau invites friends over," Alexander said. "Julia comes to dinner all the time."

That was an exaggeration, but I could see he was trying to put Angela at ease. I just smiled and nodded my head.

"I'm glad to be here," she said.

"Beau tells me you write poetry," Karin said.

"I try." Angela shot Beau a look. It seemed she wasn't pleased with him for sharing that information with his mother. "I'm still learning."

"Mrs. Davis told our English class that Angela's poems are quite impressive," Beau said, keeping his eyes on his mother.

"And what do you write about, Angela?" Karin asked.

"My experiences. My emotions. Stories I've heard from my parents."

"And what do they do?"

"My father is a house painter," she said. "My mother is a cleaning lady."

"I see." Karin's expression didn't change.

"Houses need cleaning and someone has to," I said, trying to help and earning a quick nod of appreciation from Angela.

"And how long has your family lived in Princeton?" Karin asked.

"All my life," Angela replied. "My grandfather was born in Princeton, two years before Paul Robeson, the singer. They used to play hide-and-seek in the Witherspoon Street Presbyterian Church where Paul's father was the minister for a time there."

"Robeson's an impressive man, a Renaissance man," Alexander said, and paused, considering his words. "Athlete, lawyer, actor, singer. A tragedy that so many doors were closed to him, although he didn't help himself with his politics. Quite radical at times. He's no longer performing, is he?"

"He lives in Philadelphia with his sister," Angela said. "He's retired. And I'm not surprised that people become radical when they face prejudice and rejection. Paul Robeson stood up for himself and paid a price. An unfair price."

"I can't disagree with that." Alexander nodded slightly to her. "I suppose I'd be just as radical under the same circumstances."

When Jimmy asked me later how I thought the dinner had gone, I told him that Angela had been very impressive.

"I thought so, too," he said. "Beau agrees. That's not the problem, though."

"What's the problem?"

"Beau's worried about the impression my parents made on Angela."

I didn't say what I wanted to, that the Kincaids assumed that everyone wanted to join their charmed family circle. I certainly did. I didn't need any encouragement. Angela was different, and if Beau hoped for a future with her—if he wanted more than a high school romance—he did have cause for concern.

In the spring, things came to a head.

Beau announced that he had decided on the University of Virginia for college. He had been accepted at Princeton and Yale, and his choice surprised all of us. His father confronted Beau and suggested that he had been overly influenced by Angela, who was headed to Howard University in Washington, closer to Charlottesville than any of the Ivies. Beau was furious. According to Jimmy, who witnessed the argument, Beau told his father that his decision had nothing to do with Angela. In fact, they had broken up. Not Beau's choice. Hers. Then he stormed out of the house.

The last weeks of high school must have been very hard for both Beau and Angela. They avoided each other. She had been the one who ended it, at least that's the story I pieced together from things Jimmy said. With college ahead of them, she didn't see any reason to stay together.

Beau was clearly hurt. He wouldn't talk about it with Jimmy or Desmond, and he disappeared into his room for hours at a time.

After graduation, Beau took a summer job as a lifeguard in Avalon, and so we didn't see much of him in Princeton. In the fall, he packed his bags and left for Charlottesville. When he returned home at Thanksgiving, I got up my courage and questioned him about Angela.

"Have you heard from her?" I asked.

"No. No reason to."

"Are you going to see her?"

Beau shook his head. "It's done and over with, Julia."

"So that's it? You're not even going to stop by her house and see how she's doing?"

"I don't think that would be wise." He looked away, his discomfort evident. He quickly changed the subject. "Is it true that Jimmy wants to go to Columbia?"

"You know it is. Don't duck my question. Don't you owe it to yourself to see her?"

"When did you become such a fan of Angela?"

"I guess I have a soft spot for hometown girlfriends."

Our conversation must have spurred him to action, because on Saturday, by chance I spotted Beau and Angela walking together on Nassau Street a few blocks ahead of me. Angela kept her distance from him, which was a change from the past, when Beau would have his arm around her shoulder and she would have a hand in one of his belt loops.

Still, they looked great together; they were both tall and slim, the same body type. I felt a twinge of envy: what I wouldn't have given for Angela's long legs and arms. I was four inches shorter, and knew I couldn't wear the long, flowing skirts that Angela preferred.

They stopped and I could see Angela had her arms crossed, and she leaned away from Beau. He spoke to her with urgency and I could see her shaking her head. I slipped away, hoping they hadn't seen me spying on them (for that was what I was doing.)

I walked over to Lafayette Place and was listening to Beatles songs with Jimmy and Hanna when Beau arrived. He motioned for me to join him in the kitchen.

"I ran into Angela," he told me, keeping his voice down.

"And?"

"It didn't go well."

I didn't say anything, waiting for him to continue.

"It hurt, being around her. She felt the same way about seeing me. I don't want to be her friend. I want more than that with her, and that can't happen."

"Why not?"

"She's convinced that it will never work. She believes we're too different. Angela told me that it was exhausting for her to live in my world, the Kincaid world, where she never feels comfortable, where she never feels like she belongs, where she feels judged and found lacking. At Howard, she doesn't stand out. There are black people all around her. She feels at home."

I nodded. It made sense. I could wear the right clothing, say the right things, look the part, but I often felt anxious about my place in that Kincaid world. And I was white. No one ever stared at me and Jimmy when we walked down Nassau Street hand-in-hand.

"And children," Beau said. "She said she couldn't imagine having children and putting them through the pain of not truly belonging."

"Do you agree with that?"

"I don't. But I can't persuade her otherwise. I've tried. Believe me, I've tried."

"I'm sorry for you, Beau. For both of you."

"It's not meant to be."

"So now what?"

He shook his head, and didn't respond. I had never seen Beau so at a loss for words. Or so downcast. That afternoon convinced him that it was over with Angela, and there was no way back, no hope of reclaiming her. Angela saw clearly what a future with a white husband and mixed-race children might mean, and she wasn't willing to see it through. Not even for Beau, not even when the attraction between them was so magnetic.

"Angela never thought we would last," Beau said. "She told me that. That bothered me the most, that she felt that way from the start."

"Did you think it would last?"

"I was willing to give us a chance."

"Even with all the possible complications?"

"I thought it was worth it. She didn't."

Later, I wondered what would have happened if Angela had changed her mind during that Thanksgiving break. Would she and Beau have been able to navigate a long-distance romance? I tried to imagine Beau visiting her on Howard's campus in Washington and the reception he would have met, not that it would have been any easier for Angela in Charlottesville. At best, it would have been awkward. Would their relationship have survived that sort of stress? I had my doubts.

Would I have made the same choice that she did? It's impossible to say, because I'm not black, and I can only imagine what that's like.

What I think hurt Beau the most was Angela's adamant refusal to give him a chance, to give them a chance. He didn't understand her, but I did. The longer she held on, the deeper her feelings would grow, and the harder the inevitable breakup would be. She had her eyes wide open. So I can't blame her for that. Who asks for a broken heart?

NINE

They drove from Princeton to Richmond for Beau's wedding, listening to James' eight-track tapes of James Taylor's first two albums, with Julia singing harmony on "Carolina in My Mind" and "Fire and Rain." They enjoyed the car ride, the time alone; James had been working long hours at the Associated Press, and they hadn't spent as much time together as they would have liked.

Neither knew Beau's fiancée very well, a young woman named Hillary Spencer. They had met Hillary when Beau brought her to Lafayette Place to meet the family. A tall, slim blonde, Hillary was sharp and poised with a finishing school air. She was an editor on the Law Review, where she and Beau had met, and she ranked near the top of their class.

Beau's visit home had been a brief one, two days with a trip to Philadelphia on the second day. Beau had never brought a girlfriend to Lafayette Place during his college years, so Julia assumed that it was a serious relationship. James and Julia could only stay for lunch; they had to get back to New York. Beau walked them the few blocks to catch the Dinky at the Princeton Station. There, he told them that he planned to propose to Hillary when they returned to Virginia.

"Congratulations," Julia said, giving Beau a quick hug. "Do you have an engagement ring?"

"Not yet. If she says yes, we'll go to a jewelry store in Richmond on our way back. She can pick out a ring that she likes."

"She'll say yes." Julia smiled, confident about the outcome. "She'd be crazy not to."

On their drive to Richmond for the wedding, Julia had claimed that Beau couldn't have picked a woman more unlike Angela Jackson if he had tried.

"What do you think Beau sees in her?" she asked James.

"She's smart," he replied. "She's pretty. And she's confident. They'll have the law in common."

"But she's not sexy. Not like Angela. How do you think Hillary compares in bed?"

"You surprise me, Jules," James said. "Comparisons like that are more of a male thing, aren't they?"

"Wondering if someone is good in bed? Trust me, women think about it, and we even talk about it with our friends. Good friends." She gave him a sly look. "So what do you think? About the comparison."

"Who knows? There are plenty of reasons Beau might find Hillary sexually appealing. Conquering the ice maiden, making Miss Prim and Proper moan and gasp."

"And now you're talking dirty," Julia said, laughing.

"Maybe she played hard to get. That would be relatively new territory for Beau. He hasn't had to do much chasing, has he?"

"Other than Angela? No, he's had it easy with girls. This time he chased Hillary until she caught him."

Beau's relationship with Hillary was a topic James could, and would, never raise with his brother. Beau had dated casually in college, rarely staying with a girlfriend for very long, and his romance with Hillary had been unexpected. Did Beau wonder about what his life would have been like if it had worked out with Angela? James remembered how in love they had been. Beau's breakup with her had been a hard one. If James had a say in the matter, which he didn't, his choice of a wife for Beau would have been a woman more like Angela than Hillary.

The rehearsal dinner the night before the wedding was more formal than James and Julia had expected. It included a four-course meal and brief toasts from the members of the wedding party. As best man, James spent most of the evening by Beau's side. Alexander and Karin made small talk with Hillary's parents while Hillary was surrounded by a cluster of her college girlfriends.

Julia was happy to catch-up with Hanna and Desmond; she hadn't seen much of them living in New York. Hanna told her in a whisper that she was surprised that Beau was getting married—she had expected he would hold out until he was in his thirties.

After the rehearsal dinner, James joined Beau in his hotel suite and they shared a bottle of bourbon and talked late into the night.

"My intended's a bit on edge," Beau said with a smile. "It's been tense. Hillary wants the perfect wedding. And she's pushing me about the flying lessons. Doesn't see the purpose and thinks it's too dangerous. She wants me to stop. I don't want to, Jimmy. I feel so alive when I'm flying, when I'm in the air."

"What are you going to do?"

"I guess I'm going to keep making her unhappy."

"What about law school?" James asked. "How are your classes?"

"It's a trade school," he said. "There's not much intellectual rigor. The Professor wouldn't be particularly impressed with the curriculum."

"Do you like it?" James asked.

"I understand it. The law. I see the logic. The logic-splitting. I'm good at it, which shouldn't come as a surprise, not after all those years in the Kincaid Debating Society. But I wish I could find a greater purpose to it. I'm a lot happier in the cockpit of a Cessna than I am grinding away on case law."

"Promise me one thing," James said. "You won't lose Beau."

"What does that mean?"

"I don't want you to turn into Wilson Kincaid, Esquire. So serious and conventional that I don't recognize you anymore."

"That won't happen."

"Promise?"

"Promise."

Wilson "Beau" Kincaid and Hillary Jean Spencer were married at St. James Church, the oldest church in Richmond, the site of Patrick Henry's famous "Give me liberty, or give me death!" speech. It was a traditional Book of Common Prayer service. As Beau's best man, James brought the wedding ring to the altar, a Tiffany diamond ring, in his vest pocket. Desmond was a groomsman along with two of Beau's college friends. The maid of honor was one of Hillary's sorority sisters, as were her bridesmaids. (Julia dubbed them the "Stepford Wives in Waiting").

Hillary's parents looked on with broad smiles. Her father owned an insurance agency located in the center of the city, and her mother spent much of her free time at the country club playing golf with her friends. They seemed pleasant enough, although James suspected his parents were far from impressed with the Spencers.

James knew he had angered Hillary by keeping Beau up late, leading him astray, although it hadn't taken much to convince Beau to keep drinking. At the reception, she took it out on James, keeping her distance, making no attempt to talk with him or Julia. There was a moment when Beau, who could see what was going on, said something to her and she made a face and whispered fiercely back at him.

James and Julia were on the dance floor, when she asked him whether he remembered Beau slow dancing with Angela at a high school event. "They looked so right," she said. "Like they were meant to be together."

James glanced over at Beau and Hillary, which he knew was what Julia wanted him to do.

"Can you see how stiff she is?" Julia asked.

"They look fine together. You're imagining things." James shook his head. It had been more than five years since Beau and Angela had broken up. Julia thought of them as star-crossed lovers; he had to remind her that it was a high school romance that ended like so many after graduation.

"No, I'm not imagining things."

"Beau has made his choice," James said. "He sees something

special in Hillary. You don't, Jules. But it's his call. He's the one marrying her. We need to support him."

"It's a match made in the law library, not in heaven," she said. "She'll never make him happy."

"Keep that thought to yourself," he said. "We have to hope it works out for the better."

"Hope all you want. I see what I see."

Beau's marriage lasted eighteen months. He turned up unexpectedly one Saturday night at James and Julia's rented house in Princeton. King was sleeping quietly in his crib. James was reading the Sunday *Times* in the living room when he heard a knock at the back door and then Julia call out Beau's name in delight. His brother embraced James tightly when he joined them in the kitchen, and explained he was back for the weekend.

"I might as well get the bad news out of the way," he said. "Hillary and I have separated. We've agreed to divorce."

Julia had him sit at the kitchen table and poured Beau a cup coffee before she told him she was sorry. James followed suit. They waited for Beau to continue.

"It was inevitable." Beau took a sip of coffee and sighed. "I'm not cut out for the life she had planned for us."

"You don't need to explain," Julia said. She shot James a quick glance.

"There's nothing scandalous," Beau said. "No other woman, and she wasn't seeing anyone on the sly either. It just wasn't going to work out." He shrugged. "That's one thing we agreed on. Hillary didn't put up much of a fight after we talked it through."

"So you initiated the break?"

"I guess you could say that. Some big changes ahead. For starters, I'm leaving law school. I've decided to enlist in the Army."

James and Julia exchanged another quick glance.

"As an officer?" James asked.

"Officer Candidate School after Basic. Then, the Army's flight school for helicopter pilots. Fort Rucker. I've been through all this with the recruiter in Virginia." He looked down at his hands. "Hillary made it clear that if I went ahead with this, we were done."

"You're sure this is what you want?" Julia asked.

"I am. I want to fly and to serve my country. This lets me do that."

"And the law?" It was James.

"It will be there when the time comes. If it comes. I'll need to complete my final year and then pass the bar exam."

James didn't say what he was thinking. The Army offered Beau an escape from the mistake of his marriage. James wondered what he would have done if Hillary had accepted his abrupt decision to abandon law school, had agreed with his plans to become a military aviator. Beau had to know that would never happen. Hillary had mapped out their future, and her plans required a thoroughly domesticated Wilson Kincaid, climbing the professional and social ladder in Richmond.

Why Beau had ever considered that respectable future was somewhat of a mystery to James. It might have well been a mystery to Beau. Many of his classmates had opted for law school after college, and to Beau, it must have seemed the path of least resistance. Beau had been comfortable at Mr. Jefferson's University, and with decent grades and an excellent LSAT score, he was able to remain in Charlottesville for law school. James thought his brother must have been regretting his decision for some time. It was clear that Beau hadn't found his professional calling in college—as James had with journalism—and at some point he must have realized that his true passion was flying, not the law. That he could do that in the military, at the same time serving his country, must have convinced him to walk away from the life he had been constructing.

And Hillary? Had he loved her? Not enough, James guessed.

Was Beau being selfish? He had veered off course and James had to give him credit: it took courage to do what he did. Then again, courage was a quality Beau had in spades.

"Have you seen Mom and Dad?" James asked.

"I came here from Lafayette Place. They weren't pleased. Not hard to imagine why. A divorce by a Kincaid. My abandoning law school for the Army. But I'm sure they weren't completely surprised at my screwing up—I've always been a disappointment to Dad."

"No, you haven't," Julia said.

"Thanks, but in his eyes I have. I'm not in graduate school working toward my doctorate, following in his footsteps. The curse of the first son. Living up to expectations you never agreed to."

Julia turned to James. "Do you feel the same? About the expectations?"

"Not in the same way as Beau. There's the expectation that you make something of yourself. But we all have that. Except maybe Hanna. I think my parents ran out of energy by the time Hanna arrived. But it doesn't matter in one sense. Beau can do whatever the hell he wants. Just as I can. We have to find our own way, whether it pleases my father or not."

"Do you want to stay the night here with us, Beau?" Julia asked.

"Thanks, but I'll head back home." Beau pulled on his coat, and lingered by the back door.

"I'll call once I've got everything squared away on my end," he said. He lowered his voice. "Dad's angry about this. You know how it is, he gets that look that I've always hated, like he's tasted something sour."

Julia turned to James after Beau departed.

"She wasn't right for him," she said. "I take no pleasure in being right about that. I don't think your brother would be easy to live with. Too many sharp edges. But Hillary didn't put up much of a fight to keep him. I doubt that she even considered becoming a military wife. She wasn't about to drop her career and follow him around."

"I'm sure Hillary would say that wasn't what she signed up for. They were supposed to be Richmond's new power couple, and Beau went way off script."

Julia shook her head. "Like I said, she wasn't right for him."

Even though James believed that Beau had made the right decision, he knew ending the marriage had to be painful. No matter what front she might put up, Hillary had to feel betrayed. Knowing Beau, he probably hadn't said anything to her until near the end. James hoped Beau had at least told her that he was having second thoughts well before the breakdown of their marriage.

"The silver lining is that he'll be doing something he loves."

"Do you worry for him?" Julia asked. "Flying helicopters? There's an element of risk, isn't there?"

"He's always wanted to fly," James told her. "Steve Canyon. Remember the comic strip? Beau loved it. He'll turn out to be a damn good pilot. He'll follow the rules. The checklist. It's the sort of thing he's very good at. It's always like that when Beau puts his mind to something."

James' instincts were correct: Beau thrived in the Army. Commissioned as a second lieutenant, he cycled through Infantry Officer Basic Course before entering helicopter training at Fort Rucker in Alabama. He proved to be an excellent aviator, graduating at the top of his class. A natural leader, by all accounts he earned the respect and trust of the soldiers he commanded and his superiors took notice. After he completed flight school, the Army sent Beau to Germany to fly Cobra attack helicopters and he earned an early promotion to the rank of captain.

For the first time, Beau put some distance between himself and his family. He returned to Lafayette Place only on his brief leaves, and when he did, it took some time for him to drop his guard and seem more like the Beau of old.

TEN

JULIA

I remember the May sunlight moving on the windowsill in the Kincaid's second-floor guest bedroom, the linen curtain rippling in the breeze, on the afternoon I lost my virginity. I remember thinking that I had crossed a threshold, that I had become a woman, which was absurd because I had just turned sixteen.

It was the spring of my sophomore year and Jimmy and I had the house to ourselves that late afternoon; his parents were at a conference in Boston, and Des and Hanna were out playing with friends. My parents were at work, and they didn't keep close tabs on me—they thought I was studying with Adrienne Harris at her house.

We didn't mean to go that far that afternoon. We had been experimenting that spring, kissing, making out, "petting," pushing the boundaries. The air was warm and filled with the smell of blossoming flowers, and it should come as no surprise, I felt sexy. Jimmy was eager to fool around—he was a teenager with the typical raging hormones of a boy that age. I surprised him, I think, by my willingness to explore the boundaries set for us by our parents and by society. In his mind, good girls were more than a bit reluctant, but I was in love.

When we slipped into the bed, naked, and began kissing and

hugging, one thing led to another. When Jimmy began to enter me, I gasped but didn't stop him. To my surprise, it didn't hurt as much as I had anticipated, and I loved the feeling of his naked body on top of me. The first time was a mix of pain and pleasure.

Afterward, Jimmy began making apologies, but I told him that I loved him and that I wanted him to be my first lover. I didn't tell him that I wanted him to be the first and *last* man to ever make love to me, because I didn't want to scare him off.

We were both worried until my next period arrived, but we weren't about to stop making love, now that we had experienced what it was like. Jimmy got up his courage and bought condoms at the local pharmacy. From that point on, we took every opportunity to make love.

We thought it was our secret, but later I learned that most of my friends assumed that Jimmy and I had become intimate.

"I could tell that the two of you were sleeping together," Adrienne, my closest friend, told me later. "The two of you seemed connected at the hip, and I just figured you were connected elsewhere."

"You never said anything."

"What was I going to say? I figure you wanted to keep it secret."

"We did. I guess we didn't do a very good job at that."

A year later, I worried that I might lose Jimmy when he went off to Columbia. But I was determined to keep him—I did love him—and I worked out how I could visit him on the weekends. Jimmy loved college and the energy of the city; he was intoxicated by Columbia's first year Humanities A course, which explored the great works of Western literature and philosophy: Homer, Dante, Plato, Virgil.

Morningside Heights was a day trip from Princeton by train and subway. I visited Jimmy there nearly every other weekend. My parents let me go, no doubt assuming that our romance would fizzle out by Thanksgiving. They were wrong—the only competition I faced for Jimmy's attention came from his fascination with the *Daily Spectator*, the student newspaper. Jimmy had time only for his classes, the newspaper, and me—and I liked it that way.

I limped through my senior year of high school and decided I would stay close to home for college so I could continue my weekend trips to see Jimmy. So I began taking classes at Rider College in Lawrence, and I figured I had the best of all worlds. The Rider campus was only a few miles from Princeton.

After graduation, Jimmy's college newspaper stories—his clips—were strong enough to land him an interview at the Associated Press. We celebrated with a dinner at Sardi's in Times Square when he was hired as a city reporter. By then, I was bored by college and wanted to be with him all the time, not just on weekends, so we moved in together in a small apartment in the West Village. Jimmy would take the subway to Rockefeller Center for work. His hours were terrible—I hated when he worked the graveyard shift—and we had little money, but we were happy. I found a job as a waitress at a neighborhood restaurant, working breakfast and lunch so I'd be around when Jimmy was off in the late afternoon and early evening. While the daytime tips weren't great, every nickel and dime helped.

It was a golden time for us, a young couple in the Big City. I remember wandering around the Village, taking in the Washington Square Park scene, with its chess players, and drug dealers, and NYU students. It was a bit sketchy at times, but I developed that sixth sense you need living in a big city. It was a casual, uninhibited time for sure, with gays coming out of the closet and artists and actors gravitating to the Village like they always had. I remember once walking down a side street one afternoon and discovering a small group of people of all ages dancing to the beat of "Rosalita," the Bruce Springsteen song, not a care in the world.

Jimmy threw himself into his job, soaking up as much insider knowledge as he could from the veteran reporters and editors, learning his craft. We were enjoying the here-and-now and didn't talk much about the future. There was the unspoken understanding that we were in it for good, for the long haul, which (in my mind) meant marriage and children.

On a cool, sunny day in October, I felt suddenly dizzy at the end of my lunch shift, but I didn't think much of it. When I got sick the following morning, I figured that I might be pregnant. Diaphragms aren't a full-proof form of birth control, it turned out. My gynecologist confirmed matters two days later.

I'd always imagined having children, and having them with Jimmy, but confronting the reality of a sudden pregnancy was different.

That night at dinner, I told Jimmy I was pregnant. I didn't know what he was going to say, but I had decided I would let him take the lead. He came over and put his arms around me.

"Well, then we'll need to get married," he said.

"You want me to have the baby?"

"Of course I do. Sooner than expected, but that doesn't matter." He looked me in the eyes. "Do you want the baby?"

"I do," I told him. "I'm scared, but I want him. Or her. A little Kincaid."

"I do love you, Jules," he said. "And I'll love our little one."

We were married at New York City Hall on a crisp, sunny autumn day, a Friday.

I didn't want a church wedding, I just wanted to get married. Jimmy agreed. We told Jimmy's parents that next day in Princeton. We accepted their congratulations and then went to lunch with Des and Hanna at PJ's Pancake House. Hanna admired the simple gold wedding bands that we had purchased from a jeweler in the Village.

Two months later we packed up a battered U-Haul truck and moved back to Princeton, to a small rented house in the Borough several blocks from Nassau Street. I wanted to have my baby at home. Jimmy began commuting to the city, leaving before dawn, taking the Dinky to Princeton Station, and catching one of the earliest trains. Some nights he wouldn't be home until ten o'clock and we only had a few hours together before he'd have to catch some sleep and begin the grind all over again.

He never complained, but he always seemed to have a coffee cup in his hand. On his days off, we saw his family or mine. I had a relatively easy pregnancy and I didn't start showing until the seventh month.

We were lucky because Jimmy was home when I went into labor just after midnight. I had felt growing pressure in the hour before my water broke. I called out to Jimmy to warn him and tell him it was time to go to the hospital.

I was grateful for the spinal block at the very end of my labor. King was an early-morning baby, arriving at 6:23 AM. Doctor Donahue, my obstetrician, announced that we had a boy moments after my final push.

Jimmy had wanted to name our son "Teilhard King Kincaid" after his hero, the French Jesuit theologian, but I wasn't about to saddle our child with that first name. We compromised on "King Teilhard Kincaid."

Both sets of parents came to welcome their grandchild the next day.

"He is adorable," Karin said in her cultured accent. "And you look lovely, my dear."

She and Alexander had arrived as I was breastfeeding King. I confessed to her that I was exhausted and relieved.

"There's something about a baby boy," Karin said. "Such a brave little man, yet so dependent on their Mommy. They never lose that neediness."

"Is that so?" James asked.

"Without a doubt. You just don't want to admit it."

"He certainly looks like a Kincaid," Alexander said to James. "Reminds me of Beau, when he was a newborn."

"I would hope there's a family resemblance," James said dryly. "Considering that I had something to do with it."

"Of course," Karin said with a hint of annoyance. "You shouldn't joke about that."

James hoped King wouldn't inherit any of the Kincaid moodiness, which he blamed on his mother's Swedish genetic heritage. "Long nights near the Arctic Circle," he explained. "Generations without enough ultraviolet light. We've got mood swings as part of our genes."

Desmond and Hanna were delighted to welcome their first nephew. "He's so cute," Hanna said. "A perfect little boy."

Jimmy sent a telegram to Beau in West Germany announcing King's birth, and mailed a copy of the best photo he had taken of me and King. A month later Beau's gift arrived in the mail—a Camouflage baby jumpsuit with "ARMY" stenciled on the chest.

When I look back on those days as a young mother, I remember how I was scared and tired and overwhelmed, but I was also deliriously happy. That's the clearest memory: I remember how happy I was, how I was so in love with the two boys in my life, in King and in Jimmy.

My mother wasn't as supportive as I had hoped. She and I clashed over how to raise King. I had found a wonderful book by Penelope Leach about child rearing, and I trusted it more than I did my mother's advice. Karin was more helpful. She told me to trust my instincts, that it would be easier over time, that I'd figure it out for myself.

I imagined having more babies. A brother or sister for King to play with. I think I had first gravitated to the Kincaid boys because I was an only child and I envied their closeness.

Karin asked me directly when King was four whether we were going to have more children, and I gave her a vague answer. That night I picked a fight with Jimmy. "You need to tell Karin that you're the reason," I told him. "She acts like I'm somehow to blame. That I'm reluctant to have another child because I'm selfish."

"You're getting worked up over nothing, Jules You're too sensitive."

"Am I? Your mother had a child every two years. That's what she expects from me. From us."

Jimmy shrugged and ended the conversation the way he always did—promising that once he was more established at work, he'd be ready for another child.

He must have had a conversation with Karin because she never asked about our having more children again.

It was not to be. I thought we had all the time in the world before we had our next child. Jimmy wasn't ready, and then, when he was, it turned out the delay carried a cost with it. I had developed endometriosis, and a second pregnancy wasn't in the cards.

In every marriage there are wounds inflicted, hurts and injuries, scars that last. For the longest time, I blamed Jimmy—we had waited because of him—and I nursed that resentment. But I also blamed myself, hated the betrayal of my hopes by my body. It didn't seem fair—I had done nothing wrong. I could be considered selfish, I imagine, for there were women who couldn't bear any children—and I had King—but that didn't make the regrets any less painful.

ELEVEN

HANNA

Princeton, 1977

It's a silly family myth that as the youngest child I've had it the easiest. No way.

Try living up to your overachieving siblings and then tell me that it's easy. It isn't. So I won't.

Sure, maybe Mom and Dad have had a lighter touch on discipline with their little girl, their one and only daughter. So Des and Jimmy claim. It may be true with that Beau and Jimmy had a tighter leash, but Des hasn't had lots of rules to follow. Mom has been stricter with me, as a girl. I have a curfew, and she wants to know who I'm hanging out with and where, although Mom has nothing to worry about. After seeing the high school heartbreaks of my siblings, I've steered clear of romance.

Mom doesn't like the way I dress, of course. I'm always in jeans and a flannel shirt or t-shirt. She'd prefer to see me in dresses or skirts and blouses, but I just don't feel as comfortable in girly clothes. I'm not a tomboy but I don't care to primp and preen. So Mom and I will fight over it. I will reluctantly put on a dress for church, but that's about it.

Of course as the youngest, I've represented the last best hope for untapped achievement: Mom hoping I'd be artistic and Dad hoping I'd pursue science as a career. I wiggled out of both of those dreams. Their dreams!

After years of lessons—painting, sculpture, piano, tap dancing, and ballet—it became crystal clear that I didn't have the talent, or interest, for Art with a capital A. I was happier pruning roses in our backyard garden than performing on a stage or slapping paint on a canvas. And when it came to science, while I found biology interesting, I didn't care for the dry theories and equations I was supposed to master.

At some point, my parents realized that I wasn't going to be a superstar in anything. And so what? I wouldn't trade places with Beau or Jimmy. When have they ever had a chance to stop and smell the roses? (I do like gardening!) I think I have a much better chance at happiness by just being myself.

As the last in line, I've watched what it's been like for Beau, Jimmy, and Des in dealing with my parents' expectations for them, and at times it hasn't been pretty. From the outside, the Kincaids seem like the perfect Christmas card family. We're far from it. Trust me.

I had a front row seat for the drama around Beau and his romantic ups and downs with Angela Jackson, the stupid dispute with Dad over college choices (who cares? does it matter?), and then Beau's enlistment in the Army. Talk about mistake on top of mistake! And Beau was supposed to be the Chosen One!

Jimmy was always competing with Beau. I'm glad he went in a completely different direction, because the watchful observer, the journalist, suits his personality. And marrying Julia, (which I know my parents weren't wild about because she wasn't sophisticated or worldly), and having King, have all been good things.

I'm closest with Jimmy. I think of him as my big brother, the one who looked after me when I was little. There's a big age gap with Beau, and he never paid me much attention. Des is sweet, but he has always lived in his own world. A bit strange that world, actually.

Des has struggled. We all know that. Mom and Dad have focused on his issues with mental health, finding the right doctor, the right treatment. As it should be. When he has one of his episodes, everything at home comes to a grinding halt until he's better. That's fine by me, because it's meant that I've been left alone for the most part. I'm not complaining. Trust me. I'd rather stay under the parental radar.

When I've been cornered by my parents, I've told them that I just don't know what I want to do after high school. I don't have any idea. They humor me, convinced that I will end up like the rest of my classmates and do the safe, expected thing, the well-worn path to adulthood that begins with a college education and degree.

It's easier to say what I'm not, than what I am. I'm not a stoner or a jock. I'm not particularly artistic or musical. I'm not Boy Crazy. I'm not wild about the idea of sitting at desk in an office job as my future. I hate the idea of being trapped indoors. So I'm not sure what I want to do.

I figure I have some time to figure things out. I guess I don't mind being the one Kincaid without a grand plan.

TWELVE

The signs of Desmond Kincaid's mania first surfaced when he was fourteen years old. His mother noticed his restlessness and impulsive behavior. Desmond was easily distracted, and he had trouble sleeping.

His mother thought it was a phase, something triggered by the hormonal change for a teenage boy. Every child was different, she told herself. Yet she somehow knew something was more fundamentally wrong.

Desmond had always been a dreamer. He told his brother James that he had decided to become an inventor, that he was destined to win the Nobel Prize for unlocking the secrets of fusion and harnessing it to create unlimited power. In his sophomore year of high school, he begged his father to introduce him to the head of the Princeton Fusion Lab, which Alexander Kincaid agreed to if Desmond achieved an A in his pre-calculus course. But Des missed two weeks of school because of a lingering cold that turned into pneumonia and didn't do well on his make-up exam.

By then, Karin Kincaid had become alarmed about Desmond's hyperactivity and mood swings. When he began complaining about a sense of sadness, and suddenly couldn't stir from his bed in the morning, they asked their pediatrician to examine him. He referred Desmond to a child psychologist, who in turn brought in a psychiatrist, a Dr. Crossland. He diagnosed Desmond with manic depression, and prescribed the drug lithium supplemented by talk therapy.

After a month or so, Desmond's symptoms improved. While his depression had lifted, he complained that the lithium made him feel like he was swimming underwater. Dr. Crossland tried adjusting his medication, but Des grumbled that he was still not feeling like himself.

"My shrink gave me all sorts of tests," he told Julia. She always lent a sympathetic ear. "Apparently I'm quite brilliant. Who would have known? But then he drugs me like I'm one of Odysseus' sailors in the Land of the Lotus Eaters."

"You seem fine," Julia replied. "Like the Des we all know."

"I wonder. Who am I? Maybe the true Des is manic. Maybe taking these drugs is a mistake. Did you know they say Samuel Taylor Coleridge and Winston Churchill and Beethoven were manic depressives? They didn't go on lithium. Look at what they accomplished."

"Des, I think you should listen to your doctor. Take the medication he has prescribed."

Desmond frowned. "And when does it end? When can I stop? Dr. Crossland won't answer that question. At some point, he needs to. It's only fair."

In his senior year of high school, Desmond embarked on a project to catalog all of the stone gargoyles and tigers on the Princeton campus. He created a thick scrapbook that included a map of the locations of the statuary with photographs, descriptions, and a brief history of their origin.

He shared the scrapbook with Julia, who was impressed by Desmond's thorough and careful research.

"You have a flair for this," she said. "Have you thought about a career involving research? Perhaps at a university?"

"You're sounding like my father. What do I want to do when I grow up? I like the idea of research, of being a scientist, but I don't want to be a professor."

"You don't? Why not?"

"I would never want to make the sacrifices."

"It can't be that bad."

Desmond looked at Julia and smiled as if he knew something she didn't. "Have you heard the one about the Devil and the assistant professor? The Devil approaches him and offers him a deal. The assistant professor's career will soar. He'll publish groundbreaking research. He'll gain tenure, a fully-funded chair, and senior professor status. He'll even win a Nobel. But, the Devil says, at the end of all of this you'll have a ruined family life, a wife who detests you, children who you never see, and not a friend in the world. 'How about it?' Satan asks. The assistant professor takes his time thinking about the offer. Finally, he speaks. "OK,' he says. "Give it to me straight. What's the catch?'"

Julia never thought to ask why Des was so interested in the University's statuary. She had become used to Desmond's intense and unrelenting focus on whatever topic or idea that caught his interest.

She remembered the time Desmond had insisted on attending the New Year's Eve ball drop in Times Square. She and Desmond had met James in New York and found a spot at the fringes of the crowd. Desmond hadn't explained why he wanted to come so much. He gazed around Times Square, at the thousands of people gathered near them, all staring up at the lighted ball.

"Isn't this something?" he asked. "All these people here to worship."

Julia shook her head. "It's a celebration. No one is here to worship."

Des smiled and shook his head. "It's just like sun worship," he said. "They're looking up at a shiny ball in the sky. An annual worship service." He turned to James. "I'm glad I got to see this in person. It's very strange. Can we go now?"

"You don't want to stay and watch the ball drop?" Julia asked, surprised.

"Not really," he said. "I saw what I came for. But we can stay if you like."

Later, James laughed about the absurdity of the situation; the three of them making their way through the densely-packed streets to Times Square and once they'd found a vantage point, Desmond satisfying his curiosity and then pronouncing himself ready to move on.

"That's Des," James told Julia. "He hears a melody the rest of us don't. He could have been one of the members of the stringed quartet on the deck of the *Titanic*. He'd be playing away, enjoying the music, as the ship went down. But he'd be happy, because it was the song he wanted to hear."

In the spring of his senior year of high school, Desmond stopped taking his medication. His mania spiraled out of control, and he had to be hospitalized. He spent three weeks in the psychiatric ward and missed his high school graduation ceremony. The episode convinced his parents that he needed to stay at Lafayette Place where they could keep an eye on him. When his health stabilized, they could make plans for his future.

Alexander Kincaid arranged for borrowing privileges for Desmond at Firestone Library. He loved spending the day there, piling up a stack of books in his study carrel. He would tell anyone who asked that he was an independent scholar.

When James and Julia moved back to Princeton, Desmond gravitated to their rental place, spending hours drinking coffee in their cramped kitchen, explaining his latest project—researching a way to survive a nuclear war. They listened, fascinated and (in Julia's case horrified), as he laid out what he had learned. "Sorry, but the Northeast is possibly the worst place to be," he explained. "Washington and New York will be primary targets, possibly Boston, too. Along with the missile silos in the Dakotas. I thought about trying to find a place that isn't near military targets. Maybe Vermont or New Hampshire along the Canadian border. But that won't work. Too many Soviet missiles are going to get through. Then what? You can't hide in the basement. The gamma rays will get you when the radioactive particles land on your roof because you need something really dense to stop them, not wood floors. No, the best place is somewhere with few targets."

"Where would that be?" his brother asked.

"Somewhere in the Southern Hemisphere. Latin America."

"Are you learning Spanish?" James asked. "I thought you took French in high school?"

"I can get by," Desmond said. "But even in Chile and Peru, there may be significant competition for resources after the war ends.

Refugees from all over. I've thought this through carefully. I think I have a solution. A clever solution."

He paused, waiting for his brother to respond. "I'll bite," James said. "What's your idea?"

"A sailboat," he replied. "A cruising sailboat. The idea is to sail to the Southern Hemisphere with a store of food and water aboard. You can supplement that with fish that you catch and water that you desalinate. Even if there's radiation in the atmosphere, it won't have reached the fish yet. We can bring seeds and look for small islands where we can grow vegetables."

"It sounds like you want us to live like Robinson Crusoe," Julia said.

"For eighteen months to two years. Then, we can sail to wherever order has been restored. We'll know where that is by listening to shortwave radio."

He appeared after dinner one night and explained that he had made progress on his plans.

"I've chosen the name of my sailboat," he said. "Fair Winds. From 'fair winds and a following sea.' Do you like it?"

"I like it," Julia said.

"If you and Jimmy and King come, we'll need a bigger boat," he said. "I've already started on the calculations. For adequate food and water."

"Thank you for the invitation." Julia stood up and hugged him. "Don't forget the diapers for King."

Desmond brightened. "I hadn't thought of that. Cloth diapers. They can be rinsed with seawater. I'll make up a checklist of what King will need, and you can approve it."

"Maybe not right now," James said. "Let's wait until you've worked all the other details out."

"Sure, Jimmy," Desmond said. "We can wait, but not for too long."

Desmond stopped taking his lithium pills on the second day of March, not long before his twenty-first birthday.

As in the past, the symptoms of his illness surfaced in the days that followed. His father was in Miami at an academic conference, James and Julia had taken King to visit friends in Philadelphia, and Karin was slow in recognizing that Des was slipping back into depression.

When she confronted him, he claimed he felt better when he wasn't taking his medicine. Karin shook her head. "You promised you wouldn't stop. Does Dr. Crossland know? Have you told him?"

"I'm seeing him in two days. I planned on discussing it with him then."

A day later, Karin went to wake her son and knocked on the door to his bedroom several times, calling his name. When he didn't respond, she opened the door and stepped inside his room. She saw him lying in his bed, a down comforter pulled up by his shoulders. There were two empty bottles of sleeping pills on his night table next to an empty water glass.

She touched him on his shoulder, and when he didn't respond, she felt a moment of fear. When she placed her hand on his cheek and found it cold, she knew that he was gone. Karin quickly looked around the room but found no note or message.

The funeral was delayed to allow Beau to return home from Germany. They held a private service for Desmond at Trinity Church only with family members in attendance. Afterward, at Lafayette Place, Alexander retreated to his study, Karin to her studio, and Julia and the Kincaid siblings congregated in the living room.

"I can't believe that he's gone," Julia said. "I expect Des to come in through the door and start explaining his latest crazy project."

Hanna shook her head, tears welling in her eyes. "This past year he struggled so. I couldn't do anything to help him. He insisted that he was fine."

Beau and James left them and sat out on the patio and finished off a bottle of Jack Daniels.

"I didn't realize that he was in such deep trouble," Beau said. "Any signs near the end?"

James shrugged. "When he was taking his medicine, he was stable. He seemed to be doing well, but he fooled everyone. His doctor. Mom and Dad. Then he stopped taking his meds and that was disastrous."

Beau shook his head. "I've lost men in my unit. We had an accident in training. Night ops. Helicopter rotor hit a power line. Both pilots killed. They left behind young families. It's damn hard to take, but when it's your own flesh and blood, it's different, deeply personal."

"It won't be the same without him," James said. "This house. The family."

"But you have to go on," Beau said. "That's really all you can do. That and saying a prayer or two for him."

THIRTEEN

JULIA

Desmond's death hit Karin the hardest, I think. She had always been protective of her third son, the troubled one, the most sensitive of her children. While she would have denied it, Des was clearly her favorite. He had an innocence, a sweetness about him, that touched something in her. We could all see it.

Until I had King, I didn't understand the fierceness of a mother's love. King taught me about that. I believed the apocryphal story about the mom who freed her child trapped under an automobile by lifting up one end.

A month after Des's memorial service, Karin surprised me by telephoning and inviting me to Lafayette Place for lunch. "Please bring King with you," she said.

While it was a chilly day, I decided that I would put King in his stroller and we would walk over from our rental place to the Kincaid's house. It wasn't far, perhaps twenty minutes on foot. The wind was stronger than I had expected, and halfway to Lafayette Place, I was regretting my decision. I peered at King in the stroller—his cheeks had turned a bright red from the cold, and he gave me the most adorable little smile. I hoped that he wouldn't catch a cold.

Once inside the Kincaid's house, I found myself apologizing to Karin.

"I should have canceled," I said. "My mistake. It's too cold today for King to be outside."

"He's fine," she said firmly. "People in Stockholm think nothing of taking their children outside in weather much colder than this." She kissed King on his cheek and my rosy-cheeked son grinned up at her. "See? He's none the worse for the wear. A little Viking."

She made hot chocolate and we sat on the living room floor, taking turns holding King on our laps. I could see how King softened her.

I had always wondered what she really thought of me. Did she think I had trapped Jimmy into marrying me with the pregnancy? Did she think Jimmy could have done better than his childhood sweetheart? I had no fancy degree, I wasn't a career woman. But I hoped that she could see that I was a good wife and a good mother. That had to count for something.

When King dozed off in my arms, Karin had me transfer him into a small crib that, she told me, had last been occupied by Hanna.

"While King is sleeping, I want to show you something," she said. "It won't take a moment."

I glanced over at King; he was sleeping soundly in the crib. If he did wake up and cried for me, I was sure I would hear him even if I was on the other side of the house. I nodded, willing to leave him alone, which I considered quite a concession.

Karin led me to the north side of the house and took me into her studio. I had been there only once before. A white sheet draped over an easel covered a square canvas, hiding it from view. I could smell turpentine and paint.

"I wanted you to see this," she said. She carefully removed the sheet, exposing an oil painting. It was a portrait of Desmond and I gasped at the sight.

It was so unlike any of Karin's paintings, which typically were scenes from the Scandinavian sagas, with dark tones and bold figures. In her portrait, her son was seated under a sun-dappled tree, with a half-smile. I studied the painting for a long moment.

"It's amazing," I managed. "It brings him back."

"If only it did."

"His memory, I mean."

"Yes, his memory." She paused and replaced the sheet over the canvas, hiding the painting from view. "I can't look at it for too long," she said."You have a son. You brought him into the world. You nursed him and loved him and now you're watching him grow. Imagine losing him. It's a terrible thought and a terrible thing. It violates the natural order. We are meant to go first, not our children."

I couldn't say anything to her in response. I felt a sudden chill. The idea of losing King was terrifying, the stuff of nightmares, and like many first-time mothers, I worried that every sniffle and cough of my baby might signal the start of some terrible illness.

Karin turned to me, tears in her eyes. "When a baby is born, you're relieved when there are ten toes and ten fingers. That they cry loudly. For all of my children, there was no concern. But they can't test the baby's mind, the chemical balance in the brain. Something in the chemistry was wrong. In Sweden, they say joy and sorrow are next-door neighbors. It's true. Desmond brought so much joy for all of us." She blinked back her tears. "Now he brings sorrow."

I was surprised by the sudden intimacy of the conversation. I had always been wary of my mother-in-law with her studied reserve, her penetrating gaze. We had never had such a deeply personal conversation. I took her hands in mine and squeezed. She gave me a small smile.

"We've been away from King long enough," she said. "Let's have lunch."

I studied her face for a moment, noting the tiny crow's feet around her eyes, a few gray strands in her hair, and realized that the woman I had always thought of as ageless had grown older. No doubt the events of the last few weeks had weighed heavily on her. I felt another surge of sympathy. She seemed very alone at that moment.

We returned to the living room. I felt a sudden rush of emotion, of love, when I saw King's little swaddled body in the bassinet. I sat cross-legged on the floor next to him, and Karin joined me.

"Once you've become a mother, it transforms your life," she said. She gently stroked King's cheek. "I wonder what my life would have been like if I had stayed in Stockholm and painted. Made art my life. I do paint, now, but for so many years I could not. I never could make the time, with the children and with Alexander. You know that I was young when I met Alexander? Very young. It was just after the war and America seemed a wonderland, a land of dreams. I had no idea what being a wife and mother would mean, certainly not what being Alexander Kincaid's wife would mean."

"The road not taken," I said, aware that it was a cliché, but true nonetheless.

"Yes. On that road I would have inherited my parents' summer cottage, just outside the city. It looked over a small lake. We used to pick lingonberries, cloudberries, and blueberries in the forest and meadows. I was happy there as a child."

I had to wonder: did Karin regret her choices? She had become a wife and mother before the feminism of the 1960s when few women of her class worked outside the home or chose the less traditional path of a career. Or had Desmond's death caused her to question her choices? Losing a child had to turn things upside. The manner of his death had to tear at Karin and Alexander.

"We have kept Desmond's passing quiet," she said, as if she had read my thoughts. "When people ask about him, we say it was a sudden illness. It was. He was sick. No healthy person takes their own life. He was sick. It bothers Alexander greatly. I know it does. He won't talk about it, but I can see it in his eyes, the deep sadness. We must bear some of the blame. The things we didn't do." She paused. "Desmond was not the only child we lost. I miscarried once. Eighteen months after I had Desmond. It was nothing like this, the hurt. I never knew that baby, never held him, changed his diapers, sang lullabies to him. Not like Desmond."

"He knew that you loved him, Karin. We talked about it once. He hated how he had become a burden."

"Desmond was never a burden. Not to me. Never. I found him, you know. It was if he was peacefully asleep, curled up in his bed."

She rose to her feet. "There are sandwiches waiting for us in the kitchen. And hot soup. Just the meal on a cold day."

In the end, I like to think that it was my little King who helped pull Karin out of the darkness enveloping her after Desmond's death. That, and time, although I believe Karin never stopped grieving after her son.

After our heart-to-heart during that morning visit, I brought King to Lafayette Place almost every day, rain or shine, pushing him in the fancy stroller that was a gift from Jimmy's Aunt Priscilla. I found myself looking forward to our visits. Jimmy was puzzled by the sudden closeness between his wife and his mother, but I told him it was all about Karin's embracing her role as grandmother.

Karin loved holding King, bouncing him on her lap, playing with him. He was a happy baby, gurgling and cooing. Children that age have a magical aura about them—they respond to love and attention; quickly fed and diapered, they're not difficult or overly demanding. A mother can believe that her bond with her son or daughter will never be broken, that all will be as it is. That's not so, of course, but who doesn't want to cling to the illusion that the sweetness of early days will last and last?

I don't know what happened to Karin's portrait of Desmond. She never invited me to view it again. After she died, Alexander locked the door to her studio. When Jimmy and I cleared out Lafayette Place, I told him about Karin's painting of Desmond. I looked high and low and never found the painting. Had either she or Alexander destroyed it, finding it too painful to keep? I think it was Karin. I was disappointed for the portrait had captured Des as I remembered him, at his most relaxed, a smile on his face.

FOURTEEN

ALEXANDER

January 12, 1980

Dear Pri,

Thank you for your kind note. I'm sorry I wasn't particularly communicative on the phone. It's been difficult to talk about what happened.

I'm told some people deal with their grief by talking about it. I find it painful to do so.

Desmond's service at Trinity Church was private, with only the immediate family attending. Karin hadn't slept for several days, and she sat there in the pew in stunned silence. It was devastating, Pri, to witness her grief, to see how deeply affected she was.

Beau flew back from Germany on leave. He stayed with us for five days, and then had to return to his unit.

I'm no stranger to grief, nor are you. It was a shock when we lost Mother and Father and I mourned them, but it wasn't anything like this.

Children shouldn't die before their parents—it's a terrible distortion, a violation of the natural order of things. The circumstances of Desmond's death make it even more painful. I have tried to understand the urge for self-annihilation but to no avail. Am I too much of an egotist? Too caught up in myself? Nonetheless, it's a mystery to me why anyone would want to cut their life short, to cease to exist before their allotted time.

I know that throughout history a small but consistent percentage of humans commit suicide. Some believe it is part of the price we pay for our evolved consciousness. But there's some evidence that we're not the only species capable of suicide. A Roman author wrote a brief book on the question, chronicling what he claimed were accounts of animals deliberately choosing death. The recent thinking is that animals can't, that suicide is a uniquely human act. I'm not so sure. Primates have emotions—glee, anger, sadness. I've seen it firsthand. If animals can feel, there must be times when the pain becomes too much for them to bear? It must have been that way for Desmond. Too much to bear.

We had seen his highs and lows before, and in the past, he had always responded to drug therapy. It's clear now that he stopped taking his medication, always a problem with those suffering from his form of depression.

I can rationalize what happened, but I failed Desmond, and in turn, Karin. There had to be more that I could have done. I shouldn't have relied on the doctors here. I should have taken Desmond to Boston, to McLean, for treatment. It would have been disruptive, but at least I wouldn't have these second thoughts.

Does Karin blame me? She won't discuss Desmond. She has retreated into silence. She tells me she doesn't want to talk about it, ever.

The one glimmer of hope is Karin's attachment to King. She loves spending time with him, and Julia has welcomed having a doting grandmother living nearby.

Hanna has also been deeply hurt by this. Beau and James have been out in the world: Beau, hardened by military life; James, by what he has seen as a working journalist. It's not that they don't feel the pain, but they haven't reacted with the same intensity. They've seen the unfairness of human condition.

Losing Desmond has been a reminder of what awaits ahead. Death. It's been on my mind, the end of my life. We are selfish creatures, aren't we, to consider things from our personal perspective. My mortality? It's something I push away, try not to think about, and then something like this happens. I've found some comfort in reading the Stoics and their musings on death and grief.

And then there's the immediate family and what this means for us, to Beau, James and Julia, and Hanna. It's a wound that will never fully heal. Will a day pass without something to remind us of Desmond?

We can only hope that some of that pain will fade over time. It won't ever go away completely and we'll just have to live with it.

Your loving brother, Alex

PART THREE

FIFTEEN

HANNA

11/12/80

Dearest Jimmy,

It's hard to believe that I'm actually here, living in San Francisco. Go West, young woman! Sorry for the delay in writing to you, but I decided to wait until I was more settled and had some positive news to share.

I love this city. Who wouldn't? It has hills and cable cars and neat old buildings and a mesmerizing view of the Bay. I could sit and gaze out on the blue expanse of the water for hours and hours. And there's something about the light here, it's crystal clear and warm and inviting.

I've been exploring the city on foot, taking my trusty camera along so I can snap photos of the cool things I encounter. I'll send some of them to you in my next letter. Of course, I'll need to get to a One Hour Photo and have them develop the three rolls I've already shot. Stay tuned!

People are different here, they're warmer, open to newcomers, open to everything, it seems. Not like the East Coast. It's been thirteen years since the Summer of Love, but there are still hippies and free thinkers and stoners here.

No one asks where you went to college, or what your job is. That's not what they judge you on. That's more than fine by me.

My tiny apartment is in the Mission Dolores neighborhood. What a cool place! There's this amazing historic gold-painted fire hydrant on the southwest corner of Dolores Park that firefighters used to save the nearby buildings in the Mission District after the earthquake of 1906. The people who hang out in the park are quirky and eclectic, young and old, hippies and gays, well-to-do and newcomers just scraping by like me.

I'm working two jobs. I made friends with a professional dog walker and I spell her one day a week. The dogs are a mix of breeds and sizes and they keep me on my toes. Then, I'm waitressing four days a week in a Greek restaurant. The owner, Mr. Karras, and his wife, Olympia, are very nice, even if they're a bit old-fashioned. I have to wear a uniform with a skirt that comes below my knees. I can't wait to get back into my jeans after my shift ends.

Moving here has liberated me to try new things. You know I've always wanted to try singing in front of an audience. It was very scary but exhilarating to step out and sing at a local club during the open mic time. I do love writing songs, but I'm not wild about performing. I learned it makes me anxious, and I don't need any more of that in my life.

I don't have much of a social life. Not yet. One of the other singers, a young guy from Oregon named Brett Scott, asked me out on a date of sorts, but we didn't hit it off. He struck me as the jealous, controlling type and why would I ever sign up for that?

That's the news from this California Kincaid.

I know Mom and Dad aren't happy with me. A Kincaid abandoning college after two years? That just isn't done. But I felt that I wasn't learning anything, just treading intellectual water (that's a strange metaphorical image) and I'm glad that I dared to make the break.

After what happened with Des, and the silence and the grief, I had to get away from Lafayette Place. I don't regret my decision to leave, not for a moment. Mom and Dad wanted me to stay with them there, but I couldn't stand it. Mom was so grim, hiding in her studio and painting those dark pictures. It's macabre. I know she feels somehow responsible for what happened. But she's not. No one is. Certainly not Des.

And the month before I left it did seem as if I had become the target for her moods. I got tired of being judged and coming up short. She never wanted to let me live my own life, choose my own way. It wasn't easy being the only girl growing up in our family, and Mom didn't make it any easier. I could never be pretty enough or smart enough and she hated my music. Is it any wonder that I was rebellious? Who wouldn't be?

You and Beau have your escapes. You have Julia and King and your reporting job, and Beau has his toy soldiers and his helicopters.

I'm going to find my True North, Jimmy. It just may take some time.

Is there any hope that you and Julia and King could come and visit? I know it's hard to travel with a little one, and you may already have a vacation planned somewhere else (Boca Grande, no doubt), but I would love to see all of you.

I've decided not to come back to Princeton for Christmas. Not this year. Mom and Dad won't understand, but you will.

I had a dream about Des the other night. It was the four of us, and we were playing cards, Hearts, sitting on the porch at the Boca Grande cottage. Des was telling us a story, one of his funny stories, and we were all laughing. He kept trying to shoot the moon, but you and Beau were too clever for that. Then the sun began to set and Des left the card game and walked out toward the Gulf. I called for him to come back to the house, but he ignored me, he just kept walking out into the water. I felt incredibly sad. Then I woke up. My therapist—who bills herself as a Jungian—said it's my way of trying to process his loss, although I hardly need to pay her hourly rate for that interpretation.

Hugs and kisses.

love,

your one and only sister, Hanna

SIXTEEN

Princeton, Fall 1981

From nearly half a block away, she could make out the Garbers' living room, bright with lights, a beacon of sorts on the quiet suburban street. Adrienne tugged on Beau's arm and pointed out their destination. As they drew closer, they could hear the sounds of animated conversation and the soft strains of Pachabel's Canon. For once during their walk, she didn't have to struggle to match Beau's longer stride; he had noticeably slackened his pace as they walked up Murray Place and moved closer to the Garbers' house.

Adrienne had enjoyed their stroll down Nassau Street and their detour through Princeton's hushed side streets, the still-colorful maples and oaks forming a brilliant autumnal canopy above them. Beau had reluctantly agreed to attend the Garbers' dinner party only as a favor to Adrienne. She'd asked him to substitute for her boyfriend, Hugh, who had to stay over in Chicago another day to finish some involved business negotiations.

Anyone watching them make their way down the street would think they were a handsome couple, she decided, a well-matched couple. Next to Beau, she didn't feel that her legs were too long. It made her wish Hugh had Beau's lanky frame, and then she felt guilty for entertaining the thought. A friend of hers, a fellow dancer, had once observed, with more than a touch of jealousy, that Adrienne had been blessed with a Balanchine body, elongated but sinuous. But those same long legs had made Adrienne prone to injury, and a stress fracture in her right foot that never healed properly had ended her career as a performer and left her to make a living as a teacher and choreographer.

Beau had been in town for a week on a rare visit to his parents. Even though she hadn't seen him in two years, she didn't hesitate in asking him to accompany her. They'd always been direct with each other, and, unlike some of her friends, she had never been intimidated by Beau.

"I've canceled on Zoe Garber twice," she had explained to him, hoping that would help persuade him to join her.

"Can't you go solo?" he asked. "Where do I come in? Why do you need me to go?"

"Because it's a dinner party with couples," she said. "There's the Garbers, Zoe and her husband, Levi, who's a journalist. He's on a sabbatical of sorts to write a book on Congress and Zoe's very active in local politics. And then there's another couple, Derek and Gillian Hawthorne. They're English. He's a visiting professor, in mathematics, I think, and she designs jewelry. We'd be the third couple."

"But we're not a couple."

"We are and we're not," she said. "You're not my boyfriend, but you'll balance the table. You know, boy-girl, boy-girl. So I need you as my dinner date. Please, Beau, as a favor."

"I don't think I'll really fit in with your friends. I'm not part of their world."

She remembered that Beau had never had much patience for

academics—probably a reflection of his troubled relationship with his father.

"It will be just fine," she said. "Please come. It'll take your mind off things."

"What things?" he asked. "I didn't realize I needed to be distracted."

"I know it's difficult when you come back," she said. "With your parents."

He paused for a long moment. "It can be tough. I don't know how Jimmy and Julia handle living so close to the Professor. I can't believe I'm the only one he picks arguments with."

"It's probably because he misses you," she said. "Maybe you're the only one who will joust with him. Escape for the night. Come to the dinner with me. I promise you won't be bored."

In the end, he agreed. When she called Zoe Garber, Adrienne explained that Beau was an old Princeton friend, that he was well-traveled, had broad interests, and could more than carry his end of a conversation.

It was Zoe who met them at the front door. A thin, intense woman in her early thirties, she wore her light red hair pinned in a bun. Her lightly freckled face made her look much younger than her husband, Levi Garber, who had grown a beard to compensate for his receding hairline. Levi shook hands with both of them in welcome, nodding to Beau. Zoe hugged Adrienne, complimenting her dress, and offered her hand to Beau, openly appraising him.

Zoe then introduced them to their other guests, the Hawthornes, who stood awkwardly by the door with half-empty wine glasses.

"Beau! What a marvelous name," Gillian Hawthorne said. She wore a white peasant blouse and a dark wraparound skirt. Silver and turquoise bracelets and a silver choker necklace completed her outfit. "Beau Kincaid. I don't think I've met a Beau before."

"That's not his given name," Adrienne said. "Just his nickname. His real name is Wilson."

"So how did you come to be called Beau?" asked Zoe, turning to Beau.

Beau smiled. "I'm sure Adrienne can explain. She'll tell the story much better."

"Beau is the oldest of three brothers," Adrienne said. "Remember the brothers in the movie *Beau Geste*? In the movie Beau is the oldest, always leading the other two. I think it was my friend Julia King who began calling him Beau. It certainly fit him better than Wilson. And she's Julia Kincaid, now. She married the second brother, Jimmy."

"So there you have it," Beau said. "All of my secrets exposed in the first five minutes you've known me. Thank you, Adrienne. Perhaps we can turn to a topic more interesting than my childhood."

"Beau, you'll always interest me," Adrienne said. "Even your childhood interests me."

"So you have known each other for a long time?" It was Levi Garber, curious about their easy familiarity.

"Since high school," Adrienne said. "Everyone in town knew the Kincaids."

They had briefly dated the summer before Beau went to law school. She remembered how she had been attracted by his toughness and irreverence—so different from the other college boys—and by his unabashed maleness. Beau was definitely out of step with the times, a throwback. She remembered how Julia had warned her not to get too attached to Beau. The only reason they had stayed in touch over the years was because her best friend, Julia, had become a Kincaid.

Levi appeared at Adrienne's shoulder and offered her, and then Beau, a glass of Sauvignon Blanc. Zoe encouraged them to move into the living room and sit down. It was an inviting room, comfortable in a spare way. On the far wall, light oak built-in bookshelves were crammed with hardback books—serious books, biographies of world leaders, political memoirs, a few volumes on journalism, and an embossed crimson-and-gold set of the *Harvard Classics*. A thick braided rug covered the gleaming polished oak floor. Beau and Adrienne sat down on one of the two Scandinavian-style couches and the Hawthornes occupied the other. Levi and Zoe sat facing them in armless teak chairs.

Derek Hawthorne broke his prolonged silence by asking Levi to finish a story he'd started about covering Congress as Washington bureau chief for a newspaper chain based in the Midwest. Derek had a neatly-trimmed mustache and he wore round, wire-framed glasses. Levi smoothly picked up his narrative, explaining how he'd exposed the taxpayer-financed Caribbean junkets of a Wisconsin Congressman who was stupid enough to take his wife and mistress to the same hotel in Jamaica on consecutive weekends.

"He signed them both in as Mrs. Gustafson," Levi said. "When my story broke in his hometown paper, he was more worried about what the real Mrs. Gustafson would do than about any action by the House Ethics Committee."

"Is he still in Congress?" asked Derek. He had what Adrienne would have described as an Oxbridge accent, clipped and precise, clearly upper class.

"Of course," Levi said. "His constituents were very forgiving. More than Mrs. Gustafson. Representative Gustafson had delivered a federal building project or two to the district."

"What did his wife do about it?" Gillian asked.

"Divorced him. And then signed on as the campaign manager for her ex-husband's opponent in the primary. Gustafson came within five hundred votes of losing his seat. But he held on."

"What about the other woman?" It was Gillian again.

"She disappeared. At least from public view."

His story completed, Levi excused himself to check the progress of dinner. "I'm the chef tonight," he explained.

"You don't realize how lucky you are," Zoe told them. "Levi's clearly the best cook in the Garber household."

The conversation shifted to an extended vacation the Hawthornes were planning to take to the Greek islands in the spring.

"Mykonos," Zoe said. "Be sure to visit Mykonos. And Tinos and Syros and Santorini, too, if you can spare the time."

"Have you been to Greece?" Derek asked, including both Beau and Adrienne in his question.

"I have," Adrienne said. "But to Athens, not the islands."

"Can't say I have," Beau said.

"Oh, you should go," Gillian said emphatically. "I get so many ideas for my jewelry by traveling to new places. If you can open yourself to newness, there is so much to discover."

Adrienne couldn't help but giggle at that. "Have you opened yourself to newness, Beau?"

"I'm working on it," he said, amused, enjoying her sudden playfulness. "I've got to learn some new tricks."

"What's wrong with the old tricks?" asked Gillian, trying to keep pace. Adrienne noticed that her accent was broader than her husband's and she swallowed her vowels more.

"Nothing," he said. "Except Adrienne knows them all."

"That I do," she said. "I guess they're not as effective for Beau as they were in the old days."

They were interrupted by Levi's return; he invited them to bring their drinks and move into the dining room. Zoe seated Beau and Gillian on one side of the table and Adrienne and Derek on the other; she and Levi occupied the end chairs.

"There was this ghastly parade in London last week celebrating the Falklands victory," Derek began as Levi served them the appetizer, an Asian salad with tangerines. "If you can call it that. All those poor blokes killed for a stupid island at the end of the world so Thatcher can boast that we still have an empire."

"My brother told me that the crowd was estimated at half a million," Gillian said.

"It's a sad commentary on what we celebrate," Derek said.

"Speaking of sad commentaries," Levi said. "Did you hear that the University has invited Al Haig to visit Princeton as a lecturer?"

Derek shook his head. "You'd think the administration would

realize how offensive that is to many in the University community. Not only are his politics amoral, but the man has no academic credentials to speak of."

"He's that awful 'I'm in control' man, isn't he?" asked Gillian. "When Reagan was shot. It had the ring of the putsch, didn't it? 'I'm in control.' Quite horrid."

"That was Al Haig," Levi said. "Now he's out of the administration. Forced out, I hear."

"What do you think?" Zoe asked Beau directly. "About the Haig invitation?"

"I hadn't been following it that closely," Beau said.

"I try to avoid politics if I can," Adrienne said. "It makes me mellower when I do."

"I am political," Zoe said, proudly. "More so than Levi, who is supposed to be objective, whatever that means."

"I'm somewhere in between you," Gillian said. "I do have my causes, like the environment and peace. But I don't care for politicians at all."

They had finished their salads and Levi brought out the main course of chicken breasts in Alfredo sauce, with pasta and baby carrots. He beamed when they complimented his cooking.

Derek hadn't finished with politics. "I'd be gratified—and I think most Europeans would be gratified—if you would come to your senses and get Reagan out of the White House," he began. "It's something I just don't understand about this country, why Reagan engenders such support."

"We'll have another chance soon enough," Levi said. "I think that if Anderson hadn't run this last time Carter could have held on.

The country will have a clear choice in the next election. I think the Democrats can take back the White House."

Derek frowned. "But in the meantime, the rest of us have to live with the consequences of Reagan's brinkmanship. This madness with the Cruise and Pershing missiles in Germany. You can't blame the Soviets for seeing the American position as a provocation. You can understand why the nuclear freeze movement has swept throughout Europe. We have no desire to be held hostage by the macho cowboy policies of Washington."

"You know many of us in this country are just as dismayed," Levi said.

"We're not all Neanderthals," his wife added.

"And this amazing gambit with Star Wars," Derek said, warming to his topic. He could see he had an appreciative audience in the Garbers. "Billions of dollars for a concept no credible scientist thinks can ever work and that further exacerbates Soviet paranoia."

Levi nodded. "I'm afraid there's been a lot of wounded American pride to repair," he said. "The Iran hostage situation. The Japanese passing us by economically. Rattling the sword makes some people feel more secure."

"It's just bullying," Zoe said. "No different than kids in a schoolyard."

Levi saw that Beau and Adrienne had yet to join the conversation and he made an effort to draw them in. Adrienne could see that Beau had leaned away from the table and she wondered whether Levi would recognize the clear message he was sending with his body language.

"So what do you think, Beau?" Levi asked. "What are your views on these foreign policy issues? I suspect even non-political types may have opinions on America's role."

"Beau is in the military," Adrienne said with defensive haste. She hoped to keep Beau from being drawn into the conversation. "A pilot. I probably should have said something earlier."

"No problem," Levi said. "I've met some very progressive people with service backgrounds. Admiral Gene La Rocque, for instance. He's supporting the nuclear freeze."

"I'm not," Beau said. "I guess I'm not very progressive."

"You're not," Levi said, hesitating. He looked over at Adrienne, unsure of himself for the first time that evening. "And you, Adrienne?"

"I don't have an opinion," she said. "One way or the other."

Gillian leaned forward, her face flush from the wine, her eyes fixed on Beau. "Are you a cold warrior, then?" she asked, an undercurrent of hostility in her tone. "You look to me like a true blue warrior. It's the way you carry yourself. I can tell."

Beau looked at her curiously. "I'm not sure what you mean," he said gently.

"I divide the world of men into several camps," she said. "Warriors fall into one of those camps. They have a long history. Perhaps the second oldest profession." She laughed. "They have tough faces and big muscles, always ready for conflict. They're representative of the earliest stage of human evolution."

Derek muttered something about rubbish under his breath.

"Gillian has her theories," Zoe said. She gave Adrienne a quick glance. "It appears Beau does have the muscles."

"I'm an aging warrior," Beau said lightly. "At best."

"Ah, you could switch camps," Gillian said. "To become a man of letters, or even to become a lover." She giggled. "Not a bad trade, that. Isn't that what they do with successful racehorses? They go from warrior to lover. They put them out to stud, I think that's the term."

"That's enough conjecture for tonight, dear," Derek said. Adrienne could see he was embarrassed by his wife. "I think Beau should be left alone in whatever camp he prefers."

"What *do* you think?" Zoe asked Beau, clearly annoyed at Derek's interruption. "About the situation in Europe."

"The situation in Europe," repeated Beau. He considered his response for a moment, clearly reluctant. "That's a complex question."

"Not that complex," she said, a slight edge in her voice.

Beau glanced over at Adrienne, looking for help. She sensed that he was willing to dodge the issue, to steer the conversation back to lighter topics, if that was what she wanted.

"They are all ears," she said to him. "Wouldn't want you to let down the side—the warrior side, that is."

"It's easier on the domestic front," Beau said. "I'm not crazy about President Reagan's domestic policies. I can do without them. But I can't quarrel with his approach toward Ivan."

"Ivan?" asked Gillian.

"The Russians," her husband explained, looking at Beau. "Beau is a cold warrior, it seems."

Beau glanced across the table at Adrienne and shrugged. She

suddenly regretted having brought him—it was a mistake. They should have gone to dinner alone.

"I mean, don't you agree it's time we moved beyond this male fixation with power before it leads to a catastrophe?" Gillian asked, fixing her eyes on Beau.

"I wouldn't know where to begin with that," he said. He turned to Adrienne and opened his hands in a gesture of resignation, ignoring the others. "This is why I don't come back here very often. I told you I don't fit in here."

"You seem to be holding your own," she said.

Derek wanted to continue the discussion. "Does that mean you agree with the cowboy tactics of Reagan?" he asked Beau, his voice pitched slightly higher.

"President Reagan," Beau corrected. "I don't endorse everything he's done. But from what I can gather, he's right about the Pershing and Cruise missiles. The Soviets have been testing us with the deployment of the SS-20 in Eastern Europe. Three-warheads each missile. If they'll forgo them, then we won't put the Pershings in. Seems like a fair trade to me."

"I disagree," Derek said. "There's the inescapable fact that the Americans are introducing theater nuclear weapons. The Soviets have offered to freeze the situation, to keep nuclear weapons out of continental Europe."

"That's Soviet propaganda," Beau said. "They started the escalation with their SS-20s."

"No," Derek said, his voice wavering slightly. "I can't agree with that."

Derek seemed caught off guard by Beau's willingness to contest his views. Adrienne guessed that Derek wasn't used to being contradicted. He reminded her of an almost-famous choreographer she had worked with years before, a Russian named Gregor who wouldn't listen to suggestions. Adrienne knew the troupe, knew what they could and couldn't do gracefully, but Gregor expected his steps to be danced his way, without any modifications.

Derek's face was flushed. "I suppose you're fine with Star Wars. Pure folly. It will never work."

Beau paused for a moment, considering his response. "I'll confess I have my doubts about the technical aspects of SDI, what you're calling Star Wars, but hell, if it's fatally flawed, then why are the Soviets so frantic to stop it? If it isn't going to work, then you'd think they would be happy to let us spend ourselves into bankruptcy."

"You're serious," Zoe said, incredulously, clenching her fists. She looked over and made eye contact with Adrienne, arching her eyebrows in disgust. Adrienne glanced away, refusing to acknowledge the gesture, feeling that to do so would somehow be an act of disloyalty to Beau.

"You're serious," Zoe repeated.

"Of course I'm serious," Beau said. "President Reagan may not make the career diplomatic types at the State Department happy, but it seems to me that he's a hell of a negotiator."

"If we make it through this period of madness," Derek said, "historians will look back and assign the majority of the blame for the Cold War, and this insane arms race, to America."

"Why don't we talk about something else?" Adrienne asked. She turned to Zoe for help. "I don't think anyone's going to change their minds tonight. There's no point in becoming emotional over this. We can agree to disagree, can't we?"

Zoe remained silent, apparently willing to let the argument continue. Adrienne thought that it might be because Beau seemed to be more than holding his own and Zoe didn't want to end the conversation until he had been fully refuted. Gillian spoke up, choosing to ignore Adrienne's suggestion.

"It all comes down to perspective," she said. She waved at Beau, her bracelets clacking. "I don't see any country's military as a positive force. They're really vestiges of a past we can't leave fast enough behind us. Those warriors I was talking about. They need to become lovers. I think the world would be safer, and saner, if it was a place without any nuclear weapons, without any armies, without the U.S. Army."

"With all due respect," Beau said coolly. "You and your husband would be speaking German tonight if it weren't for the U.S. Army. All of Europe would. Avoiding that was a positive outcome, however primitive."

"No one is questioning that," Levi said. "The military follows the policy set by our civilian leaders."

His wife shook her head. "But it's all part and parcel of the military-industrial complex," Zoe said. "I don't think our politicians really have much say so. They have to answer to Lockheed and Boeing. That's where the problem begins. The Army is part of the problem, not part of the solution."

"It may seem that way in a comfortable Princeton living room," Beau replied softly. "But not in the real world."

The room fell silent. Derek had fixed his gaze over Beau's head, avoiding eye contact. Levi and Zoe Garber sat in awkward, stunned silence. Gillian, strangely, didn't seem fazed in the least; a slight smile played at the corners of her mouth.

"If you'll please excuse me, Mrs. Garber," Beau said to Zoe, rising to his feet, towering over the table. "I'd like to step outside for some fresh air."

"I'll join you," Adrienne said and turned to the Garbers and their guests. "Please excuse me, too."

Adrienne led Beau by the hand through the kitchen which was outfitted with the latest appliances and boasted a gleaming wood floor. From the living room, they could hear a hushed conversation between Zoe Garber and her husband. The Hawthornes were silent.

Adrienne and Beau stepped out the back door onto an extensive redwood deck. She took a package of Camels from her sweater pocket and offered him a cigarette, her hands shaking slightly from the emotion. He shook his head. She went ahead and lit up, exhaling her first long drag into the night air. Beau leaned next to her on the railing of the deck.

"I shouldn't lose my temper like that," he said. "But I can only listen to that crap for so long. That comment about how historians would believe that we were responsible for the Cold War was just too much. If this country is so screwed up, what the hell is that Brit asshole doing living here?"

"Please keep your voice down, Beau," she said. "I don't think Derek would appreciate being called a 'Brit asshole.'"

"I don't believe he'd think any less of me. I'm sure he considers me as an ill-mannered Jack Tripper type. Ready to nuke the Evil Empire back to the Stone Age."

"They're coming from a different place."

"You can say that again," he said.

"Shush," she said. "Don't waste the energy."

"You're right."

"I can't take you anywhere. I'd forgotten about your temper."

"I haven't," he said. "Forgot about my temper, that is. I wish I had better control of it. I'm overreacting, I know." He exhaled deeply. "I hope I haven't made things untenable for you with your friends."

"They're not my friends," she said. "They're Hugh's."

She didn't want to say anything more, but she knew that when she told Hugh about the evening he would be angry with her. Hugh despised public confrontations and he would blame her for having invited Beau to the Garbers. Hugh had met Beau only once and hadn't cared for him, and this night would more than justify his initial negative opinion.

"I'll apologize to them when we go back in," Beau said. "I just need a moment or two more here outside."

"Thank you," she said. "Part of me wishes you wouldn't apologize, but it will be awkward if you don't. For me."

"Hugh?"

"Yes, I'm afraid that he won't be pleased with me."

"I'm sorry."

"Once you've made your apologizes we should go," she said. "It'd be awkward to stay."

"I'm afraid I've ruined your evening," he said. "It's my fault. I should have kept my cool. I hate what we've come to, the conflict with the other side, more than they can know. I've seen the consequences. I hate talking about it. In there I just reacted reflexively to their smugness. I guess you can only take so much. You can see how it ticks me off when I hear them attacking our motives."

"You just have to ignore it." she said.

He paused, struggling with his emotions. "I wish I could take them up with me in a Cessna or a Beechcraft and head West. Fly across the country, under the cloud cover, and then have them look down and see what the landscape looks like from up there. The farmland and small towns with their baseball diamonds and water tanks and grain silos and railroad crossings and the vastness of it all."

"And then what?"

"I'd have them pick any place, any town, at random and we'd put down at the nearest airport and find the town center and start asking the locals why they think our military is still in Europe. Why we're still there forty years after the war. I know what we'd hear. They're not happy about us being there, but the last time we left we had to go back and at a terrible cost. There's certainly no territorial ambition. What would we want with Europe? Hell, look around. We don't need the rest of the world. We could be self-sufficient and close our borders and not miss a beat. So no one wants our people there, or in any other foreign place, a minute longer than necessary. I only wish the Garbers and the Hawthornes could hear it firsthand. Then they might understand."

He stopped, lost in his thoughts, his face a study in intensity. She recognized, and not for the first time that night, Beau's resemblance to another difficult man, his father, the Professor. They shared a rigidity, an unwillingness to compromise, on what they saw as matters of principle and neither could leave well enough alone; they seemed incapable of letting a challenge pass. She could imagine that, in his time, the Professor had roiled a comfortable Hodge Road dinner party or two with his blunt, direct opinions.

Looking at Beau, his arm brushing lightly against hers, she remembered the fierce desire she'd felt for him the summer they'd been lovers. She wished she had been older, closer to his age, more experienced, more aware. She might have found a way to keep him longer as a lover. The truth was that she was still attracted to him, she knew, despite herself, despite the intervening years. In fact, she couldn't imagine a time when she wouldn't find Beau Kincaid desirable.

She started to say something to him but realized that, for the moment, Beau was lost to her. He was looking up from the deck at the stars above. She studied him for a moment, wondering what he was thinking. Was he soaring above the wingless and the earth-bound, above all of those who, like her, could never understand what it might be to fly alone in the clear, clean dark night sky?

SEVENTEEN

There had been warning signs, hints of trouble ahead. Alexander Kincaid ignored them. One younger editor at his New York publishing house had twice questioned Alexander about passages in his new book, *Hierarchy*. She had suggested watering down some of his more provocative musings about modern mating strategies and potential genetic explanations for the academic and professional success of Asian-Americans. He had rejected her proposed revisions, convinced that—while not central to the thesis of the book—his commentary on those topics would be of interest and value to his readers.

Then, after his publisher had sent out review copies of the book, one of his friends, Atticus Coolidge, a professor of biology at MIT, had called him and after praising *Hierarchy*, said he had heard some disturbing rumors.

"Apparently there's a point-by-point criticism of your book circulating," Atticus explained. "A left-wing critique, of course. A sociologist at Brown is the organizer. I haven't seen the document, but I understand it's quite rough on you personally. The people behind it are trying to gather signatures for a public letter of some sort. Condemnatory of the book and condemnatory of you."

"When and if this letter surfaces, I'll respond," Alexander said. "I appreciate that you thought to alert me."

"Tread lightly, Alexander. These people are politically savvy. They can make considerable trouble for you."

"That's the beauty of tenure. There's nothing they can say or do that can touch me."

"I hope you're correct," Coolidge said. "They're the type who egged on the Red Guards."

"Remember what Mark Twain once said? How he admired the cool confidence of a poker-playing Christian with four aces? I may not have the aces, but I'm confident. I can refute whatever allegations they make. The facts are clear. And my publisher is confident that the reviews will be quite positive."

That didn't prove true. The reviews were mixed—and a common criticism was that the book strayed too far from the available evidence in comparing and contrasting human and animal behavior. Then, two weeks after *Hierarchy*'s publication, the Open Letter first surfaced. One of the student reporters at the *Daily Princetonian* called Alexander for comment. He sent his secretary, Mrs. Rutherford, to pick up a copy of the letter from the offices of the student newspaper. Alexander read it slowly. It was signed by some thirty-five academics, nearly all of them sociologists or social psychologists. The letter claimed that *Hierarchy* advanced false and damaging ideas about women and racial minorities and the signers demanded that Princeton's Biology Department disavow Alexander's work and the University publicly censure him.

Alexander told the *Daily Princetonian* reporter in a brief telephone call that the Open Letter was a political statement and that he wouldn't dignify its ridiculous charges. "I'm disappointed by the tone of the letter," he said, speaking slowly so the reporter could take down his words. "Their quarrel is with the reality of evolution, not with me. Too many of my fellow academics lack any understanding of human nature and its deep evolutionary roots or are even willing to consider it. They will eventually face a professional reckoning. They can't hide from the truth."

The front-page headline in the *Daily Princetonian* the next day was calculated to stir interest on the campus: "Kincaid Book Excites Fierce Controversy." The story's opening paragraphs quoted extensively from the Open Letter, noting its call for the Biology Department to disavow Kincaid's latest book, and for the University to censure him. The article did include Alexander's response—and he was quoted accurately—but the tone of the story favored his critics. To their credit, the chair of the Biology Department and a spokesman for the University administration rejected out of hand the letter's demands, citing the principle of academic freedom. Alexander, who had never faced public criticism, admitted to his wife that the charges in the Open Letter had stung.

"I thought I could shrug it off," he said. "But it's my reputation in question."

"No one who matters will believe any of these lies," Karin said. "Not your friends. Not your colleagues."

"It's not in me to let this go unanswered."

She shrugged. "You will only call more attention to it. That's what they want."

"They're wrong. They're wrong in their claims, and in the way they've attacked the book, and me. I need to respond, or it will look like there's something to what they say."

James Kincaid arrived at Lafayette Place on Saturday, a copy of the *Daily Princetonian* in hand. Alexander greeted his son with a half-smile and, eyeing the newspaper, suggested they retreat to his study to discuss the situation.

Alexander settled into his desk chair and James took the captain's chair opposite him.

"I was lucky to scare up a copy," James said, tossing the newspaper onto the desk. "Only a few were left at the convenience store on Nassau Street."

Alexander folded his hands together and frowned. "When I was a child in Boston, they said your name should appear in the newspaper only three times—your birth announcement, your wedding, and your obituary. There's something to be said for that. But I enjoyed the positive newspaper reviews of my first book, so I guess I'm obligated take the good with the bad."

"It is bad," James said. "You never want your name and the word 'racist' in the same sentence, no matter the context. Whoever is behind this Open Letter is out to damage you badly. Do you know how widely it's been circulated?"

"Widely enough that I've gotten calls from the *Times* and the *Washington Post*. I suspect the organizers sent it to all of the major newspapers. And I understand there's a brief Associated Press story that includes the quotes I gave to the student newspaper."

"You haven't returned those calls?"

"Not yet."

James exhaled. "Good."

"I've written a response to the Open Letter. It refutes the accusations point-by-point. I planned to make that my response for now, ask Mrs. Rutherford to fax them to the reporters who called. Then, there's this interview request. A writer from the *Times* Sunday magazine. She wants to come here and meet me and talk." Alexander picked up a slip of paper and read from it. "Jennifer Rabin. Do you know her?"

"I don't. My advice? Politely decline. You're better off not talking to her."

"If the major newspapers cover this story, I would like my side to be told. Accurately."

James shook his head. "In any magazine profile you're at the mercy of the writer and I doubt you'll get fair treatment. She'll have you on defense the entire time, explaining why you're not a racist and a sexist. The longer you talk the more likely it is that you'll say something that will hurt your case."

"My case? That sounds like I'm on trial."

James picked up the newspaper from the desk and waved it.. "They went easy on you. They're students. It won't be that way with the professionals."

Alexander laughed. "Wait a minute. You're one of them, a professional journalist, and you're telling me not to talk? What about setting the record straight?"

"If you agree to an interview, I suggest you meet the writer for lunch at Conte's. Pizza and beer."

"Really? I thought the Faculty Club or Lahiere's would be better."

"No. You need a setting that humanizes you. Mention that Pete Carril, Princeton's basketball coach, also likes Conte's. After lunch, walk back to Nassau Street and then give her a tour of campus. Talk about your love of teaching, of exploring new ideas with students."

"So you're suggesting I manipulate this reporter."

"I'm not," James said. "You like Conte's pizza. You love the campus. It's a side of you that she needs to see. Details that she can weave into the story that put you in a better light. Trust me, she's going to quote from the Open Letter, and she'll talk to all of your academic critics and they'll paint you as the villain, an elitist, an ancient snob, a racist. You need to give her a different point of reference."

"I'm sixty," Alexander said. "I don't think that makes me ancient."

James hid his amusement at his father's vanity—he seemed bothered more by being considered old than characterized as racist and sexist.

"This writer won't have much of a scientific background," he told his father. "She'll turn to one of your critics to help in simplifying the debate. That's just the way it is. You need to keep it simple and factual. Point to the evidence. And then let's hope for a little fairness."

They spent the rest of the afternoon in mock interviews, with James playing the role of a hostile questioner. He peppered his father with leading questions, questions designed to put him on the defensive. He caused Alexander to flush in anger at least twice.

"I doubt she'll be as tough as I was," James said after they'd finished the session. "But don't be fooled if she starts with softball questions. She'll be probing, looking for signs that you're the evil reactionary that your critics claim you are."

"Some of your questions." Alexander shook his head. "Hostile, to say the least. Will she ask them? You'd think I was advocating race war."

"If you want peace, prepare for war. She probably won't go that hard at you, but who knows? By the way, steer the conversation away from race if you can. If she presses you, repeat what's in your prepared statement. Keep it short."

"I stand by what I wrote. There's nothing racist about it, at all."

James shook his head. "It's the third rail, Dad, and anyone who touches it gets zapped. I didn't think what you wrote about IQ added anything to the book. A tangent. All it did was make you a target."

"We'll have to agree to disagree about that," Alexander said. "I pray that the day never comes when I censor myself for fear of becoming a target."

Alexander waited impatiently for the arrival of Jennifer Rabin, at Princeton Station on a crisp October morning. He had agreed to meet the feature writer there, tour the campus, and then take her to lunch at Conte's on Witherspoon Street. He was slightly uneasy—he had thought about his son's warning, but he believed that he could convince her that he wasn't the reactionary that his critics were making him out to be.

A diminutive woman with curly dark hair and wire-rimmed glasses, Rabin was far from confrontational. Alexander showed her the campus, a tour he had given many times before to guests, and they made the walk to Conte's talking about his latest research project on great apes. She smiled at some of his jokes. He thought he was making headway.

At lunch, the atmosphere changed. Once she opened her reporter's notebook, he noticed that her tone became more formal.

Alexander explained that he had agreed to the interview because he wanted to directly address the accusations in the Open Letter. He handed her his neatly-typed three-page response. She took it from him, folded it in half, and placed it in her handbag.

"Why do you think so many professors signed this letter?" she asked.

"Simply put, they didn't like what I had to say in my book," Alexander responded. "It represents a challenge to their ideological worldview. None of them are in the hard sciences—chemistry, physics, astronomy, biology. I'm a scientist, a biologist. I begin with my research into primates and then I've looked for similarities in human behavior. My critics apparently believe in a blank slate. I don't. I recognize this makes some people uncomfortable. Darwin did, too." He paused. "I'm not suggesting I'm in the same realm as Darwin, God knows, because I'm clearly not, but their reaction reminds me of how the Establishment first reacted to the theory of evolution."

"Does their reaction give you pause?"

"I'm human. Who likes to be called names?"

"They've made some serious claims. Do you think they would do so frivolously?"

"I can't speak to their motives," Alexander said. "I can't say who acted in good faith, and who didn't. Many of my critics appear to be quite ideological."

"Don't all of us start with an ideological framework?" she asked. "You have an ideology, even if it isn't stated."

"Well, I don't know about that. I approach things through the scientific method. I also believe that we shouldn't decide beforehand what should be ruled out for further experimentation. I have supported Professor Jahn's right to run the Princeton Engineering Anomalies Research laboratory. Many of my colleagues did not. It's not that I believed in ESP or telekinesis—I don't. But Professor Jahn's a respected scientist. Attacking his right to conduct his research is an assault on scientific inquiry. Yes, it was eccentric. But why not investigate the paranormal? Design experiments, generate the data, invite others to replicate the results. Extraordinary claims demand extraordinary evidence. By the way, if he's proved correct, he'll join Newton and Darwin and Einstein in changing how we see the world."

"But you doubt that will happen."

"I do."

Rabin dabbed at her lips with a paper napkin. "Do you consider yourself rich, Professor Kincaid? Wealthy?"

"Most people would consider me well-to-do. I've been fortunate in that."

"A member of the elite?" she asked.

"Aren't tenured professors members of the elite almost by definition?"

"So that is a yes? You're part of the elite. Do you think that membership might make you more prone to view the established order as somehow natural? As the way things should be? God's in his heaven, all's well in the world. And that might influence the conclusions in your book?" She studied his face.

"That's a fair question. In my book, I write about the way the quest for status shapes society. Not just ours. Can't say I've encountered many cultures without a pecking order, without hierarchies. That includes our primate cousins."

"Your critics believe that you have twisted research to arrive at some quite reactionary conclusions."

"I know full well what they believe. They're wrong. I understand the allure of Utopia, a world without hierarchy. My critics believe in complete human malleability. But the delusion that we can change human nature, a delusion shared by the Nazis and the Marxists, has cost humanity dearly."

"It is 1983, Professor Kincaid. And we seem quite a ways from Orwellian territory."

Alexander shook his head. "Perhaps not as far as we should be."

She shook her head slightly, and wrote something in her notebook. The rest of the interview was pleasant enough, but Alexander could tell from the questions that she sided with the critics of *Hierarchy*.

James had warned his father to be prepared for a negative profile. After the interview with Jennifer Rabin, the only question was how negative.

The article appeared a month later with a sinister-looking black-and-white photo of Alexander and a headline that proclaimed: "Princeton's Problematic Professor." In the piece, Jennifer Rabin made a distinction between the man and his ideas, suggesting that it was tragic that the personally charming Alexander Kincaid seemed oblivious to the damage that *Hierarchy* could do for the cause of social justice for women and minorities.

On Princeton's leafy sun-dappled Gothic campus, Alexander Tarkington Kincaid lives in a bubble, divorced from the inequalities of American life, the grinding poverty and limited opportunities for the disenfranchised, the poor, the marginalized. He admits to being an elitist but claims that he doesn't favor the powerful. No matter that disclaimer, his critics see his views on status, authority, and hierarchy as the tired old "survival of the fittest" argument, an argument supported by shaky research findings and logical leaps.

Kincaid also claims, somewhat disingenuously, to be surprised at the intensity of the reaction to Hierarchy. He shouldn't be. There's no outright smoking-gun evidence that he's a racist or misogynist, but his world view appears to be stuck in the past. Some of his colleagues see him as a tragic figure, a Boston Brahmin now out-of-touch with how the country has changed. Yet his pronouncements from the ivory tower have consequences. He may believe his intentions are pure, but Kincaid's conclusions lend a veneer of respectability to reactionary political claims and toxic eugenic theories.

Over lunch at Lafayette Place, Alexander admitted to James that granting the interview was a mistake.

"You were right," he said. "I should have stayed silent. Your mother thought so, too."

"It could have been worse," James said. "At times, the article was almost sympathetic."

Alexander shook his head. "I could do without the sympathy."

"I did warn you."

"Rabin was right about one thing," his father replied. "It's a different world, today. Imagine signing a letter like this one, a letter filled with the most vile charges? Who lends their name to that? Are they so afraid of my ideas that they'll stoop that low?" He shook his head. "I have tenure. I don't worry about my position. But what of those just starting out? These attacks are a warning to younger faculty about what can and cannot be considered. The opposite of what a great university should encourage."

"You're past the worst of it," James replied. "Things will settle down."

"Cold comfort," Alexander said. "There's damage to my reputation. I'm not blind to that. So I've decided to let things quiet down. Get back to my research. I don't want to spend any more time defending myself, certainly not in the popular press."

"I think that's wise."

"Your mother quoted a Swedish proverb to me. Something about how speech is silver, but silence is gold."

"Under the circumstances, that sounds about right," James said. "I know it goes against your nature, but moving on from this is the best course."

"Perhaps so," Alexander said. "But I stand by every word I wrote."

In the days and weeks that followed, Alexander Kincaid remained silent, refusing to engage any further with his detractors. He had never been very political—he regarded his views as mainstream, he considered himself to be open-minded and tolerant, and he was mindful of the freedoms and liberty afforded to him living in a liberal democracy. He had been surprised by the outright venom in the Open Letter, and wondered if it represented a new, darker trend in academia. He hoped not. It seemed that the radicals—and that's how he termed them—wanted to declare some topics off-limits to research and conjecture, largely because (he believed) they feared what the conclusions might mean for their Utopian project. They would fail. They had to fail.

He did not emerge unscathed. Over time, he sensed a wariness, a new reserve, among some of his younger colleagues. There were fewer offers to collaborate on research, fewer speaking invitations to conferences. He worried about the impact in the classroom. Did his students see him in a different light? Did they think the charges against him had any validity? He tried not to feel defensive. He found himself shying away from some of the faculty social functions he used to attend and spending less time on campus and more time in his Lafayette Place study.

He told himself that he had made the right choice to insist on keeping the controversial passages in *Hierarchy*. But he wondered, considering the price, had he?

EIGHTEEN

ALEXANDER

December 6, 1983

Dear Priscilla,

It seems that I only take pen to paper and write to you when there are dark clouds overhead. But naturally, I turn to my older sister, for reassurance when things have taken a turn for the worse. When I was little, a scolding from Dad? Skinned knees as a boy? As an adult, the slings and arrows of outrageous fortune? It's comforting to know that Pri is there to listen.

This time, it's a bruised ego. Mine. I've been under a coordinated attack for what I wrote in *Hierarchy*. A number of leftist sociologists and psychologists (a redundancy, I know, to note they're leftist) ginned up an Open Letter attacking Yours Truly for all sorts of Thought Crimes. I would be repulsed by their description of Alexander Kincaid if I didn't know how false the charges are.

They have seized on one paragraph in the book where I mused about the IQs of Chinese and Japanese immigrants and their professional success. Even though I also cited the work ethic and traditional commitment to education by these groups, the Open Letter mob seized upon that and branded me as a racist. And my other Thought Crime was to suggest that men and women pursue different mating strategies.

James recommended that I not grant interviews, that I keep my response to the criticism as brief as possible. Apparently, there's something called the Barbra Streisand effect, where publicly refuting an attack just calls more attention to it.

I disagreed with him on that. I wanted to refute the lies. James wasn't happy with that, but he did advise me on how I should deal with the press. We did a mock interview and he was quite rough with me, asking leading trick questions, interrupting me, trying to get under my skin. I felt better prepared when the magazine writer came to Princeton to interview me.

While I appreciated James's help in prepping me for the interview, I couldn't shake the feeling that he has reservations about my work, particularly as to how it relates to human behavior. I think I understand why. His personal theology is a mixture of Jung and Teilhard de Chardin, and he regards me as a hopeless skeptic on the question of transcendence. Where I believe great beauty can be the product of randomness, James cannot.

I don't know whether my *Sunday Times* magazine profile changed anyone's mind. The writer, a woman named Jennifer Rabin, did quote me accurately (more or less) but throughout the article she made her sympathies clear, suggesting that I was an out-of-touch elitist and letting my critics, the leftist sociologists and psychologists, have the last word.

In short, Alexander Tarkington Kincaid did not emerge smelling like roses.

Until this episode, I led a charmed professional life. There were the occasional academic spats, but I was unprepared for the ferocity of this latest assault. I believed that I was thick-skinned, but learned my skin isn't nearly as thick as I thought.

Still, I don't regret having written *Hierarchy*. The ideas deserved to be voiced. I had something worthwhile to say, and I don't regret publishing the book.

For now, however, I think it's best if I disengage from the debate. I don't want to become a lightning rod for controversy. I've learned that it's nigh impossible to mount a successful defense of bad faith attacks on one's character. I was naive about this, and I won't make this mistake again.

James was kind enough to send a brief note quoting the Psalms, Isaiah 54: "No weapon that is formed against thee shall prosper; and every tongue that shall rise against thee in judgment thou shalt condemn." I copied it onto a note card and have posted it on the wall above my desk where I can see it.

Your battered and beleaguered brother, Alex

P.S. I just read what I've written, and I'm appalled at how whiny I sound. With all that is going on in the world, with our Marines being killed in Beirut and protests over Grenada, it's more than a bit self-centered for me to complain. I was tempted to rip up this letter, but I'm sending it anyway, knowing you'll understand.

NINETEEN

HANNA

9/25/84

Dearest Jimmy,

I promised in our last phone call that I'd write a long letter, and the new and improved Hanna Kincaid is following through (although I may run out of energy and see this turn into something shorter than intended).

Did you know that I kept a diary for a while during middle school and high school? I've been recording my thoughts in a journal again, and I've found it surprisingly calming.

As I told you on the phone, I've been here in a small rental, in Sebastopol, for several months now. I had no intention of leaving the city, but then I spent a weekend touring the vineyards here and I fell deeply in love with Sonoma Valley, the sheer natural beauty of the place with its rolling hills and lush valleys, and the relaxed, laid-back lifestyle. There's something about the atmosphere, something serene and golden that just called to me. Not completely rational. I just knew that I wanted to live here. And now that I'm here, I have a sense of belonging. It's a place to come to.

As I write this letter to you, I can see the dark-blue Pacific stretching out in front of me, wave after wave washing over the beach. Quite a sight! I'm in Bodega Bay, spending the weekend housesitting for a client. It's an amazing place, and the owner has hired Kincaid Landscape Design—that's what I'm calling my business—to work on the grounds. I still have to have a licensed landscape architect sign off on my designs, since I don't have my own license yet, but I'm lucky to have connected with a very generous man, Ted Gray. He has been wonderful. Ted is an older guy who has forgotten more about plants and trees and landscaping than I'll ever know. He's been generous with his time and his advice.

Back to the house I'm staying at—it's quite something. The owner is a financial wizard type and this is his weekend place. He wanted a terraced garden with flair and he had seen some of my landscaping work at a friend's house. Darla, the friend, had given him my phone number, and he had called and asked for me to come by the following week, see his place, and draw up a plan. When he suggested I could stay here, I made it clear I would only if I was by myself—and he thought that was hilarious because he explained that he's gay.

No, I never imagined that I'd run a business. Remember how I wanted to be a singer-songwriter, the next Carole King? That didn't go as planned. In truth, I didn't care for performing in person, and I was never quite able to capture that lightning in a bottle when I wrote songs. Designing landscapes is a different matter. I'm actually pretty damn good at it, and I still can't believe that I get paid to do something I love.

I credit Mom. She's the one who got me interested in trees and plants. We'd walk around Princeton together and she would teach me about the various species. Remember the backyard rose garden at Lafayette Place? I didn't realize how much I learned from Mom about gardening until I started this job.

I've been reading tons of books on landscape design and taking courses on horticulture, site plans, landscape irrigation, and arboriculture at the local community college. I'll need a degree and will have to take an exam before I can get my license, but it won't be too long before I have it.

I'm making new friends. No man in my life at the moment, but I don't need the distraction when I'm trying to get Kincaid Landscape off the ground. I don't need a lot to live on. I figure a few jobs every month will pay the rent and keep food on the table. I've saved enough money to tide me over for quite some time.

It sounds like King is a handful, a wonderful five-year-old handful. I promise I will move heaven and earth to get back East this year so I can hug my adorable nephew. Send me a list of some toys that he might like for his birthday. And nothing educational! Something fun, that he'll enjoy.

I feel guilty that I haven't been as connected with family as much as I'd like.

my love to Julia and King and to my Jimmy,

your one and only sister, Hanna!

P.S. What are you hearing from Beau these days? How much longer will he be stationed in Germany? Do you think he'll return with a pretty Fraulein in tow?

TWENTY

JULIA

Why did I become curious about religion? It happened gradually: the Kincaids were churchgoers and I used to tag alone with Jimmy to services. He was my initial guide to the mysteries of faith, and he had some interesting insights about the people who turned up in the pews around us on Sundays.

"Some come out of habit," he said. "Some come for the sense of community, and some for the spirituality. And there are those who come to be seen—someone once said that Episcopalians were the ruling class at prayer. And some come because they believe."

"And you?" I asked.

"It reminds me that there's something more," he said. "More than the material. And I feel like I belong here."

I found that I wanted to belong. I got more serious about exploring questions of faith and belief when we moved back to Princeton after I got pregnant with King, and I began attending at Trinity Church. I joined the adult religion class and just two months before King was born, I was confirmed in the Episcopal Church.

I liked my fellow parishioners, the other young couples with children, the long-time members of Trinity, solid vestrymen in dark suits, and gray-haired little old ladies who never missed a Sunday. I found comfort in that community, the prayers and the hymns and Holy Communion. I know it made Jimmy happy to have me and King in the pew next to him.

We had waited six months to have King baptized. We gathered at Trinity for his christening on a cold February Sunday morning. We asked Fred Bond, a friend of Jimmy's, and Hanna to be his godparents.

King cried when the minister sprinkled water on his forehead but quickly settled down when he was swaddled and back in my arms. I hugged him close to comfort him and gave him a kiss on his cheek.

Alex and Karin looked on with smiles, and my parents stood by awkwardly, clearly feeling out of place.

As a child, my father had attended services at the Methodist Church in his Pennsylvania hometown, only because his parents had insisted. He decided that I wouldn't be subjected to Sunday School. My mother didn't object—she had never been much of a churchgoer herself. They did have me baptized at the insistence of my grandmother King (who died when I was two years old).

I think that Jimmy was the one Kincaid whose faith grew as he aged. None of his siblings seemed as interested in spiritual questions. There's some irony in that—a skeptical journalist chasing after a supernatural God. But it made sense to me. Jimmy saw some terrible things covering crime stories in New York City and it made him consider deeper questions about life and death. He told me that questioning helped pull him back to church.

"I figure I have a choice," he said. "What am I to think about all the pain and unhappiness in the world, The terrible things we're capable of doing to others? Do I think we're alone, no rhyme or reason, to our existence? Some days it feels that way. Shit just happens. But I'm not a nihilist. There has to be some deeper meaning." He paused and rubbed his eyes. "There are glimmers, traces, of how we should live. And love, *agape*. I see signs all around us. I don't think it's all in my head. I don't think it's my imagination."

"And there's King," I reminded him. "That's what makes me think there's a God. He's such a little miracle."

I think Jimmy's spiritual quest began as an intellectual exercise (later, it became more a matter of heart than head). He became fascinated by the French Jesuit theologian Pierre Teilhard de Chardin, who looked to bridge the gap between faith and science. Jimmy was fascinated enough to persuade me to make "Teilhard" King's middle name.

Teilhard was a paleontologist and his work in China and Africa had convinced him of the truth of evolution. Jimmy had me read some of his books (I tried, it was rough going), and I could see the appeal his ideas held for my husband, the deep thinker. There is something very comforting about his notion of spiritual evolution, all of creation converging on a future Omega Point, a final point of unification with Christ. Teilhard's theology was suppressed by the Roman Catholic Church, even though it could be tied into scripture—after all, in the Book of Revelation, Christ calls himself "the Alpha and the Omega, the beginning and the end." But it was the 1950s, and the Vatican clung to the Latin Mass and wasn't going to encourage free-thinking.

I liked one of the quotes from Teilhard's book: "If humanity ever captures the energy of love, it will be the second time in history that we have discovered fire."

I've never been one for deep thoughts. I'm a practical girl. For me, the Golden Rule and the simple message of forgiveness and unconditional love is enough. Love without conditions. The kind of love a mother has for her children. That makes sense to me. It always will.

Jimmy never complained about my desire to live in Princeton and raise King in the place we grew up, even though it meant he spent long hours in the car (or train) commuting to New York. We could have moved closer to the city, but it would have meant finding a new community and making new friends and neither Jimmy or I had the energy for that. And perhaps I was somewhat selfish, but I didn't want to move and leave the familiar.

I loved the continuity of staying in our hometown.

There was a cost. It meant Jimmy wasn't around as much as I would have wanted and when he was home, he was often tired. Whatever free time he had, we spent it together with King, attending church on Sunday, stopping by Lafayette Place for lunch, and taking long walks with King safely strapped into his stroller.

There were some changes in our life.

My parents surprised us by retiring to Fort Lauderdale. They were drawn by the balmy weather and the lower cost of living. My father retired at the age of sixty, and my mother was confident she could find a part-time job to supplement their savings.

"You have the Kincaids," she said. "You'll be fine. Come visit us when you need some sun."

From the start, she had questioned whether my relationship with Jimmy would last. She was wrong, and I think she secretly resented that our marriage had endured. That's a sad and terrible thing to think about your own mother, but I'm afraid it was the truth. I never felt close to her. She wasn't an affectionate woman by nature, and while she didn't mistreat me, I never felt fully loved, never felt much warmth. It wasn't in her nature. My father couldn't fill that emotional vacuum. He was quiet and distant, worn down by making a living.

Perhaps I overcompensated with King, loving him as fiercely as I did. I tried not to dwell on any slights from my past. I had Jimmy, I had King, I had a comfortable home, and I felt loved. That seemed more than enough.

There was one shadow on my happiness, one nagging concern—my fear of the Kincaid curse of moodiness and depression, the disorder that often weighed down Karin and that cost Desmond his life. Had it been passed on to King? I could only hope that he had been dealt a better genetic hand.

I watched him carefully for any signs of depression. Thankfully, he was a cheerful, happy-go-lucky child, and that made me less anxious, although I could never completely relax. I had read enough to know that depression often surfaced in the teen years.

When he was around, which wasn't nearly often enough, Jimmy was a good father. He played catch with King in the backyard, read bedtime stories, took him fishing when we spent vacation time in Boca Grande at the Kincaid beach house. But there was always another reporting assignment that would take him away from us for days or weeks at a time. I knew that was the life of a journalist, but that didn't make it any easier. And yes, I resented it, fair or not. I wanted him home more, and he didn't try hard enough to make that happen—at least that's how I saw it.

I learned how the years fly by when you're raising a child. Play dates. Nursery school. Doctor's appointments. And then the moment when your baby boy starts kindergarten when you no longer control their day, and you realize that the world, with all of its bumps and scrapes, awaits him.

King was a bright child. Independent. He was curious, like his father, and eager for new experiences. In that, he was a Kincaid.

TWENTY-ONE

JAMES

Reykjavik, Iceland, October 1986

I had always hoped to cover a big story—every journalist worth his or her salt does—but I never imagined that my break would come unexpectedly in such a strange place.

In an attempt to derail tension between the superpowers, President Reagan and General Secretary Gorbachev had agreed to rendezvous in Reykjavik with only two weeks' notice to the Icelandic government. The tiny island nation was a convenient halfway point geographically for the meeting, although its capital city was ill-equipped to handle the ensuing influx of journalists, security officers, diplomats, and government officials.

Once the news broke about the summit, I pitched the idea of covering it with my editor, Ed Donaghue. I fully expected to be turned down—I hadn't been with the Continental News Agency very long—and I was surprised when he agreed to the idea. I was excited and anxious. One of the reasons I had left the Associated Press was that I figured in a smaller outfit like Continental, I might have a shot at more important stories.

It was my first international assignment, and I felt the pressure of wanting to be both accurate and fast in my reporting. Sensing my nervousness, Ed Donaghue had assured me that I would be fine.

"In some ways, it's harder to cover a small-town city council than the White House," he told me. "It's the President of the friggin' United States. There's a well-oiled apparatus in place to brief the press with bulletins and news releases. The three big networks and the *Times* and *Washington Post* will get more access, but you'll be credentialed and included in some of the reporting pools."

He peered at me over his half-glasses. "Keep it simple. Always explain things in a way our readers will understand. Clear and concise. You can do that, yes?"

"I can do that."

"And find some angle that's different. We need to justify the expense of sending you, so see what you can turn up that will keep 'em reading to the end of the article and talking about it around the kitchen table."

I nodded. I wanted to make the most of the assignment—a chance to prove I could handle a big story. And I was curious about what it would be like to watch history being made.

I flew to Iceland four days before the start of the summit, thankful to get a seat on an overbooked flight, and relieved to find that my hotel reservation would be honored and I had a place to stay—no small thing with the hordes of outsiders descending on the city.

I did what I always do when I arrive in a new place: I bought the most detailed map I could find and took off on a walking tour of Reykjavik.

The streets were already starting to fill with visitors. I began by stopping at the traditional tourist sights, visiting the landmarks, viewing the city from the observation tower of the Hallgrímskirkja, the Lutheran cathedral that's the tallest building in the country.

The neat, simple wooden houses lining the sloping side streets of the city reminded me of those in Täby, the town outside Stockholm where my mother had grown up. I visited Täby once, with Julia, when we visited Sweden one summer between my junior and senior years in college.

I felt lucky to have a hotel room close to downtown, fairly near to where Reagan and Gorbachev were to meet at the Hofdi House, a small whitewashed mansion situated on the waterfront with a view of the mountains across the harbor. The local legend was that it was haunted by a poet who took his own life when he was spurned by a lover.

I filed two feature stories while I waited for the arrival of the U.S. and Soviet delegations. For the first, I interviewed several English-speaking Icelanders about how their views of President Reagan and found many of them were skeptical about whether he would negotiate in good faith with the Soviet leader. They had a more favorable impression of Gorbachev than I would have expected. The second article focused on the frantic preparations by city officials for the summit and how the dearth of hotel rooms, rental cars, and restaurant reservations quickly drove up prices and benefited local businesses.

I was eager for the start of the summit, even though I knew it would involve a fair amount of standing around and waiting for the release of an official statement or for a news conference where a few correspondents from the major newspapers and networks could ask questions.

Since you can't be everywhere, you learn to share information with your colleagues. Within reason, of course, but there's an expectation of collegiality.

I was lucky to meet a few more experienced journalists at the hotel bar. I took an immediate liking to a young British academic, Nigel Hawes, who wrote a column for the *Guardian*. He introduced me to Isabelle Lavalle, an older French photojournalist whose dark hair and eyes suggested that she was of Eurasian heritage.

"I'm here because I'm most interested in this fellow Gorbachev and what he might mean for the Soviet Union," Nigel told me. "He appears to represent something different, a dramatic change from the doddering Politburo types of the past. Thatcher believes the West can do business with him and the Iron Lady isn't easy to impress."

"And you?" I asked Isabelle.

"For a photographer, it's a dream come true, *un rêve devenu réalité*," she said. "After I record the history of this summit, I can spend a week taking photographs of the landscape of Iceland. Mountains, fjords, waterfalls, islands, the horses."

"I think Isabelle will take away more from this than we do," Nigel said, looking over at me. "The summit is likely to produce modest progress on arms control, at best. No breakthroughs."

I nodded. From what I had gathered about prospects for the summit, Nigel was right. Few thought the superpowers would reach agreement on reducing ballistic missiles or on intermediate nuclear force levels. And Gorbachev had, for the moment, looked like the peacemaker with his calls for ridding the planet of nuclear weapons, even though it wasn't considered a serious proposal.

"You have low expectations, then?" I asked.

"They're talking. That's progress. I think it was Harold Macmillan who said 'better jaw jaw than war war.' Jaw jaw is better, isn't it? Even my father, the resolute Tory, would reluctantly agree."

I had to smile. "My brother, the Army officer, would agree, also reluctantly. No love lost for the Russians."

Nigel nodded. "I've Polish ancestors on my father's side, so I know the sentiment. But the world's too small a place to hold old grudges. So I tell my father."

I didn't sleep much the next few days.

I wasn't going to let anyone outwork me.

I was there when President Reagan arrived at Keflavik Airport aboard Air Force One just after seven o'clock on Thursday evening. After being greeted by Icelandic government officials, he was whisked away to the residence of the U.S. ambassador, which was situated next door to the Embassy, where he was to stay during his visit. His advisors set up offices in a nearby school building.

I'd already written a preview of the summit and topped it with a few paragraphs about the President's arrival, and then filed the story with New York.

I was waiting outside the Hofdi House the next morning, angling for a spot in the scrum of journalists where I could see the front door. I was surprised by how much larger President Reagan seemed than Gorbachev when they met in person at the steps of the mansion. They shook hands, smiled for the cameras, and went inside, followed by members of their delegation and their security details.

This wasn't their first encounter—they had met in Geneva in November of 1985, and by all accounts it had been an awkward meeting with little accomplished.

So then the waiting began. What was going on behind closed doors? Anything substantive? Did they have, in the diplomatic jargon, a "frank and useful discussion" or were they actually negotiating?

A comprehensive account would have to wait until the day, long in the future, that the transcripts of the conversations were released, when historians could review the oral histories and the (self-serving) memoirs of the participants.

For the working press, the best we could hope for was to report the basic facts with as much color as we could conjure up. We weren't getting any help from the White House communication staff—they were trying to lower expectations about the summit.

I filed a story describing the face-to-face meeting of the leaders and reviewed the key issues—in simple terms—and the prospects for agreement, which were slim.

There were hints that something more substantial might be going on—arms control experts from both the U.S. and the Soviet delegations had returned to the Hofdi House and were apparently in an extended working session.

I knew that it would be hard to find anyone in the U.S. delegation who would talk to me, on or off-the-record. I had one card to play: Continental News syndicated articles appeared in several small newspapers largely in the Middle West that were friendly to Ronald Reagan's brand of conservatism.

Moira Featherstone, a college friend, knew a State Department official, Lydia White, who was on the Secretary of State's staff. As a favor, Moira had called her before the Summit and asked her to meet with me in Iceland. White reluctantly agreed to a brief background interview.

When we met at her hotel, White was gracious but made it clear I couldn't quote her.

"All not for attribution," she said. She paused, pursing her lips, and waited until I nodded.

I asked her whether it was hard to negotiate with the Russians.

"At times," she said. "Many of them have lived in the West. They know that their country has been crippled by the arms race. And crippled by their ideology, if they're intellectually honest. They're hard men. Their system has made them hard. We deal with them because we must."

"Do you think Gorbachev can be trusted?"

She shrugged. "An intriguing fellow. His biography doesn't suggest he's anything more than a lukewarm reformer with a half-decent tailor. Lukewarm because he won't actually challenge the system. He's a Party man. But their economy is in tatters. He knows it can't continue like this."

I asked her whether President Reagan was willing to make an arms deal or was only trying to soften his image before the midterm elections.

"I think that you're wrong about him," she said. "The President's sincere in wanting to reduce the potential for an Armageddon. Sure, some progress with the Soviets would help with his favorability ratings. But I'll let you in on some inside baseball.

The Pentagon is worried that the President may concede too much to the Russians."

"The Pentagon? Who in the Pentagon?"

"The hardliners. Our Secretary of Defense thinks that the White House is too eager for a deal."

"That's certainly not Reagan's reputation," I said. "Isn't he the last of the Cold Warriors?"

"Don't believe everything you read," she said. "Certainly not the caricature of the President that appears in the *Times* and the *Post*. They don't understand him. They never will. But he wants peace and he wants to rid the world of nuclear weapons. Fancy that." She smiled. "I'm afraid I have a meeting I need to attend.

I thanked her for her time and watched as she exited the room.

There wasn't much I could use from the interview, except perhaps for her description of Gorbachev as a "lukewarm reformer with a half-decent tailor." Yet I found it intriguing that she was willing to reveal that the hardliners were worried about Reagan softening his stance. Was that true? Or an attempt to cast the President in a favorable light in advance of the midterm elections?

Then, in a move that surprised all of us watching, the summit took a strange turn. The two leaders extended their meeting time on Sunday and there were rumors that some significant announcement, perhaps even a breakthrough on arms control, might be in the offing.

But the abrupt end of the summit—with both Reagan and

Gorbachev publicly expressing frustration over a lack of agreement on the thorny question of Reagan's pet project, the Strategic Defense Initiative—dashed expectations.

I attended the Soviet news conference where the Russians openly expressed their displeasure, and then went back to the hotel and where I found Nigel and Isabelle in the bar. They waved me over.

"I'm not quite sure what has happened," Nigel said. "It's a bit of a bloody mystery, isn't it?"

"What do you mean?" I asked.

"If what we're hearing is true, Reagan did something no one expected. The Cold War cowboy agreed in principle to significant arms reductions, but he wouldn't budge on his beloved Star Wars and that's what killed any deal."

"Reagan looked very disappointed when he was leaving the Hofdi House," Isabelle said. "Tired and angry and disappointed."

Nigel waved to an empty chair. "Join us for a drink?"

I explained that I had to immediately file my story. "That's the problem with working for the wire services," I said. "You have to feed the monster."

"And what will you say?" Isabelle asked.

"A lost opportunity," I replied. "A missed chance to change the terms of engagement. But some hope. From what I can gather, they did Nigel's jaw jaw."

"I'm going to surprise you," Nigel said. "I think your President came in good faith. I think he wanted to reach an agreement with Gorbachev. That's a positive in my book."

"Are you planning to share that opinion in your column?" I asked.

"You're also going to surprise your readers who faithfully vote Labor and can't stand Reagan."

"I can't very well criticize the man for not engaging with the Soviets and then attack him when he does, can I?" Nigel grinned. "This may be one of the few times when I've had to revise my opinion about a politician. Could it be we've misjudged him? That Ronald Wilson Reagan is a secret peacenik? That he represents a threat not to world peace, but to the American military-industrial complex? Wouldn't that be a twist of fate?"

I flew back two days later, the conquering hero (in my own mind) eager to return home. I was drained but excited. I felt I had acquitted myself well. It was the biggest story I had ever covered, and I was still on an adrenaline high.

I took a cab from Kennedy Airport to the Continental News' office in Manhattan. I hadn't slept much and I'd imagine I looked pretty ragged.

Ed Donaghue greeted me with a handshake and a crooked smile.

""Your stuff was good," he told me. "Just what we were looking for. Go home. Take a few days off."

I thanked him and fell asleep on the train from New York to Princeton. Julia picked me up at Princeton Junction, with King asleep in his car seat. I kissed both of them.

"So how did it go?" Julia asked. "They're saying on the television news that the summit was a disappointment. Nothing accomplished."

"I don't know what to think," I told her. "I went there convinced that it was a dog-and-pony show for political reasons. But I think Reagan was sincerely trying to find a way."

"Could that be possible?" Julia asked. "I'd rest better if they just do something. Baby steps. Agree to something, build fewer bombs."

"They may have made a start, I think."

"Wouldn't it be wonderful if King could grow up not having to worry about a nuclear war like we did as kids?"

"Who knows? Nixon went to China. Maybe Reagan can deliver where a liberal couldn't. I didn't think he was serious about doing something about arms control, but now I do."

Julia sighed. "I hope and pray that you're right, Jimmy. I really do."

Years later, I found my reporter's notebook from the Reykjavik summit buried in a cardboard box. As I leafed through it, the scrawled names (Shultz, Poindexter, Nitze, Perle, Adelman, Shevardnadze, Dobrynin, Yakovlev) and abbreviations (START, INF, SLCMs, LRINF) brought back a raft of memories. It had been a consequential time for a world desperately hoping for a thaw between the superpowers, and for a young journalist covering the biggest story of his career.

Reading my notes prompted me to dig up the newspaper clips of my coverage of the summit. To my surprise, they held up fairly well. I had managed to make some sense out of what was happening and had suggested that there was a glimmer of hope about possible progress. My reporting might have been narrowly focused, and incomplete, but it got the basics right and I found myself proud of the job I had done.

But in characterizing the Reykjavik summit as a failure, which I came close to doing, I got it wrong. Most of my colleagues missed the mark as well. They say journalists write the first draft of history, and sometimes we think we know more than we really do. I sensed something shifting during that weekend in Iceland, but who would have believed it was the beginning of the end of the Cold War?

TWENTY-TWO

HANNA

2/20/87

Dearest Jimmy,

Thank you for sending the newspaper clippings of your reporting from Iceland. (I think it's really cool that Continental collects articles from all your client newspapers). Seeing your byline above an article about the Reagan-Gorbachev Summit made me so proud. I envy that you could be there as a witness to history.

It's a shame that they couldn't reach a real agreement on doing something about these horrific weapons that both sides have stockpiled. Why is it so hard for men to drop their war clubs and get along? Does anyone think a nuclear war is winnable? Sometimes I can't believe how childish they can be. And it is a male thing.

Speaking of men, I've met someone. Sort of. One of my clients, Karl Vance, asked me to dinner after I finished landscaping his property, creating an elaborate Japanese garden. Yes, his property. He has an oceanside estate. Karl made his money in something he describes as router software, selling his company to Cisco Systems.

His place is amazing. The main house is a dark wood structure recessed into a hillside with a view of the Pacific. He wanted a full-scale *karesansui* garden, incorporating a "dry-style" contemplative area in one section with sand, stones, and scattered rock islands. My design included a granite bridge, four-feet long, that leads to a main rock island. He also asked for a pond, which he'll stock with koi.

Yes, this cost him a pretty penny.

And I said yes when he asked me on a date. (This time I wasn't fooled. He's straight!) I know what you're thinking—I'm like Elizabeth Bennett in *Pride and Prejudice* when she visits Pemberley and once she sees his massive estate decides that perhaps the arrogant Mr. Darcy might have redeeming qualities. (Jane Austen understood women quite well, I think.) But Karl interested me and I haven't been out with anyone for a while. What did I have to lose?

He took me to dinner in San Francisco to a fancy French restaurant. Quite the gentleman.

Karl is a driven man. He works out two hours a day. Inside his mansion is a complete gymnasium with the latest equipment, Nautilus and Cybex machines, and a heated lap pool. For a man in his early 40s, he's in great shape. (I'm blushing a little.)

At dinner, he opened up to me, explaining that he had married young, a mistake that ended in a divorce. I give him credit for honesty. His wife left him because of his workaholicism. They were both software engineers, but she coded to make a living while coding was his life. She couldn't deal with his intense focus on work. He had learned from the experience, he said, and realized that he needed to add more balance in his life after he sold his company.

He's fascinated with the concept of Tao and how it's at the center of the mysteries of life. Karl began his study of Eastern mysticism, traveling to India and Japan, reading the ancient classics, practicing meditation. It's why he wanted a Japanese garden. I know this must seem so West Coast to you, Jimmy, but I like the idea of exploring new ideas.

I also like a lot of things about Karl. I've seen him three times now. I'm not sure that we're suited for each other. Remember the story about how Dad met Mom in Sweden and knew she was the one? And she felt the same way? I haven't felt that about Karl. About any man. Is that sad?

Too much about me. When are you sending the latest photos of King? And you and Julia?

Love, your Hanna

P.S. It's been a week since I wrote this letter and didn't get around to mailing it.

So there's more to report. A bit of a bummer. I broke it off with Karl. When I saw him a day after I wrote this letter, he proposed to me. I had to say no. Karl wants children, and I'm not wild about the idea, at least not yet. He was kind and sweet and a bit weird and it was never going to work. Marrying him would have meant embracing a traditional relationship. It certainly would have meant financial security. But I couldn't. I didn't love him. I didn't desire him.

I suppose there might be a man out there that I could love and desire, but I haven't met him. Not yet.

TWENTY-THREE

JULIA

Princeton, 1989

Karin's stroke caught all of us by surprise. It came out of nowhere, like a bolt of lightning on a quiet, blue sky afternoon. An unexpected catastrophe. I was shocked for Karin was only fifty-eight, and she had no health issues to speak of, or at least any that Jimmy or I were aware of. She didn't smoke, or drink to excess, and was quite fit—I had always envied her slim figure, and she looked years younger than her age.

According to her doctors, the specific origins of her stroke were unknowable. That's hard to take. I've always wanted cause and effect to be clear when bad things happen. I don't want it to be so damn random.

I wonder about the underlying reasons. There was the wear-and-tear of giving birth to four children. And there was the stress surrounding the loss of Des. Karin always seemed so poised, so composed, but underneath I think she pushed down her deepest feelings, suppressed them, and that must have taken a hidden toll.

Alexander told us that he realized something was wrong at dinner that Thursday night. Karin complained of fatigue and a sudden slight numbness in her face, and he noticed that one side of her mouth was drooping. When he asked her how she felt, she answered with a pronounced slur in her voice, unaware that anything was wrong.

He was alarmed enough to insist they immediately go to the emergency room, over Karin's protests. There, the young ER doctor immediately began administering drugs to dissolve any blood clot through an IV.

Once it was clear that Karin was out of danger, Alexander called Beau and Hanna and told them the news, that their mother had experienced a stroke but her condition was stable and improving. He asked them not to come immediately to Princeton but to wait until she was feeling better.

Karin spent three nights in the hospital. Alexander remained by her side, reluctant to leave her when visiting hours ended. Jimmy and I spent time at Lafayette Place, making sure that a distracted Alexander had a meal or two before he went back to the hospital.

The neurologist warned that because of damage to the left side of her brain, Karin would most likely have speech and memory problems. When Jimmy and I visited her in her hospital room, she seemed pale and wan, but she struggled to hold up her end of the brief conversation.

It was a different Karin, an altered Karin, who came out of the hospital and returned to Lafayette Place. She struggled during the early days of her recovery with a low-grade headache and memory problems. Alexander hired a woman to cook and clean and lessen the load of household chores.

I visited almost every other day. Jimmy came with me when he could. I didn't bring King at first. He loved his grandmother, and I wanted to wait until she was less confused.

Karin wasn't the same. Parts of her memory seemed to have been erased, and that frustrated her greatly. She couldn't match familiar faces with names. She didn't remember recent events. Her gaps in memory weren't logical or predictable. She could recall stories from the distant past but not something that happened a year ago. At times, I'd see her tear up as her balky memory failed her.

For the first time, I saw her lose her temper, something the Karin of the past never did, at least publicly. She was abrupt with Alexander, often dismissive, sometimes raising her voice to him.

Had she suppressed her emotions in the past? I knew that as people aged their inhibitions often dropped. Had the stroke, an insult to her brain, made her more impulsive? It seemed that way.

Jimmy and I talked about the changes in his mother. Were we seeing aspects of her personality that had been there below the surface all along? Feelings that had been submerged, controlled by what the doctors called the executive function of the brain? It was a mystery, and a sad one at that.

The idea of a small luncheon honoring Karin with a display of her paintings was mine. My mother-in-law wasn't receptive at first, shaking her head.

"Who would care to see my art?" Karin asked. "I'd be embarrassed. Wouldn't it seem like I was showing off?"

"Your paintings are striking," I told her. "They tell an amazing story. People will admire what you've done all these years. I'm sure of it. You've been hiding your light under a bushel basket. Whatever that is."

Karin laughed. "A bushel basket? That's silly."

I didn't give up—I recruited Alexander and Jimmy to help me persuade her. I don't know what they said to Karin, but she eventually relented and agreed to a gathering of family and friends where her paintings would be shown.

Alexander reserved Palmer House, a small historic house on campus that could be rented by faculty or alumni for catered events, and began working with Karin on an invitation list. My vision for the party was to place her paintings on easels in the parlor and solarium, both on the first floor, and serve guests lunch after they'd had a chance to admire her artwork.

We spent an hour or so in her studio and Karin chose ten of her saga paintings, and a few family portraits, for the display. I arranged for easels and frames from a local art store.

"Are you sure this is a good idea?" Jimmy asked. "She's quite fragile."

"It's the first time since the stroke that she's been so focused and energized, Jimmy. And there's more to it. She sacrificed her artistic career to have children. She couldn't do both. This will show everyone how talented she is. A chance for her to be the center of attention, for once."

"I don't think she regrets the choices she made. She's never said anything to me about it."

"Would you expect her to, Jimmy?"

"I guess not. She never complains."

"Trust me," I told him. "She made sacrifices for her children over the years. Karin could never devote herself to her painting. What she has created is wonderful. She deserves her moment to shine."

The day of Karin's party began with a cool morning breeze and dark clouds and I worried that it might rain. The weather forecast on the all-news radio station was reassuring. The sky was supposed to clear with the prospect of late-afternoon sunshine.

I arrived early at Palmer House and made sure that everything was ready for the guests. The room was filled with her paintings, easels set up against three of the walls. I had a program printed up that included Karin's biography, the names of her paintings and the year she had painted them. There were twenty-one paintings on display; there could have been more, but Karin had rejected twelve or so canvases that she didn't want seen. One of those was her portrait of Desmond, and I was glad that it wasn't going to be shown—it wasn't a day for painful memories.

My only concern was that Karin might not react well to a full room of people. She struggled with connecting names with faces, and became frustrated when she recognized a friend but couldn't recall their name. It was a common challenge for someone who had survived a stroke.

Thankfully, the party went well. Karin wore a long, flowing dress and she had tied her hair back. She had lost weight since the stroke and was painfully thin. I hoped that it wouldn't prove too taxing for her. She greeted the guests gracefully with a smile, and she watched intently as they circulated throughout the room, admiring her paintings. Jimmy or I stayed by her side.

Karin scanned the room several times. "Where is Hanna?" she asked. Hanna had flown in from San Francisco for the party.

I spotted Hanna by the front door and waved for her to join us. Hanna slipped through the crowd and made her way to where we were standing. She had stayed with us the night before and we had got caught up. King had taken to her, and they had played with his train set and other favorite toys. She had a few errands to run before the party and came separately to Palmer House.

"Hi, Mom," Hanna said. They embraced and kissed.

"I'm so glad to see you," Karin said. "All the way from California for this. Thank you."

"When Julia called I knew I had to be here. I'm sorry I've been out-of-touch." Hanna made a face. She was embarrassed. While she stayed in touch with Jimmy, she didn't communicate much with her parents.

Karin nodded, smiling. "It doesn't matter. It doesn't matter. You're here."

I left them to chat while I answered a question from the caterer. Hanna pulled me aside minutes later. "Mom seems distant," she said. "Vague. A bit confused."

"She's better than she was," I told her. "It's going to take time."

Hanna shook her head. "It's hard to see her like this. She's so different."

I took her hand and squeezed it. "She will be fine."

After thirty minutes, Alexander clapped his hands and announced it was time for a light supper.

He thanked everyone for coming and explained that Karin hadn't wanted any long speeches, but he did want to say a few words. "The my best decision I've made in my life was to ask Karin to marry me," he said. "As you can see from her paintings, I married not only a marvelous mother and wife, but an amazing artist." He raised his champagne glass.

"To Karin Johanson Kincaid!"

We all toasted her in turn, and I could see Karin struggling with her emotions. She pulled me close and whispered a thanks. I had never thought the day would come when I would feel completely accepted by my mother-in-law, but it had and it made me very happy.

I know that I wasn't the wife she would have picked for Jimmy—I was the neighborhood tomboy of his childhood and I wasn't poised or polished—but perhaps she recognized that I had been good for her son and grandson. And I had.

I'm glad that I insisted on the gathering for Karin. It was the moment for her to shine, for all of us to honor her talents and celebrate her art. She was more than a wife and mother, she was an artist.

Later, she told Jimmy that she hadn't expected to enjoy the party, but she had. I was so delighted to hear that. I'm glad we didn't wait.

For we didn't have her with us for much longer.

TWENTY-FOUR

JAMES

October 28, 1989

Dear Beau,

I'm going to give you call tomorrow, but I wanted to put some of my thoughts down on paper on this historic day.

I watched Tom Brokaw reporting from Germany last night on the fall of the Berlin Wall. Never thought I'd write those words. Thrilling words.

Hope you were able to catch the images of the joyous crowds. The party to end all parties! The strange thing is that the East German authorities may have opened the gates to West Berlin by mistake….one of their bureaucrats jumped the gun on approving visas and once word got out the checkpoints were overwhelmed with East Berliners looking to cross over.

It's only been twenty minutes since I finished a special news analysis column for Continental and our client newspapers about the impact of this development. It's too early to say that Germany will reunify, but with the Wall down it seems inevitable. That may give the Kremlin second thoughts, to say nothing of the rest of Europe. I imagine the French have mixed feelings about this development. The dark memories of the Third Reich are still strong.

From what I've been able to gather, Gorbachev either isn't willing or doesn't want to send in the Red Army to restore the old order, and he won't support Honecker or any of the other autocrats in using force to put down the demonstrators. He wants the East Bloc nations to reform along his lines—*glasnost* and *perestroika*—and he's refusing to prop up failing regimes. I applaud that, but I think he's underestimated how unpopular figures like Honecker and Ceausescu and Jakes are.

Based on what's gone on in Poland and Hungary the remaining Communist Party-backed governments in Eastern Europe are shaky. Will they be forced to accept multiparty governance? That might be the death knell for the current leadership for I doubt the CP candidates would attract a majority in free and fair elections.

It's to Bush's credit that he's being careful in what he says and does, now. No victory dances in the end zone. The rest of us can celebrate the fall of the Berlin Wall, but it's wise not to poke the bear!

I imagine it must be very strange for you. You mentioned that you'd visited Berlin a few times when you stationed in Germany. Thank God you and your men never have to defend the Fulda Gap against invading Red Army tanks. It's one thing to be the point of the spear, another to be the tripwire.

On the home front, Mom seems to be better. She still is too frail. Julia stops by Lafayette Place with King as often as she can, so we're keeping an eye on the situation. I know Dad is worried by her condition, although he hasn't said anything about his concerns. Stiff upper lip, like he's an Englishman of the 19th century.

Any chance of you meeting us in Boca Grande in early December for a week or so? It's been awhile, brother! We could go back bay fishing in Charlotte Harbor and take King with us. He will love the idea—what ten-year old wouldn't want to spend the day on the water with Uncle Beau and his Dad?

Looking forward to our call, and to seeing you (in Florida? Princeton?) in the not-too-distant future.

James

TWENTY-FIVE

ALEXANDER

February 19, 1990

Dear Priscilla,

Thank you for your lovely note about Karin. She did bring grace and light into all of our lives.

Is she really gone? I struggle with that reality. It doesn't seem real.

I barely made it through the service without breaking down. Thank God the Anglican tradition calls for a brief funeral service, for I couldn't have stood it much longer.

Even though I know how unlikely it is that there's a heaven—I am a scientist, after all—I found myself wishing it were true. A place where one day I could be reunited with Karin. It's a wonderful fairy tale, isn't it? I do understand why we so want to believe it. We want life to go on and on. It's such an elemental desire.

I wish you could have been here with us. You have had to face your own losses of late, with the passing of Dolores (has it been two years?), and I know your health issues are troublesome and very concerning and a trip to Princeton would not have been wise.

I never imagined that Karin would die before me, just as I never imagined that we would outlive any of our children. I was wrong.

That's the terrible randomness of life. We expect the next day will be as routine as the last, and we're jarred when we discover that isn't always so.

It has been different with losing Karin. After her first stroke, the doctors told us that she was at a higher risk of another. Although you're never fully prepared for the worst, her death wasn't as shocking as Desmond's.

Karin told me a year ago that she felt she was on borrowed time.

I miss her. We had wonderful years together. Not a perfect marriage, but what marriage is? We had our moments, luminous memories. When I met her in Stockholm all these many years ago, I never could have imagined how our life together would unfold.

After Hanna left us for California, when we became empty nesters, Karin turned to her painting as a release. She seemed to have recaptured some of the joy and passion of her art student days. She spent long hours in her studio, and I think created some of her best works. They were darker in tone, at times, but they made a memorable connection to her beloved sagas.

I'm not sure what to do about Lafayette Place. What do I want with a dusty old house, now that Karin is gone? But it's home, and I want it to remain in the family. If I stay, if I continue to live here, my hope is that James and Julia might consider joining me. At the least, it's a place for them when they come out from New York. And there are always the holidays, when we can gather at Lafayette Place, when Hanna might be enticed to come back East.

I'm determined that this sadness will not last. Karin used to say that I had to balance her native gloominess with my optimism about the future. At the moment, it's hard to imagine when that day will come, but I know it must.

I've taken to playing Samuel Barber's Adagio for Strings on repeat on my stereo. Something about the soaring nature of his composition speaks to me, calms me, begins to bring me some comfort.

love, your brother

Alexander

PART FOUR

TWENTY-SIX

HANNA

January 1st, 1991

Dearest Jimmy,

Happy New Year! A day for making resolutions, hopes for the year ahead, turning over a new leaf, etc.

It's silly, though. Why should the first day of January be any different than the last day of December? We continue to give it way too much symbolic weight.

I'll confess that New Year's Eve brings back bittersweet memories for me. This year I shared a bottle of champagne with a girlfriend, Jacqueline. She's quite interesting: a French-Canadian from Quebec who fled to California to escape a traditional and judgmental family (sound somewhat familiar???). Where we're completely different—she likes girls, not boys. She may have a bit of a crush on me, but I've made it clear that we can be friends. Just friends.

We got a little tipsy and I told Jacqueline your story about taking Des and Julia to Times Square on New Year's Eve and how, once he had surveyed the crowd and satisfied his curiosity, he announced that he was ready to leave. That's so like Des. Marching to the beat of his own drum. Jacqueline was amazed at the story. I tried to explain about Des but I'm afraid I didn't do him justice. I do miss him so. There was an innocence to him, an openness, a way of seeing the world as a child does, what the Zen masters call the Beginner's Mind.

I've only dabbled in Zen. Read a few books about it, and talked to a friend of mine who's a Buddhist. I like the idea of the interconnectedness of creation, of the universe, and that seems close to what your hero, Teilhard, believed. Sorry, Jimmy, but I confess I never fully understood his Noosphere—did I spell that right? Something about the evolution of human spirituality. Anyway, the rest of Zen, the denial of ego, seems a bit much, but I give them full credit for trying to figure out the meaning of life.

I guess if you're going to ponder philosophical questions, it makes sense to do so on the first day of the New Year. First principles, right? (I remember that much from my freshman year philosophy class, but not much else.)

One firm resolution for 1991: I'm going to take it slow when it comes to anyone new in my romantic life.

I'm still looking for that one good man. After Karl, I didn't date for a long while, for more than a year. I was wary. And for good reason. I had one boyfriend who lasted a month until I discovered he was seeing someone else and he became abusive when I confronted him. As if I was at fault! I exited stage right as fast as I could.

Since then, I've kept it casual. I didn't have time for romantic complications. Kincaid Landscaping has kept me occupied, and I have a great group of friends. I don't feel terribly lonely.

Yes, I'll confess there have been times when I wished I had someone to come home to and share my challenges and victories.

Many women my age are worried about their biological time

clock ticking. They're in a rush to find a man, get married, and have their babies before it's too late.

I'm not there. At least, not yet. I'm not ready to settle for that emotionally bruised guy coming off a divorce. Or for some arrogant playboy. I'm willing to wait. I'm in no rush. It will happen when it's supposed to happen.

When it comes to love, I don't just want someone I can live with, I want someone I can't live without. Is that too much to ask for? I hope not.

Another resolution: I want to stay in better touch with family this year.

I haven't fully come to terms with losing Mom. Somehow I have this idea that if I came back to Lafayette Place, I'd find her in her studio painting away. I guess it's hard to believe she's gone. I assumed that Dad would go first. But then I should know better—Des left us long before he should have.

I wish my feelings about Mom, and about Dad, weren't so ambivalent. I guess the years of being judged by them left a mark or two.

Please give all my love to Julia and King. I did call Dad on Christmas Day afternoon to wish him well, and we had a brief chat. I consider that progress.

love, your one and only sister, Hanna

TWENTY-SEVEN

JAMES

New York, Spring 1991

It was early May when Beau joined me for lunch in Midtown Manhattan. The sun was out and the streets were crowded with office workers eagerly welcoming the spring warmth. The city's lovely young women had donned bright colors and short skirts. (Yes, of course I noticed—I'm a typical male, in many ways.)

Beau wasn't in uniform, but his closely-cropped hair and erect bearing made him stand out—a soldier, a warrior. And he was back from war, the Gulf War, Operation Desert Storm.

The hostess at the French bistro sat us in a corner where we could have some privacy. Beau seemed tense, on edge, with a grim look on his face.

After we were served, he picked at his salad, and we made small talk: the prospects for the Yankees (dismal), the latest Space Shuttle launch, and the winding down of the Warsaw Pact. It took twenty minutes before Beau got around to what was bothering him.

"Did you see that the United Nations Security Council has adopted a truce resolution?" he asked. "So I guess our nasty little war is over. A brilliant campaign in terms of tactics. Coalition of the willing, and all that. But damned one-sided. I've come to believe that the rules of engagement are meant for our sake, not the enemies, designed to encourage the better angels of our nature. That's Lincoln's phrase, and he got it right. It's a check and balance against the horrific things we might otherwise do in the heat of combat." He ran his hand through his close-cropped hair. "And even with those boundaries, those rules, war can be a terrible, terrible thing."

"It seemed more like a video game than a war the way it was presented on cable television," I replied.

"In truth, on the ground, it was like something out of Goya," he said, shaking his head. "Do you know the Black Paintings? Saturn devouring his son. Nightmarish. I thought about that when I flew for miles along Highway 80, the route the Iraqis tried to use to flee. The shooting was over by then, but it was all one-sided. They were defenseless. Tanks, armored vehicles, trucks, destroyed on either side of the road. Bodies on the road and in the nearby desert. In the vehicles, carbonized bodies. The Highway of Death. It was beyond grotesque."

He rubbed his eyes suddenly. I was surprised—was Beau blinking away tears? It was clear that my older brother was struggling to control his emotions.

Beau leaned forward and lowered his voice. "The Republican Guards were the bad guys, Saddam's thugs and butchers. The men we killed on that highway were cannon fodder. Innocents. Farmers and cab drivers and clerks. Forcibly drafted into the Army. You know I've never had much use for religion, but I found myself praying for those poor bastards and their families. They died for nothing. They died for the vanity of politicians, old men who never see the reality of combat."

I said quietly that it seemed that the war had been fought for a number of reasons, some of them commercial, some of them geopolitical.

"I see that," my brother said sharply. "A war to secure Europe's oil supply. Saddam couldn't be allowed to take over Kuwait. Nothing particularly noble about that. Of course, we're supposed to forget that Saddam was once our ally. A bastard, but our bastard. Then he wasn't and we had to stop him. That meant war and what happened on Highway 80. Remember what General Sherman said? 'War is cruelty, and you cannot refine it.' Soldiers know that better than anyone."

I hadn't seen Beau like this, not since our childhood. He had let his anger surface, the near-volcanic anger he had brought under control as a young man.

We had both seen things in our professional lives that were best forgotten. But his description of the carnage along that highway was chilling. I can't imagine anyone seeing it would ever be the same.

"The only smart thing we did was to stop after we booted the Iraqis out of Kuwait," Beau said. "Give Bush credit for that. I know some of the hardliners in Washington wanted us to push on to Baghdad, to invade. That would have been a colossal mistake. At least we avoided another Vietnam."

He sighed slightly and changed the subject, asking about Julia and King and my work. I told him that all was well, still troubled by his obvious distress. It wasn't like Beau.

"I've been thinking about leaving the Army," he said abruptly.

I was surprised. I knew how much my brother felt at home in the military, how he had taken to the life of an officer. He had loved serving his country. It gave him a purpose, a higher calling.

"Has your recent experience played a part in this?" I asked.

"Some. Germany is reunited. Eastern Europe is free. The Cold War is over, for all intents and purposes. I feel like I've done my part. Time to move on."

"Do you have any idea of what you might do next?" I asked.

"Not sure, yet. I could finish law school, pass the bar, and hang out my shingle. Someplace warm. San Diego, maybe. If I stay in the Reserves I can keep flying."

"What about settling down here, on the East Coast?"

"Not a chance. Too damn cold in the Northeast, and I don't like Florida. Too hot and humid. San Diego is sunny and filled with retired military. I think I'd fit in better there."

"Could part of this settling down include marriage?"

"I've thought about it," he said.

"And children?"

He nodded. Beau had told me once that he was reluctant to become a father while he was on active duty, flying helicopters in night-time exercises and in nasty weather. He didn't want to leave a son or daughter without a father and a wife without a husband. I thought he might be overly cautious, but I respected his approach.

"I didn't quite expect this," I told him.

"Neither did I," he replied. "Moving on from the Army has been on my mind. What I should do with the rest of my life." Beau shook his head, giving me a crooked smile. "Not that I've made any firm decisions. Not yet. Still thinking it over. I don't know that I'll make much of a civilian."

I found myself grinning, enjoying my brother's embarrassment. "I'm looking forward to the suburban dad version of Beau Kincaid. A respectable citizen. Pushing kids around in strollers. Little League. Hen-pecked."

"Don't jump the gun," he said. "I'm still a free man."

"It's just a matter of time, now," I said.

"Not yet."

"Better late than never."

My brother smiled again, more like the Beau of old. "Better than never."

TWENTY-EIGHT

HANNA

To: jkincaid77@aol.com
From: hannak@aol.com
Date: May 10, 1994
Subject: big news

Hey, Jimmy! I was so pleased to share my exciting news during our phone call!

It's strange to follow up by an e-mail, but it's the wave of the future, isn't it? Gotta believe that the Post Office's days are numbered. But it's weird to click a button and send words winging their way across the country and showing up on your computer seconds later thousands of miles away.

As I told you during our call, I met Nate Sorensen by chance at a lazy Sunday afternoon picnic with friends. Nate works for one of the local vineyards as general manager/jack-of-all-trades. We hit it off from the start. He's funny and smart and—this is the amazing and unexpected thing—sees the world the way I do. The only awkward factor is that he's a bit younger than me, by five years. I'm not going to let that bother me if it doesn't bother him. (No cradle-robbing jokes, please!)

I think you will like him, Jimmy. He's no intellectual...but neither am I. And it's taken me years, but I'm no longer defensive about that. We're alike in that we both feel drawn to the outdoors and the natural world, and we like to get our hands dirty in our work.

We ended up talking almost exclusively with each other at the picnic where we met. Then, Nate took me on a dinner date that Friday night and one thing led to another and we spent the weekend together. When Monday came, it seemed natural for him to bring his stuff over to my place and we haven't been apart since.

Nate is from Minnesota, the son of a Lutheran minister. He had the typical teenage rebellion against his father's overly stern authority. I guess we also have that in common. He left home and moved to San Francisco when he was eighteen and then found his way north. He split time between taking college classes and working in wine country at several different vineyards. He can fix anything mechanical, and he's learned an amazing amount about soil and grapes and how to make excellent wine.

Even better, there's no ex-wife in his past. No kids, either. No heavy baggage, which is a relief.

Is it too early to admit that I can imagine having children with him? I can see growing old with Nate. He has a wonderful calming influence on me. I don't get anywhere near as anxious with him around.

Do I sound head over heels in love?

I guess I am!

Love, Hanna

To: hannak@aol.com

From: jkincaid77@aol.com
Date: May 11, 1994
Subject: Re: big news

Hanna, you never cease to amaze.

Wonderful news! Can't wait to meet Nate.

He sounds like a keeper, as the saying goes.

E-mail doesn't feel as strange to me. I've been inputting copy into computer networks/messaging systems for years and years, ever since my days at the Associated Press. The lesson learned was that you don't type anything you wouldn't want the world to see. There was a young woman at the AP who thought she was forwarding her boyfriend (another AP reporter) some explicit ideas for what they might do in bed that weekend, and mistakenly sent the message by the internal system to every AP bureau in the network. Needless to say, she became a legendary figure at the wire service. A cautionary tale as to what you want to put into these electronic messages.

It hasn't been the easiest time for me at work. Continental has been facing some financial issues and they're pinching pennies. Not many opportunities to travel on assignment. I've been asking myself some difficult questions. Am I living to the fullest or just existing? Am I doing something worthwhile?

Julia thinks I should count my considerable blessings. And I guess I am being selfish, navel-gazing when I've got so much going for me.

Yes, this is what happens to men in middle age. I look at my college classmates, other men of my vintage, and wonder if they made better choices. What do they say, comparison is the thief of joy?

love, James

P.S. Beau will be completing his law degree at the end of this semester! Then he's threatening to move to the West Coast, most likely San Diego…Two Kincaids in California!

To: jkincaid77@aol.com
From: hannak@aol.com
Date: May 12, 1994
Subject: Re: Re: big news

Dearest Jimmy,

Don't apologize for asking questions about your journey through life. They're too damn important to sidestep or ignore.

And I can't wait for Beau to move to San Diego. Maybe living here will loosen him up a bit and he won't be such a fierce wooden soldier!

I think back East people are more likely to plow ahead and not take the time to consider who they are and what they are doing. There's an openness to that self-discovery here that's refreshing, even if it's mocked by the rest of the country.

No one is going to ask those questions if you don't. And only you have the answers.

It can be painful, but that's part of the journey.

So keep on keeping on.

Love, your one and only sister, Hanna

To: jkincaid77@aol.com
From: hannak@aol.com
Date: May 21, 1994
Subject: We did it!

Dear Jimmy,

We're married!

Nate and I tied the knot yesterday with a few of our friends as witnesses at Town Hall. We spent the night in a nice hotel in Santa Rosa, and now it's back to work and life. (Nate won't go within a mile of a church. Given his negative experiences with his father and religion, I get it.)

I'll call Dad and Beau to let them know. Doubt they'll be surprised…it's a Hanna-type thing to do, yes? Just slightly more respectable than eloping! I just wish I could tell Mom. Maybe she's watching from above? If only that were so.

Can't wait for you to meet Nate.

love, Hanna

TWENTY-NINE

JULIA

August 1996

I kept my emotions in check during the long drive to Washington, chatting with Jimmy and King, watching as the miles flew by, trying not to tear up when I thought about this trip and its meaning. Dropping off your child at college represents a milestone in any parent's life. Certainly in my life. At least King had chosen Georgetown, not one of the California schools that he had briefly considered, so we would be relatively closer.

The drop-off was well organized. Jimmy parked the car near King's dorm, and we unloaded his luggage and helped him move into his room. We met his roommate, a nice young man from Virginia with a freckled face who looked like he was twelve years old. I could see King was excited, eager to begin his college life. He walked with us back to the car, and he shook hands with Jimmy and let me hug him. We said our goodbyes and I watched as he left us, striding back to the dormitory and his new life. No longer my little boy…

I found my eyes filling with tears, and I climbed into the passenger seat, fighting back the urge to cry. I knew that my life would never be the same. This was one of the rites of passage—my son was leaving home, and we would return to an empty nest. A future without him there every day.

I won't lie—along with the sadness, there was some resentment mixed in. If Jimmy had been willing to have more children when I had so wanted them, King wouldn't have been an only child. I could have had a full house of kids and maybe seeing King go off to college wouldn't have hurt as much. But he was my one and only child.

I tried not to let that bitterness get the better of me. I gave Jimmy the cold treatment for several days after we'd returned from Washington. I think he understood my mood, but I wasn't about to tell him how I felt, the resentment I had bottled up for years: *You kept us from the family we should have had.*

Was it fair to blame him? It wasn't completely his fault, I guess. I didn't assert myself the way I should have. I was too passive. But he had argued that we should wait until he was better established in his career before we had more children. I should have fought back. We shouldn't have waited.

Of course, there was nothing I could do about it now, no time machine to take us back to 1981 or 1982.

I was fortunate to have my store, Nassau Gifts, as a distraction. The routine of opening and closing, of ordering inventory, of helping customers pick out the right gift, and keeping the books up-to-date, became a welcome distraction. I liked being in control, and I was good at it (if I say so myself).

I'd be lying if I said it was easy with an empty house, with King in Washington and Jimmy hiding from me at work. I missed King. Jimmy missed him, too.

It wasn't a happy time for Jimmy. A newspaper chain in the Midwest had suddenly dropped its contract with Continental

News Service, and Jimmy worried that there might be staff cutbacks. The owners of Continental had covered financial shortfalls in the past, and the hope was that they would find new investors to help offset the gap. Just another thing to worry about. More stress for Jimmy and more stress for me. And our marriage.

I knew marriages had their ups and downs, and I couldn't deny that mine had hit a bad patch. The worst of it was that we didn't acknowledge the pain we were both feeling. We didn't talk. I thought that if I was patient, it would get better. I loved Jimmy. He loved me. Sometimes it was hard to remember that.

THIRTY

New York, 1997

She lay on the hotel bed, naked, face down, the sheets draped across her body. James Kincaid watched her sleep, her chestnut hair spread out on the pillow. She was so lovely, he thought, studying her profile, the curve of her neck, the slight dusting of freckles on her shoulders. Then she stirred, rolled over, and rewarded him with a lazy, contented smile.

Not for the first time, he wondered how he had ended up in Room 202 of the Carlyle Hotel on a weekday Manhattan afternoon, a married man, alone with a woman not his wife. He had always questioned the French notion of a *coup de foudre*, the irrational thunderbolt of attraction between a man and a woman. He knew better, now. He felt drawn to Orit, aroused and enthralled, in a way he had never felt before. And, if anything, his desire for her had grown more intense the more time they spent together in bed, a desire so intense that it hurt.

He never expected that he would become an adulterer. A cheater.

But that was before he met Orit Silver.

James remembered distinctly the moment when he first spotted her at a crowded book party in New York. She was wearing a long skirt with a slit that gave a glimpse of one tanned leg. On both wrists, multiple sliver bracelets, stacked. A simple silver necklace. Her layered chestnut-colored hair touched her shoulders.

"Look at her," his friend Harold French had said with a soft whistle.

"She's something," James replied.

"Out of my league," his friend said. "But I'm going to try. Nothing to lose. Wish me luck."

Harold left and walked over to the woman and said something to her James couldn't hear. She smiled and they began to talk. James found himself envying Harold— as a divorced man, his friend could pursue her and James could not.

That very moment it seemed as if she had read his mind because she looked over directly at him. James felt himself flush and he quickly glanced away.

When he looked up, he saw that she was making her way through the crowd toward him. Over her shoulder, he could see Harold with a puzzled look on his face.

She stopped in front of him. "You're James?" she asked, with a slight smile. "Your friend Harold told me your name. I was curious."

Her eyes were hazel, with shades of light brown and green. In a certain light, they appeared almost gold in color.

He nodded. "I'm James Kincaid."

She looked at his left hand, at his wedding ring. "You're married, James Kincaid?" She had an accent, vaguely British.

He didn't say anything.

"I see," she said.

"What does that mean?" he asked.

"You haven't been looking at me like you're married."

"I couldn't help myself. Take that as a compliment. It's the effect you have on men. You must know that."

She shrugged. "Harold says you are a journalist."

"I am. Freelance these days."

"Journalists have the most interesting stories. Do you have interesting stories, James Kincaid?"

She moved closer to him and he caught the scent of her perfume. Later, he discovered she wore Chanel No. 5, and he could never again encounter that fragrance without thinking of her.

"I imagine that I do. It's my job, after all. Telling stories that interest the reader. These days if you don't hook the reader quickly, you'll lose them. Too many other distractions."

"And how do you hook your readers?"

"You look for ways to make your story relevant to them. Or you expose them to the contradictions in what you're covering. And you try to do that in simple, direct ways, like you would if you were explaining something to a friend over lunch."

"That's quite clever."

"It's storytelling. No different than the skald who told the story of Beowulf."

"Beowulf. A very literate journalist."

"Not that highbrow." He smiled at her. "A childhood spent reading adventure books. *King Arthur and his Round Table. Beau Geste. The Scarlet Pimpernel.*"

"That's quite a reading list."

"And your childhood books?"

"I didn't read much. Instead, I was horse crazy. My father spoiled me rotten, I'm afraid, but he did insist I go to University instead of show jumping."

"And what do you do now?"

"Art," she said. "I have an art gallery in London." She checked her wristwatch. "Time flies. I must go. Would you like to buy me a drink tomorrow? One o'clock. I'm staying at the Carlyle. We can meet in the bar."

James found himself nodding, and she smiled and leaned into him. "I love how you smell," she said. "It's quite sexy, even for a married man." Then, she walked away.

His eyes followed her as she left the room. "What was that?" James asked himself softly and then quickly glanced around, worried that someone had heard him.

Harold appeared at his side. "Well, that was strange," he said. "She shut me down quickly. Asked who you were, and then made a beeline over here. I thought I'd give you some space. Any luck?"

"She read one of my travel pieces," he said, lying, trying to make sense of what had just happened, the flirtation, the invitation to see her again.

"A bit of a prima donna," Harold said. "When I complimented her on her bracelets, she told me she wore silver because she is. Then she laughed."

"We spoke only briefly," James said. "Did you get her full name?"

"Orit. Orit Silver. British and Israeli. A foot in both places. Money, too, from her looks. I'll bet she's a handful."

James nodded, but didn't say anything more.

He knew that he should ignore her invitation to meet the following day. It was risky to continue then flirtation. But Orit Silver intrigued him and he wanted to learn more about her. He could always step back if things got too intense. Or so he told himself.

There was affection and warmth in his marriage, but little romance or passion, which wasn't a surprise after all the years that he and Julia had been together. They had settled into a routine. With King away at college, Julia occupied with running her store, and James hustling for writing assignments, they spent less time together. They had less to say to each other.

And now, a chance meeting with an alluring woman had brought some excitement into his life. It might not be the smartest thing, but he decided he would meet her at the Carlyle Hotel. He sensed it might be a mistake, but he told himself he wouldn't step over the line.

He had been restless for months, weighed down by feelings of alienation and discontent. For the first time in his marriage, he felt detached from Julia. Some of it was embarrassment. He had failed, lost his job, and it meant they were short on money. Without a steady paycheck, he had been forced to turn to his father for a loan for King's second-semester tuition payment, a loan he didn't think he could ever repay.

His bleak mood had been heightened by a chance encounter with Max Grey, a friend from his college days. He bumped into Max on 44th Street and learned that he had left his Wall Street job, divorced his wife, and was moving to Costa Rica.

"I woke up one morning and realized that I was desperately unhappy and that I didn't want to spend the rest of my life doing something I didn't believe in," Max explained. "When I told my wife I wanted to quit, she was furious with me. I was going to derail the gravy train! We wouldn't be able to afford the house in the Hamptons and the apartment here."

"But you went ahead anyway?"

"We don't have kids. I was more than generous with the settlement and Janice can go back to work if she wants a more lavish lifestyle." Max grinned. He had thickened with age and had a severe widow's peak. If they hadn't been classmates, James would have guessed him to be approaching his late forties.

"Why Costa Rica?"

"Beautiful weather. Beautiful *chicas*. I'm going to take some time and figure things out."

James had wished him luck. The conversation stayed with him in the days that followed. Part of him envied Max for the bold changes he was making in his life. Of course, Max had made enough money to finance a midlife adventure, but he was taking chances, and James admired that.

It made him wonder what he might be missing; had he become too stuck in his ways? Too willing to accept the status quo? He had responsibilities, a wife and son, but there had to be more he could do to deal with his restlessness. Could he find a way to break out of his rut? Experience more?

He had tried talking about his feelings with his father on a long walk in Princeton on a balmy Sunday afternoon.

"When you were my age, did you ever feel restless?" James asked.

Alexander shook his head. "I had my work," he said. "There was always another field trip coming up, another paper to author. And although your mother bore the brunt of raising you and your brothers and sister, I had that responsibility as well. Not much time to get restless."

"You were lucky, then."

His father remained silent.

"I've been questioning things," James said. "I'm not as sure about my direction as I have been in the past. I've been unsettled."

"We all have our moments when things feel out of kilter. Challenging times. Mine came with your mother's death. And that damn Open Letter. There's no avoiding the dark days, James. It's part and parcel of the human experience. You have to do your best to carry on." His father patted James on the back. "Things will work out."

When James entered the bar at the Carlyle Hotel, his mouth felt dry and his heart was pounding. He spotted Orit waiting for him at a corner table. She wore a pink button-down shirt, blue jeans, and dark-blue flats. She smiled when she saw him and gestured for him to join her.

"I wasn't sure you would come," she said.

He shook his head. "I don't believe you."

"I'm not that vain. While I found you quite interesting, you seemed somewhat reluctant."

"I'm here."

"That you are." She rose to her feet. "Why don't we adjourn to my room. It's much cozier there. There's a minibar if you'd like a drink."

He wondered suddenly whether it was a game for her. Meet a man, see if she could seduce him. The female equivalent of a womanizer. James hesitated.

"Second thoughts?" she asked.

He shook his head, and followed her from the bar through the lobby to the elevator bank, excited, aroused, and yet anxious and already feeling guilty. He hadn't gone too far, yet, but he didn't want to stop. They didn't touch or talk in the brief ride up in the elevator to the second floor. The elevator was sheathed in reflective metal, and James could see their faces in the mirror-like surface. Orit wore a slight smile.

Inside the room, she stood next to him, tilting her face up, and they kissed slowly. She pulled him closer and when his hands slid down the curve of her back to her bottom he knew he was lost.

She took her clothes off carefully, first the shirt, and then her jeans, draping them over a nearby chair. She had small breasts and a slim waist. He undressed quickly and they moved to the bed. He was surprised at how small she was when he took her in his arms, marveling at the feel of her soft skin on his. He kissed her again and felt her tongue dart into his mouth.

"I like your taste, James," she said. "Let's see if I like the rest of you."

She was an inventive lover and James found himself responding eagerly. They made love silently until she tightened her arms around him and gave a small cry. He climaxed moments later, moaning at the intense pleasure of it.

"Well," she said. "That was something."

"It was."

They lay side-by-side, her hand in his, their fingers interlaced.

"Are you regretting this?" she asked.

"That's a hell of a question."

"You haven't answered it."

"I don't do this," he said. "There's something about you, though. I guess I couldn't resist." He squeezed her hand. "It's like a magnetic attraction."

"I sensed it when I first saw you at that party," Orit said. "It felt much stronger as we talked."

"The truth? I don't regret acting on that feeling."

"May I see your wallet?" she asked.

"What?" he asked, confused.

Orit met his gaze with a grin. "It's amazing what you can learn from a wallet."

He couldn't think of a reason to say no and so he rolled out of bed and retrieved his wallet and gave it to her. She laughed when she studied his driver's license.

"You fooled me," she said. "I thought you were considerably younger. Maybe you're not as innocent as I thought."

She replaced the driver's license and found the old snapshot photo of King that he carried with him.

"Handsome," she said. "Your son?"

"King when he was twelve. He's in college, now. Georgetown."

She gave him the wallet back. "My detective work is done."

"What's going on here?" he asked, irritated.

"I told you I find you interesting, James Kincaid," she said. "Beyond and above the near-irresistible urge to merge, I find I'm curious about you. Don't worry, I'm not looking to overly complicate your life, or mine. This has to stay light."

"And what is this?"

"Us. Together. For as long as it lasts."

When he told Julia that he wanted a trial separation, he had lied. She asked him if there was another woman, and he lied. No, he told her, he just needed some time alone, time to sort things out. Too much going on in his professional life. Too many arguments between them. He wanted some quiet. He would stay in New York; a colleague and friend from Continental, Ted Calkins, had an assignment in Europe and was happy to let James live in his Upper West Side apartment while he was away.

Julia had cried, and James had been ashamed of himself for his shabby lies, the hackneyed prevarications that married men resorted to when they weren't sure what they wanted and weren't ready to end their marriage. How had he let himself fall into that trap? Wasn't he better than that?

Had he fallen out of love with Julia? It was confusing as hell. Orit was so different; he had no idea whether he had a future with her or whether she wanted one. He knew without a doubt that continuing the affair was a mistake, that it wouldn't end well. But at the same time, he couldn't help himself—or so he rationalized. He was infatuated.

At the start, they only met at the Carlyle, and she never invited him to spend the night. He chafed at the boundaries Orit had established—did she see him as only an afternoon fling? Nothing more?

A month after they had made love for the first time, she asked him to come to her Upper East Side apartment. James wondered if he had passed a test of some sort, that she had decided to bring him into her world, that she saw him as more than a temporary lover.

She evaded him when he tried to steer the conversation to the future, their future.

"It's best to live for the now," she told him. "This moment. Not something in the future."

He tried to learn more about her during their afternoons together. He was curious about her past, her life. It bothered him that she always brought the conversation back to him, and gave him vague answers to his questions.

She was willing to talk about her art gallery and how she scouted new artists and convinced them to show their work at her place.

"My mother was an artist," he told her. "A painter."

"And what did she paint? Landscapes? Portraits?"

"Nothing like that. Most of the time, she painted scenes from the Icelandic sagas. She was Swedish and had loved reading about Norse mythology as a child."

"I'm not a fan of Norse mythology," she said wryly. "You can imagine. Wagner and all that. *Götterdämmerung*. Midnight marches with torches."

"My mother was Swedish, not German."

"And what did the Swedes do during the war? Sell the Nazis the iron ore they needed?"

"The Swedes weren't perfect. They hid behind neutrality, it's true. But they took in Jews from Denmark and Norway. And they let the Allies use their airbases for the invasion of Norway."

"And your family? They opposed the Nazis?"

"My grandfather was an academic. A bit of a socialist. A reformer. He had no use for the Germans. When my parents first met, my mother was saying that Sweden should have fought the Nazis. That didn't make the host of the party happy. This was a few years after the war. My father had been an officer with Patton's Third Army. He admired my mother for speaking her mind. She was the youngest person at the dinner."

"I was an officer. Briefly. In the IDF."

"Were you really?" He had propped himself up on his elbow so he could see her face.

"I was. Intelligence."

"My older brother, Beau, was a major in the Army."

"What sort of name is Beau?"

"A nickname. His given name is Wilson."

She laughed. "Beau is better than Wilson."

"I think you'd like Beau. He's softened from his days in the military. A lawyer, now. He doesn't get back East every often, but we could have dinner together."

"I don't think so. I doubt I'd feel welcome. Considering our situation, it would be awkward."

"Not necessarily."

She laughed. "Sometimes you're so naive I can't believe it, James Kincaid."

Later, James realized that he had precipitated the break—he couldn't leave well enough alone. When he asked Orit if she would consider living with him, she shook her head.

"You're married," she said. "You agreed we'd keep it light."

"I'm separated from my wife."

"Are you? That's a mistake if you think that is what I wanted. I didn't." She smoothed her hair with her hands. "A mistake."

"I hate this stolen time," he said.

"Stolen?"

"You know what I mean."

"I like you," she said softly. "You're a decent man. But we would never work."

A few days later, Orit called him to explain that she had decided to return to London at the end of the week. He asked if they could meet, and she reluctantly agreed to see him at an East Side cafe, near her apartment. James arrived first and sat waiting for her.

She came directly to the table and they ordered coffee.

"When are you leaving?" he asked

"I've decided not to wait around. A flight tomorrow night. I'll arrive at Heathrow in the morning."

"I'm sorry, Orit. I didn't mean to pressure you."

"But you did. After you agreed that we wouldn't become serious."

"Did I agree to that?"

"Those were my terms."

"What are you so afraid of? Why do you push me away?"

"I told you what you want wouldn't work," she said. "I'm not good at long-term relationships. I have two ex-husbands as proof. I don't want a third."

He felt sudden anger—how could she be so nonchalant, so removed, when they might never see each other again? There had been something between them, something more than just sex.

"So that's it?" he asked. "Just like that?"

"My grandmother used to say: *Altsding lozt zikh aroys mit a geveyn.* An old Yiddish saying: 'Everything ends in tears.' Don't worry. You'll get over it. Over me." She sighed. "I'm no bargain. It's better I leave before you realize that. No drama. No recriminations."

She finished her coffee and rose to her feet and gave him a brief hug. She didn't offer her lips. She put on a pair of oversized sunglasses. "Goodbye, James Kincaid," she said.

"Goodbye, Orit Silver."

James watched her through the cafe window as she made her way down Madison Avenue, disappearing into the crowd of pedestrians on the sidewalk. He paid the bill at the front counter and left the cafe, not quite sure what had happened.

THIRTY-ONE

JAMES

The Sinai, Egypt, 1998

I arrived at the guesthouse of Saint Catherine's Monastery on a chilly March evening, surprised by the penetrating cold. Somehow I had imagined the desert would always be warm, but of course, that was nonsense. I looked up at Mount Sinai in the distance, the clear night sky above, and took a deep breath.

I could see why this harsh desert attracted prophets and pilgrims for there was a purity to its spare desolation, to its barren, rocky landscape and muted palette of sandy browns and tans, to its narrow valleys and towering mountains. For those seeking the divine, there were few distractions. In Deuteronomy, it was characterized as "the waste, howling wilderness."

My visit to Saint Catherine's Monastery came at the tail end of a trip to Cairo to write a travel magazine article on upscale hotels in the Egyptian capital. The detour into the Sinai extended my visit by three days, but I was curious about what the place might be like, and I figured there would be plenty of material for a piece I could pitch to travel editors upon my return.

The flight from Cairo to Sharm el-Sheikh took an hour. I traveled by taxi to the monastery, which was situated at the foot of Mount Sinai, *Jebel Musa* in Arabic, the spot where tradition had it Moses saw the Burning Bush and received the Tablets of the Law. The Monastery of Saint Catherine was the oldest active Eastern Orthodox monastery in the world, renowned for its outstanding collection of icons and other Byzantine art. There was plenty to write about.

But I had made the detour to the Sinai for other reasons. When I read that it was a place where hermits and anchorites sought solitude for fasting and prayer, I hoped it might offer me a chance to think, to ponder the mess I had made of my life.

I needed time for reflection about what had happened, the affair with Orit, and my separation from Julia. There were feelings of shame and guilt and bewilderment to deal with, to say nothing of my discovery that I didn't have as much control over my emotional life as I thought I did.

I wondered why Orit had chosen me, why she had decided to disrupt my life. Of course, I was no passive victim—I had been an eager and willing participant. I had found her magnetic. Was silver magnetic? I found himself smiling—Orit Silver was. At the same time, I knew that intense feeling wasn't one-sided.

I thought back to the depth of my feelings—the sense of losing emotional control, the craving for her presence, for her body. How had it happened? I had never experienced anything like it before.

It had been so impulsive, so unexpected; if I had ever been moved by a woman in such a way in the past, I might have been able to resist Orit. And, if I was honest, some part of me didn't want to stop, didn't want to forgo the pleasure and thrills of the affair.

At the same time, I knew how clichéd the entire affair would appear to the world. How would I regard it, if it was a friend caught up in a fling with a younger woman? A midlife crisis? What came next? The red sports car? The leather jacket and unbuttoned shirt and gold chain hanging around my neck?

Orit had introduced me to another unwelcome emotion—intense jealousy. My sudden possessiveness about her, a woman I hardly knew, had surprised and dismayed me. I had wondered whether she was seeing other men. I worried that she would find me lacking.

When I asked her about her past, she brushed off my questions with deliberately vague answers.

"How long were you married?" I asked her once.

"What does it matter?"

"I'm just curious."

"Curious?" She smiled. "Are you wondering if I have a commitment problem? Maybe I do. Maybe I don't. But it spoils the here-and-now whenever you worry about that sort of thing. You're like most men. You can't imagine a woman who isn't all that interested in domesticity. I don't want you to end your marriage, James. I don't want to take your wife's place. I'm more than happy to stay where I am, to live my life the way I want to."

"Have I asked you for that?"

"Not in so many words. But I know the signals."

"You're wrong," I said. It was a lie. I had wondered what it would be like if we stayed together, lived together.

"You should go back to your wife," she said. "It's where you belong."

"Then what is this? I don't belong to this?"

"This is your fling. Your fantasy come to life. But it isn't real. It won't last."

The guesthouse was located in the monastery's gardens, which were ringed by cypress trees. My room was clean and bare, what a pilgrim who had come for spiritual reasons would expect. In the morning, I took a tour of the monastery, stopping by its famed church and library. I was eager to get out and explore, to climb to the summit of Mount Sinai. One of my guidebooks claimed that, according to local legend, anyone who viewed the sunrise from the mountain's summit would be reborn with all sins forgiven. I had to smile—if only redemption was that easy.

I decided to wait until the late afternoon to make the climb when there would be fewer visitors and tourists and I could finish by seeing the sunset. I took a flashlight for my descent when it would be dark.

I took the more challenging route to the top, called the Steps of Repentance, with its steps cut into the stone. It wasn't the easiest climb, but I was in fairly good shape and I stopped twice to rest and sip from a water bottle.

At a place called Elijah's Basin, two paths met before the final 500 stairs to the summit. I had been hiking for two hours and could see that the sun was beginning to set. At the summit, I found a small chapel and a mosque, both closed. The view was striking, the peaks of the surrounding mountains clearly visible, the stark landscape stretching out before me, the sun slowly dropping down to the horizon.

I took a deep breath, surprised by how moved I was by the scene.

I couldn't say I had an epiphany. I just felt a stillness, a calm, that I hadn't felt for years. All of the colors around me felt more vivid. More alive. My problems, my worries, didn't seem so intractable. I felt awed by the beautiful desolation around me for as far as I could see.

That night my sleep was disrupted by a strange dream. I was walking through a desert landscape, looking for someone. I saw a group of people standing in the background, but I couldn't make out who they were. When I walked toward them, they moved away from me, keeping their distance.

Then I saw that one of them was Julia. Her face was sad and she wouldn't look at me. She held a young boy by the hand—my son, King. I followed them as they began to climb a nearby hill. Again, I couldn't catch up. I called out to them to stop, but they ignored me.

I woke to find myself on the narrow guesthouse bed, shivering from the cold. I must have thrown off my blankets during my dream.

The clock on the bedside table showed that it was after two o'clock. I pulled the blanket over my body and tried to get back to sleep, but I was troubled by the dream. The symbolism was crystal clear. I was worried about losing Julia. I had put my marriage at risk. I had been selfish and self-centered. My dream captured all of that.

My sleep was fitful for the rest of the night.

In the afternoon, after lunch, I returned to Sharm el-Sheikh by car for my return flight to Cairo.

When my connecting flight landed in Paris, I called Julia to let her know that I was on my way home and that I would come to Princeton to see her. I told her I wanted to talk, and that I loved her. She sighed and said that it was time we settled things between us.

The trans-Atlantic flight seemed to take forever. I kept thinking about Julia, about how badly I had treated her, and how I could make it up to her. I would tell her the truth, that I had been caught up in a madness of sorts but that I loved her and that hadn't changed.

Would she take me back? Could we repair our marriage? I couldn't imagine a future without her. She had always been there for me, a constant in my life, and she had been my best friend. I remembered her tears when I had asked for the trial separation, and I found myself cursing myself under my breath and looking around to make sure I hadn't been overheard by any of the nearby passengers.

I couldn't imagine ending our marriage and what that would mean. I hated the idea of Julia with another man. Did that make me the world's worst hypocrite? I guess it did. The classic double standard. But even if I was guilty of breaking my wedding vows, I couldn't bear the thought of Julia in the arms of someone else. I was jealous of her, too. Even more jealous.

We would start over. I would win her back. It wasn't too late, I told myself. It couldn't be.

THIRTY-TWO

JULIA

I knew that Jimmy was struggling and that he was too proud to admit his pain. Why do men keep it all bottled up? Why can't they talk about their feelings? Jimmy was surprised and rattled by being laid off, something he didn't see coming. His pride was wounded. Considering the financial issues at Continental, he shouldn't have been too surprised. Jimmy was a veteran newsman, he made more money, and there were plenty of kids straight out of journalism school willing to work for starvation wages. But even slashing costs during work: it wasn't long after Jimmy was fired that Continental went bankrupt and then closed its doors.

Jimmy wasn't the only middle-aged journalist out of a job. He began looking for a landing spot, and while he had a few interviews, nothing suitable turned up. Newspapers weren't hiring; they were shedding reporters and editors right and left. The wire services had trimmed back. My husband was in the wrong industry at the wrong time.

I ached for him. Jimmy put on a brave front. He managed to piece together a living from freelance assignments, ghostwriting a book, and other projects, but we were left without a steady paycheck. Suddenly, my store became a financial life-saver for us, a steady source of income we could count on, although at the same time we had to cut back on expenses.

Jimmy had always loved his work. Like many men, it defined him in many ways. He thought of himself as a journalist, and he took pride in his chosen profession. Now, he was on the fringes, unaffiliated, no longer inside the magic circle.

And I know he had been raised to pursue a career that had purpose. His father had made it clear that Kincaids should strive to serve others and the greater good. Alexander often quoted Woodrow Wilson's motto to them, "Princeton in the Nation's Service," as a noble sentiment. And so Beau ended up in the military and Jimmy in journalism.

It seemed to me that Jimmy began to question everything and everyone. I understood. Losing his place had been a shock.

Having King off to college didn't help. Once he was away, I realized how much our son had been a central part of what bonded us together.

His unhappiness surfaced in several ways. We argued. We didn't talk. It culminated in a separation, with him in a rental apartment in New York and me in Princeton, which was a stupid move financially, but one he insisted on.

When he first proposed it, living apart, I was hurt. I expected the worst, that this was the first step on the road to ending our marriage.

"Do you want a divorce?" I asked him.

He shook his head. "I need some time alone."

It brought me to tears. I cried when Jimmy held me in his arms, but he didn't back down. He told me again he needed time and space to figure things out. I didn't say what I wanted to—that he was mouthing clichés. Time and space? Really? He denied there was another woman, but I didn't believe him.

I told him that I would wait for him, but that I wouldn't wait forever.

"I'll want to move on at some point," I said. "If I'm going to start over, I'd rather it be sooner than later."

I could see the shock on his face. I wanted him to understand that as much as I loved him, I wasn't going to let him string me along.

We spoke on the phone at least once a week. We didn't see much of each other during the separation.

In what I regard as an ironic turn, I discovered that his father was furious with Jimmy. Told his son that he was being self-indulgent and foolish. I'd like to think that over the years Alexander had come to hold some affection for his daughter-in-law, that he respected me for the way I had raised King and how I had stood by Jimmy. Then there was the whole "Kincaids don't divorce" thing, but Beau had already broken that rule when he ended his marriage with Hillary.

I sensed that something had shifted when he called me on the way back from a trip to Egypt and apologized for what he had put me through. He came to Princeton and we talked. This time, he cried, from guilt, no doubt, and told me that he had made mistakes and hoped I would forgive him. I told him the truth, that I was hurt and angry.

He was different. Chastened? Shamed? I told him I was willing to try to put our marriage back together. We agreed to live together again. He was tentative around me when he first moved back. I wouldn't let him touch me at first, and we didn't sleep together. I wasn't ready to welcome him into my bed.

In the end, I decided not to question him about his life when we were apart. Sure, I was curious, but not so curious that I would open a door better left closed. I assumed he strayed during our separation. The truth? I'd rather not know. What's the point? If he was seeing someone, she didn't last. Whatever restlessness, whatever middle-aged craziness, it seemed Jimmy had gotten it out of his system.

As time went on, I hoped that he wouldn't unburden himself about whoever it was he had been sleeping with. I think there are some things better left unsaid in a marriage. If you've decided to make a go of it, why bring up the hurtful things of the past? And I was never part of that story. Didn't want to be.

I learned from our time apart. You can't make someone love you—isn't that how the song goes?—but you also can't ever know what another person has in their heart. I believed Jimmy loved me. I believed he was confused, lost, and the best thing I could do was to be there for him when he came to his senses. Does that mean I betrayed the feminist cause? Standing by my man? Who cares? I certainly don't. It was my life.

If Jimmy hadn't come back to me, I would have moved on and I'm sure I would have found someone new. Life would have gone on, but it wouldn't have been the same.

I didn't hide the fact that we were having trouble in our marriage. I told King. He took it calmly. I wasn't surprised, many of his high school friends had been through the collapse of their parents' marriages.

We survived. Barely. I had seen other couples around our age go through a relationship crisis and not make it through to the other side.

Jimmy asked if I wanted to try marriage counseling, and I told him no. Whatever problems we had, we could work them out together. All we needed was the closeness that we'd had for so many years. I knew we could recapture that.

Three weeks after Jimmy returned, we flew to Florida and spent a week at the Boca Grande house. We went to dinner—I wore my favorite light blue dress—and we made love that night for the first time since we had separated. I found myself clinging to Jimmy, tears in my eyes, so relieved to be reunited with him.

I could remember all the good times. Falling for Jimmy in high school, and then our early carefree days in the Village, followed by the arrival of King, who changed everything. I remembered the sweet moments of just being with Jimmy, at home, at ease in the living room, not having to say anything, content to be with each other.

While in Florida we talked about the changes we needed to make in our marriage. I wanted the closeness we once had, the intimacy, and the sense of partnership. Jimmy had been energized by living in Manhattan again, and I surprised him when I told him I was ready to move back to New York. I would miss Princeton, but we could visit Alexander on the weekends when we felt the need. I liked the idea of relocating to the Upper West Side, near Columbia. It would be a new experience, and a way to restart our relationship.

Jimmy resisted the idea at first—he didn't want me to sacrifice my happiness for his. I convinced him that wasn't the case, that I was eager for a fresh start.

I would miss my hometown more than I would ever let him know, but if we were going to make things work, we needed a clear separation from the past.

It had to be all in for us. My Jimmy isn't perfect, Lord knows, but he's been my friend since I was a little girl. My first lover, and, I hope, my last.

THIRTY-THREE

HANNA

To: jkincaid77@aol.com
From: hannak@aol.com
Date: May 17, 1999
Subject: My little sweetheart

I have such exciting news, Jimmy! I'm a mother! Finally! Officially! The adoption papers for Rose finally came through, and now my adorable two-year-old is finally my daughter...in the eyes of the state of California. Rose Kincaid Sorensen. She's such a beautiful child and I can't believe how much I love having her with us and knowing that she is ours. Nate laughs at me, calls me a bourgeois, suburban mom at heart. Maybe I am.

Never thought this would be my path to motherhood. I did try my best to get pregnant. (It annoys me when a woman will say "We're pregnant" as if her boyfriend or husband is somehow also carrying the child. They're not. Only the mom is pregnant.) But after three years of trying and failing, it just wasn't happening. I was disappointed, to say the least. I wanted to have a child, so adoption made sense.

After several years of trying, and all sorts of invasive medical procedures, Nate and I decided to give up. From all the tests, it's probably my fault more than his. Nate hasn't said a word about my not bearing him a son or daughter. It's one of the reasons I adore him, along with the fact that he's smart and funny and is willing to put up with me. No matter, Rose is here and I love her. What more is there?

It was uncomfortable being judged for our fitness to be parents by the adoption agency, but I understand why they had to scrutinize us so closely. I bit my tongue at times because I know any irresponsible eighteen-year-old skateboarder can impregnate his teenage girlfriend and they become parents without anyone looking over their shoulder. But life isn't fair, is it?

At the same time, along with the excitement is the realization that it's an incredible responsibility to take on, and I didn't feel the full weight of it until now. Did you feel the same way when you and Julia had King? Scared and thrilled at the same time? Full of love and trepidation?

It's also a bit daunting when you realize that your child has a mind of her own. Her own distinct personality. Rose can be so sweet and also so stubborn. We're learning how to set boundaries for her, but it's hard. I don't really like saying no to her. Nate is better about being tough—I think it's his traditional Lutheran upbringing and his experience with a strict mother and aloof father.

My perspective on things has already changed. I'm trying to balance the time spent with Rose with my work responsibilities. We've been able to juggle our schedules so that one of us is home with Rose, but it hasn't been easy. Nate wants us to find a nanny, but I've been a bit reluctant. Why? I'll confess that there's an element of jealousy. I hate the idea of someone else being there for Rose's first words.

I'm gradually getting used to the strange looks on the street when we take Rose out in the stroller. Her curly hair, brown eyes, and cinnamon-colored skin don't match my looks, and I've fielded some awkward questions about her father from acquaintances who don't realize she's adopted. If we were still living in San Francisco instead of near Santa Rosa, I think a white couple with a dark-skinned child wouldn't excite as much interest or curiosity.

What will we tell Rose when she's older and asks about her parents? We'll share the little that we know—that her mother and father broke up, that her mother couldn't cope with raising an infant alone, a biracial child in a small farming town in the Central Valley. But that's in the future, and for now we just want Rose to feel loved and cherished.

Here I am, going on and on about motherhood. How did your trip to Cairo and Mt. Sinai go? You never filled me in on the details. I'm jealous of all your travels around the world.

It's something to look forward to, trips with Nate and Rose to explore all those places I've always wanted to visit.

love, Hanna

To: hannak@aol.com
From: jkincaid77@aol.com
Date: May 19, 1999
Subject: Re: My little sweetheart

Such wonderful news, Hanna! No question that you'll make a loving and fantastic mother, and having Nate there by your side should smooth out many of the inevitable bumps in raising Rose.

By now you must realize that you're going to miss a lot of sleep. Hang in. It gets better.

I shared your news with Dad, at your request. He nodded and then smiled and said he hoped he would get the chance to meet your daughter someday.

It would be great if you could come East at some point. Dad turns 77 next year, and if you make it for his birthday I think we could persuade Beau to time a visit to Princeton then as well.

Dad continues to work on what he is calling his last gasp book. He seems as sharp as ever, for the most part, but there are some signs of aging. There are those awkward moments when he'll stop in the middle of a sentence searching for the words or forgetting a name.

I realize now that I've always thought of Dad as being indestructible, always in command, always present. As he has aged, that's changed. It's evident physically—his hair has thinned, he's developed a bit of a stoop, and he moves much more deliberately than when he was younger. Inevitable, I know, but somehow I thought that Alexander Tarkington Kincaid would be exempt from the ravages of time. Not that he won't fight back, you can count on him to "rage against the dying of the light."

Please send photos of you and Nate and Rose. Especially Rose!

Love, J.

P.S. The trip to Egypt and Mt. Sinai was productive and challenging. Some soul-searching. I returned resolved to be a better man, a better husband and father.

To: jkincaid77@aol.com
From: hannak@aol.com

Date: June 20, 1999
Subject: San Diego road trip

Some family news!

Nate and I took turns on our road trip to visit Beau in San Diego last week. Rose was so good on the drive! I was so worried she was going to suffer, but she was a wonderful little trooper.

Is it any wonder that I live in California? And Beau does as well?

My therapist just smiled once when I mentioned that to her. Fight or flight.

Yes, so I finally visited the Oldest Brother. It was fantastic seeing Beau in his new environment. His law office is in a strip mall, a storefront office, with a sign in the window, THE LAW OFFICE OF WILSON KINCAID, ESQ.

It's just Beau and a paralegal, but he seems to be doing quite well.

He told me he's begun teaching as an adjunct at the University of San Diego Law School.

It was awkward at first. We've talked about how I never felt close to Beau when I was a child. I was too young to have much of a relationship, and when he went off to college and law school and then the military we didn't see each other much. You and Beau always had a connection, and Des would tag along.

Then, later, I felt Beau judged me for some of my choices.

He has softened, Jimmy. He laughs more and he was wonderful with Rose. We went to a Mexican restaurant and had tortillas and burritos and quesadillas and washed it all down with pitchers of beer.

No signs of a steady girlfriend, but he's a handsome man and from a few comments he made I don't think he's lonely. Maybe he's wary after the failure of his marriage. I couldn't say, because it's not a topic I'm about to raise with him.

We encouraged him to come see us later in the year. Fingers crossed that he will.

Hope and trust all is well with you. Give my love to Julia. I'm glad you're resolved to be a better husband—I would think you're pretty good already. And I know you've been a good father. King must be close to finishing college! How time flies.

Love, Hanna

THIRTY-FOUR

HANNA

At first, I couldn't believe the signals my own body was sending.

How could it be? Yes, of course, I understand the biological reality. Every woman does. But I was sure that I couldn't conceive. Even when I missed my period, I didn't think it was anything out of the ordinary. I had been under a lot of pressure and feeling stressed had caused me to skip before. I figured that I just needed to calm down. I had stopped meditating every day, so I began that again in the mornings along with some deep breathing exercises I had learned.

I didn't even believe for a moment that I was actually pregnant. We had tried to have a child before many times and it hadn't worked out. It was the reason why we adopted Rose.

But when I felt sick three mornings in a row, I began to wonder. I didn't say anything to Nate. It would be so embarrassing if I was wrong, so I waited a few more days, and then I bought an at-home pregnancy test from the drugstore.

When the strip showed blue, I was stunned.

I waited a few hours and tried again. Blue again.

I waited until after we had finished dinner and put Rose to bed before I told Nate the news. He was surprised, to say the least. He laughed and hugged me.

I found myself crying, and when Nate asked me what was the matter, I couldn't answer at first.

I was confused. I had been so happy when we brought Rose into our lives.

My secret was that I did feel "less than." I couldn't bear a child the way other women could. I had felt guilty about that, and I had thrown myself into being the best mother possible for Rose.

Now, that had all changed.

My gynecologist, Sara Briggs, told me that it wasn't that unusual, that couples who adopted sometimes found a baby suddenly on the way.

There was a Zen-like quality to this: the universe doesn't give you what you desire until you've emptied yourself of hope and no longer strive for it. I had made my peace with being barren (an ugly word, isn't it?) and then I find I can have children.

And, if I am honest about it, a baby on the way is a mixed blessing. We're going to need to rearrange our lives. Having two little ones wasn't part of the Plan. I was still a bit embarrassed—what would friends and family think when we had just announced Rose's adoption? And I'm ancient for a first pregnancy.

That was scary: I was in high-risk territory at my age. I'm otherwise healthy, but it's uncharted territory, having a baby at forty.

It's so amazing to have this other life now growing within me. I'm connected now with this little one for the duration, which I hope will be the full nine months.

We're going to tell Rose soon. I'm not sure how she will react. I worry that sometime in the future she'll think that somehow I will favor this baby over her. It's not so, but I can imagine an adopted child might feel that way. Or maybe I'm overly sensitive about this. It could be that Rose will love the idea of having a baby brother or sister.

Nate was wonderful about the change in our lives. We began talking about names, and when I suggested Desmond if we had a boy, and Karin, if a girl, I think he understood where I was coming from.

I wasn't sure I was ready for another child. We had thrown ourselves into raising Rose, and I didn't know where I would find the extra energy. It made me happy that I had Nate by my side, the easy-going, always-calm Nate who took everything in stride. I think dealing with the ups and downs of running a vineyard had taught him not to overreact and that was a wonderful balance to my tendency to worry and fret.

It's times like these that I'm so thankful for my strong and silent husband. I'm so lucky to have him.

I have to laugh, though. My life seems to be just one thing after another, after another. So I guess I'm ready for a surprise baby.

THIRTY-FIVE

Charlotte Harbor, Florida, September 2001

They had started at first light, and spent the morning fishing for snook along the mangrove fringe by Cayo Costa. James and Beau both wore long-sleeved shirts, hats, and sunglasses for protection from the strong September sun. Beau had smeared zinc on his nose.

James was at the center console of their Back Country flats boat, a vessel that the Kincaid family kept at the Boca Grande marina.

He maneuvered the boat up current and they cast their hooks and bait—live shrimp—toward the shallows, a favorite hiding spot for snook. Beau added a float to suspend the bait in the water. Moments after his third cast, the float disappeared underwater and he got the first hit of the morning. The fish fought to get back to the safety of the overhanging mangrove branches, but finally tired and surfaced. Beau brought the fish to the boat, removed the hook from its mouth, and then released it back into the water.

They fished for two hours, catching and releasing the snook they caught. Then they paused, sitting in the boat, and drank cold water from plastic bottles.

"I got an e-mail from Hanna last week," James said. "Their baby boy is doing fine. She and Nate have their hands full now."

"Were you surprised that they named him after Des?" Beau asked.

"She loved him. It's a way of honoring Des."

"And rubbing salt into the wounds, don't you think? How do you think it must make Dad feel?"

"I don't think Hanna meant to hurt anyone. She's honoring Des's memory."

"She didn't think it through. But that's just like her. Hanna has always been impulsive."

"And you're not? You're too hard on her. It was a difficult pregnancy for her, at her age. From what she told me, the pregnancy came as a complete surprise. Thank God she and Des are fine. I wish I could have been more supportive, but I was dealing with my own issues. Trying to patch up the holes in my marriage. That had to come first."

"Is it going to work out? Are you and Julia back together for good?"

"We are. Yes, for good. In more ways than one."

"How long were you separated? You never said much about it on the phone, except that you two were struggling."

"On and off for six months. It was hard on her. On both of us. I have a lot of guilt about it, about how selfish I was. I'm lucky Julia has been willing to forgive me."

"Another woman," Beau said. It was a statement of fact, not a question. "A midlife crisis, Jimmy?"

"Something like that. My turn to be impulsive." James looked into the distance, avoiding his brother's gaze. "I've had some work to do. To figure out why it happened. Self-examination is painful. I had to face up to my failings. Particularly the way I hadn't shared how I was feeling with Julia, how I was struggling with a sense of failure. I didn't want to talk to her about it. I was ashamed. I was broke at one point. Had to borrow from Dad for King's tuition payments. Do you know what that feels like? So I pushed her away."

"You're lucky that she didn't bolt."

James nodded. "I've put Julia through a lot. Too many ups and downs. My fault." He paused. "Wounded male pride. I guess that I compensated by pursuing another woman."

Beau didn't respond, waiting for James to continue.

"I met her in New York at a party. We weren't together for very long. I had it bad for her, Beau. It was like she had mainlined something addictive into my veins. Go figure. At my age."

"Sometimes it's like that." Beau shrugged. "Hard to handle that intense feeling. Typically ends in a crash. Of course, it can be a hell of a ride."

"She was so different from Julia. A bit spoiled. Entitled. Sensual. I think that was a large part of the attraction for me. I'd never met anyone like her. The entire time we were together, I felt like that French guy who walked across that tightwire at the World Trade Center. Afraid to look down for fear I'd fall. All the while knowing she was wrong for me."

"What about her? Were you as wrong for her?"

"Hell if I know. She didn't want any entanglements in her life. She'd been married before. More than once. But then she listed all the reasons we wouldn't make it as a couple, almost as if she had to convince herself."

"How much does Julia know?"

"She told me she didn't want to know. In so many words. I damn well haven't volunteered anything. I think that's better for us. No names. No details. I was in love with Orit, the other woman, but I love Julia. There's a difference, you know."

"I'm glad you know the difference, younger brother."

"And what about you, Beau? Seeing anyone?"

"As it happens, I am," he said. "Not sure whether it will work or not. She's very independent. She's younger than me. Fifteen years. But Catalina's an amazing woman."

James laughed. "Are you going to end up with a trophy wife, Beau?"

"Who knows? It's not like that. Catalina married too young and her husband was an abusive drunk. She divorced him after eighteen months. But it hasn't made it easy for her to trust men. I think the fact that I'm older appeals to her."

"We thought that you might end up with Denise."

Beau shook his head. "Denise was on a mission to fix me. She hoped for the new, improved version. Her version. I'd been through that before, with Hillary, and I wasn't going to make the same mistake twice. That's the one saving grace of growing older. You can see the trouble coming from a mile away. Catalina accepts me for who I am. And vice versa."

When Beau suggested they head back to Boca Grande for lunch at Miller's Marina, James nodded. "I'm partial to a cheeseburger and a beer," he said.

The dock was empty when they arrived. It was cool and dark inside the dining room. The bartender and a lone waiter were standing by the bar, gazing up at the television. On the screen,

James could see a long trail of smoke rising into the air. He and Beau approached the bar.

"What's going on?" Beau asked the bartender.

The man didn't take his gaze from the screen. "It's bad. Some jet planes flew into the World Trade Center. Boeing 767s. The buildings collapsed. Another plane slammed into the Pentagon. They think it's some sort of coordinated attack. They've shut down air travel."

"Damn it," Beau said. "Damn it to hell."

"Let's go back to the house," James suggested. "I want to call home. We can watch the news there."

They drove back to the Kincaid cottage on the Gulf side of the island.

James tried calling Julia at home, but he was frustrated by the busy signal he encountered. Beau had better luck and reached his girlfriend in San Diego.

On the television, the news anchors were grimly explaining that the jetliners crashing into the Twin Towers and the Pentagon appeared to be part of a coordinated terrorist attack.

As they watched, it became clearer and clearer that the initial information pointed to a Middle Eastern connection. The hijackers were described as Arabs, and intelligence sources were already suggesting Al Qaeda, an Islamist group led by a Saudi radical, Osama Bin Laden, was behind the plot.

"That comes as no surprise," Beau said. "Remember the truck

bomb in the underground parking at the World Trade Center? The blind sheikh? The fact they went after the Towers again is telling."

"How could we be so vulnerable?" James asked.

"Suicide attacks are difficult to defend against. Remember the kamikazes at the end of the Second World War? Gave the Navy fits."

"We let our guard down. That much is clear."

"It's a terrible day for the country," Beau said. "A day I never thought would come."

"Do you think there's more coming? More attacks?"

"It seems we've shut down airspace over the major cities, and they're scrambling fighters to provide air cover. They'll intercept any questionable flights and they'll have shoot-down orders if any pilot doesn't respond and lands their plane."

"And then what?" James asked.

"We'll go to war," his brother said. "There's no question about that. It's only where and when. But who can say where it ends? Al Qaeda. Blood feuds. It's the Thirty Years War with missiles and jet aircraft."

They spent the afternoon watching the coverage on television, trying to follow the latest developments. The news reports were fragmentary and inconclusive. For now, at least, it seemed the attacks had stopped. Beau was restless, cursing softly, frustrated that he couldn't somehow respond to what was happening.

"I'm forty-eight years old," he said. "It's been years since I put on a uniform, but I'd return to the service in a heartbeat if they'd have me."

He went to the kitchen and returned with bottles of beer. He gave one to James and opened his own and took a swallow.

"You damned right we let our guard down, Jimmy," Beau said. "It's worse than Pearl Harbor."

"But you can see why. We relaxed after the Berlin Wall fell and the Soviet Union collapsed. The Cold War was over. Remember, how we were told it was the end of history? We thought we were invulnerable. The last superpower standing. So much for that."

Beau shook his head. "We need to retaliate. Hard. No hearts and minds bullshit. No nation-building. We should hunt down those responsible and eliminate them and then get out. And make it clear that if we're attacked again, there will be hell to pay. The first round of Cruise missiles should target the Kaaba in Mecca."

"That's the booze and anger talking. You can't be serious, Beau."

"The Romans knew how to respond to their enemies: *Carthago delenda est.*"

"I'd like to think we've come a long way from the Punic Wars. Or from the Crusades."

"We may have, but Bin Laden and his buddies are nostalgic types. Warriors sweeping out of the desert against the infidels. Jihad. Assassins. I don't think they're going to respond to diplomacy."

Later, they ate a hastily-prepared dinner, hamburgers and potato chips, and when they finished James suggested that they move to the front porch. They sat side-by-side in battered rocking chairs, beer bottles in hand, and watched the sun slowly drop into the Gulf of Mexico. They didn't talk much, lost in their own thoughts. Inside, they could hear the television blaring with the sights and sounds of the Towers collapsing replaying again and again.

"We started the day in a different place, didn't we?" Beau asked. "Couldn't ask for better weather, out on the water, not a cloud in sight. And we end it wondering what the hell is going on. Like the rest of the damn world."

THIRTY-SIX

HANNA

To: jkincaid77@aol.com
From: hannak@aol.com
Date: July 12, 2003
Subject: My life

We've been out-of-touch, dearest brother of mine, and I'm sorry because I meant to e-mail you last week and I got distracted. That's become way too easy for me.

Being a parent means there are never enough hours in the day. I've learned that. Des is a wonderful little boy, but he can be very demanding. Rose has been so sweet with her little brother. We'd worried about jealousy, but so far she's been his best playmate, willing to share her toys, and "read" her favorite books to him. They get along quite well.

We held a birthday party for Rose, where her friends from school came for cake and punch and balloons and games in the backyard. We had an afternoon filled with happy little girls on a sugar high. It was great fun.

Rose at six is so amazing—a wonderful mixture of innocence and growing awareness of the complexity of life. She's very observant. I think she is beginning to realize that Nate and Yours Truly don't have all the answers.

I have an update about Beau and his girlfriend, Catalina. They spent a weekend in San Francisco and drove up to see us. Beau is clearly smitten with her....she's a beautiful young woman. Her parents moved to California from Costa Rica. I wouldn't be surprised if a marriage is on the horizon, sooner rather than later. She seemed very much at ease with Rose and Des, so I also wouldn't be surprised if she and Beau decide to start a family ASAP.

There is an age gap, but I'm hardly in a position to criticize Beau. After all, I'm the older woman in my relationship.

You know I've not very political, but I did talk to Beau about the situation in the Middle East. He thinks Afghanistan has stabilized, but he's concerned about Iraq. It's very sad. I know we had to do something after 9/11, but I wish it didn't mean invasions and bombings and the trouble it has brought to the people, the innocent people, living there.

love, Hanna

To: hannak@aol.com
From: jkincaid77@aol.com
Date: July 14, 2003
Subject: Re: My life

Always wonderful to hear from you, dearest sister.

As a parent, there's nothing quite like watching a child grow up in front of you. I envy you and Nate for that, in part—I didn't see as much of King when he was six and seven and eight because of the hours I was working. Sadly, there's no going back and recovering those moments. Julia tells me not to beat myself up, that I was there for King on my days off and on vacations. Nonetheless, I feel some guilt about my absences. Cherish your time with Rose and Des.

I have some news of note as well. I've landed a full-time job as an editor at a small publishing house that specializes in travel guides and maps, Far Journey Press. They're certainly not paying me a king's ransom, but the job comes with health insurance and benefits and the company is stable. Julia is delighted, to say the least. I can take the crosstown bus to the office, which is on the East Side.

My other news is not as happy. King has informed us that he will be spending some of the next year in Iraq as a staffer in the Coalition Provisional Authority, the temporary governing body set up to oversee the occupation. As you might imagine, we were taken aback by the news. We never imagined that graduate school at Johns Hopkins could involve such a dangerous assignment. King's mentor at Hopkins has been tapped to help in developing what they're calling a sustainable civil society in Iraq, whatever the hell that means. Julia is beside herself over the situation. Neither of us supported the war—King argues that he'll be doing something to justify the intervention. Julia worries about the danger. I'd like to reassure her, but from all I can gather, the security situation there has deteriorated.

love, your brother J.

To: jkincaid77@aol.com
From: hannak@aol.com
Date: July 15, 2003
Subject: King's choice

Wonderful news about your job. Even better that your commute is an easy one. I'll bet that Julia is relieved!

I can see why you would worry about King. It must be very hard for you and Julia. No mother wants her child in harm's way. I haven't followed events in Iraq closely, but my general impression is that it isn't very stable. It seems as if every other day someone sets off a bomb in a marketplace with a terrible loss of life.

My Nate will tell you the root of nearly all the evil in the world comes from religion, and he points to the turmoil in the Middle East as proof. I don't even bother to debate the question with him anymore. He knows it's the *distortion* of religious teaching that screws things up. He also knows that belief can be a force for good. But he won't concede any of that because he's a disillusioned preacher's kid.

And I still trust in the power of prayer, so I'll be praying that King stays safe from harm.

all my love, Hanna

P.S. Nate's sending along a bottle of the Chardonnay for you and Julia to try. He thinks that it's quite special...and so do I.

To: hannak@aol.com
From: jkincaid77@aol.com
Date: July 16, 2003
Subject: Re: King's choice

King and I finally had a long talk about his plans to go to Iraq. His mentor and sponsor, a man named Ross Aubrey, has an expertise in building civil society in troubled places, like Lebanon and the Balkans, where there has been sectarian violence. I've asked around and Aubrey has a mixed reputation. Smart, experienced, and cautious about security, but a real neoconservative. Convinced that we can reshape the Arab world in our Western image.

Will King be safe? There are no guarantees, although I trust that the military and security people will move heaven and earth to keep American civilians working there as shielded as possible. The danger comes in the randomness of the violence. Roadside bombs kill indiscriminately.

We've talked about the risks, but I haven't tried to talk him out of going. (Not that it would work). King will go into this with his eyes wide open.

So Julia and I say our separate prayers and count the days until we get our son back safe and sound.

love, James

THIRTY-SEVEN

JULIA

New York, November 2003

When King told us that he was taking a job in Iraq, consulting for the Coalition Provisional Authority, I was terrified.

What mother would ever want her child in a war zone, in harm's way?

Jimmy tried to calm me down. He claimed that while there was a level of danger involved, that security for American civilians working in Iraq would be tight.

I got fairly emotional. I was pretty tough on Jimmy for downplaying the situation. He knows how dangerous assignments in a place like Baghdad can be. After the Iran hostage crisis, and the embassy bombings in Tanzania and Kenya, it's clear the terrorists see our diplomats and civilians as fair game.

I pushed Jimmy pretty hard to do something. Couldn't he talk sense into King?

It probably wasn't fair to saddle him with that. How do you convince your adult child that he is making a mistake when it's clearly the path he has chosen? What's more, there's the family tradition of service to country—his grandfather and Uncle Beau were veterans, and Kincaid men were expected to pursue careers with a public purpose. Did King believe it was his patriotic duty?

Jimmy tried. He flew down to Washington and spent a day with King. He laid out the pros and cons of King taking the assignment in Iraq. In the end, King wouldn't budge. Kincaid stubbornness.

Professor Aubrey has convinced King that Iraq is the perfect laboratory for establishing democratic institutions in the Middle East. Jimmy had researched Aubrey's background and learned he had been involved in pacification efforts in Vietnam—failed efforts—and was part of the neoconservative group in Washington that had been cheerleading for the invasion of Iraq.

I know Jimmy and King had agreed to disagree over the Iraq war. Jimmy thought it was a huge error, but King was more optimistic, arguing that the invasion liberated Iraq from Saddam Hussein and his sons and would usher in a more democratic society.

I was no expert on Middle Eastern politics. I didn't pretend to fully understand the situation there, but I read everything about Iraq I could get my hands on and I didn't find any arguments that convinced me that we should be there or stay there.

Weapons of mass destruction? Yellowcake uranium? Saddam aiding Al Qaeda? Where was the evidence? It didn't stand up to the light of day. And we went to war based on that.

They say that Dick Cheney's main argument boiled down to the 1% Principle. If there was a 1% chance that Saddam had nuclear weapons that could be used against us, then we had no choice but to invade and eliminate that threat. I don't get the logic in that. Wouldn't that mean we needed to invade every country with nuclear weapons? Pakistan, India, North Korea, Israel, maybe South Africa? (Yes, I did my research).

I got so angry when I thought about the situation. Of course, I had to respect King's decision, but that didn't mean I had to be happy about it. If I believed in the purpose of the Iraq war and its aftermath. I would have felt better. Nation-building? Wasn't that the thing George W. Bush campaigned against?

Jimmy lost patience with me, I'm afraid. He said I needed to accept that King's posting in Iraq as a fact, one neither of us could change.

He was right. I needed to try harder to stay calm.

But I knew I would worry every day King was there. How could I not? At least there was e-mail now, and satellite phones, so we would be able to stay in touch. Jimmy teased me that we'd probably hear more from King in Iraq than we did from King in Baltimore.

I found a little Catholic church near our apartment, a quiet sanctuary. I began stopping by there and saying my prayers for King most mornings. It was usually deserted. I'd find a pew and kneel and ask God to protect my son from harm. I wondered how many mothers were offering up the same prayer in other holy places.

In the one brief conversation I had with King, he told me that one way or the other, Iraq would end up with a government, and he wanted to help establish a modern, democratic one that respected the rule of law. We had helped create stability and prosperity in Japan and Germany after the Second World We. We needed to do the same in Iraq, otherwise, he argued, there would always be the threat of terrorism hanging over us, the threat of another 9/11.

I listened, and I think I may have nodded once or twice. I couldn't question his logic, but I also knew how the best-laid plans could go awry, and I had a sinking feeling that this was a case where that worry was going to be proved true.

THIRTY-EIGHT

Iraq, 2004

The winter in Baghdad proved to be mild and dry, with temperatures rarely dropping below 40 degrees and with little rain. King Kincaid had been warned that the city would grow oppressively hot later in the year with a blazing sun and shamal winds spreading dust everywhere. He hadn't been in the Mideast before, and he wanted to explore the city, one of the cradles of civilization, but he had been warned in his orientation briefing of the threat to Americans from the growing insurgency.

King found the contrast between Baghdad's Red and Green Zones telling. The names alone told the story. The Green Zone, the fortified area around Saddam Hussein's former palace grounds, was safe for Americans, considered "good to go." A blast wall encircled the four square miles that had been nicknamed "The Bubble" by its inhabitants. The Red Zone, the rest of Baghdad outside the center of the city, was not safe, judged an increasingly dangerous place for Westerners.

King had joined the other young American civilians who had come to Iraq to help fashion a new society out of the ruins of Saddam Hussein's Ba'ath autocracy. He was assisting Professor Ross Aubrey, who had taken a sabbatical consulting with the State Department on the transfer of sovereignty to a provisional Iraqi government set for the summer.

They lived at the Rashid Hotel—which had a coffee shop, restaurant, disco, outside pool, and two bars—and they spent much of their time in meetings with officials in the Republican Palace where the Coalition Provisional Authority was headquartered. King was eager to get into the field, and Aubrey believed that to properly do their job they needed to meet and build relationships with those Iraqis likely to join the government.

They traveled from the Green Zone in a convoy of SUVs with heavily-armed bodyguards accompanying them, private security details comprised often of U.S. Army or Marine veterans. Aubrey had complained that it sent the wrong signal to the locals, but he couldn't get the security requirements eased. Since neither he nor King spoke Arabic, they had to rely on local interpreters when their Iraqi counterparts didn't speak English.

They made little progress. King joked that their theme song ought to be the Bruce Springsteen single with the refrain: "One step up and two steps back." The Iraqis he met were polite but guarded. Their wariness made sense—cooperating with the Americans was considered collaboration by those militants resisting the occupation.

King pressed their translator, a wiry man in his late thirties named Kassim, to offer his insights into Iraqi society. Kassim spoke with a slight British accent and was a chain smoker, rarely without a cigarette in his hand.

"I was educated in Manchester," he told King. "I think I understand the Anglo-Saxon mind quite well. You think differently than we do. And today most of you no longer believe. It is your weakness. We have Allah and his Prophet Muhammad, peace be upon him. What do you have? What do you believe in?"

"Some Americans are Christians and believe in Jesus. Others are more secular and believe in the individual and in freedom, I suppose."

Kassim shook his head and took another deep puff from his cigarette. "It appears to us that you believe more in money and power and technology than those other things. That won't work here."

King studied him for a long moment. "You've lived in the West, Kassim. Don't you want your country to have what we have? The rule of law. Democracy. A free press."

"What I may want is immaterial, Mr. Kincaid. What do the chaps in al-Sadr's militia want? Or this Governing Council you have established? Or the new government in June? What will survive after you leave? And you will leave. And what of the violence sure to come? The chaos?"

King feared Kassim's predictions would come true. In February, he was startled early one morning by the sound of a large explosion: a suicide bomber driving a white Oldsmobile had triggered explosives at the Iraqi Army recruitment center, about a mile from the Green Zone. The blast killed more than thirty men.

As the winter turned to spring, the tension between Sunnis and Shias grew stronger, and King and Aubrey made fewer and fewer trips to the Red Zone. Their security people argued that the risks had increased as the situation in the streets deteriorated. Aubrey pointed out that their mission was to build up the institutions of civil society, and they couldn't do that if they were blocked from engaging with the Iraqis.

King could see that the Coalition had lost control of the situation, with more bombings in Baghdad, fierce fighting in Fallujah, and the revelation of the abuse of Iraqi detainees by U.S. troops at Abu Ghraib.

"Are we doing any good here?" he asked Aubrey. They had found a corner table at the hotel bar and ordered a pitcher of beer.

"Can't say I've seen anything as screwed up." Aubrey sighed. "We've hit rock bottom. The best we can hope for now is for the Iraqis to agree to the constitution and hold elections. And then we should step back."

"It will be a mess," King said.

"But *their* mess." Aubrey paused to take a sip of his beer. "I've read your grandfather's books," he said. "Much of what he has to say about status and hierarchy pertains to the situation here, you know. We can't underestimate the impact of tribalism on the social structures that humans construct—although an evolutionary focus is a bit narrower and misses some of the delightful complexity we face here. The religious factor. Islam. Tribalism seasoned with theocracy. It makes it harder to build the necessary institutions. Near impossible. Saddam did keep the mullahs at bay. With him gone, the sectarian hate is out of Pandora's box."

"I've been surprised by how the locals can tell a Sunni from a Shia in ten seconds," King said. "Same ethnicity, same clothes, but the sectarian radar works like a charm."

Aubrey laughed. "Sectarian radar? That's quite good. Visit Belfast and you'll find the same thing. To an outsider, no clue as to who's a Protestant or Catholic. But they know. The locals *always* know. There are subtle tells, like in poker." He put his mug down. "I'm done, both With drinking tonight and with this consulting gig. I'm sorry it hasn't worked out. We'll wind it down next month."

"What about Kassim? By working with us he's put a target on his back. He has a wife and son."

Aubrey shook his head. "He's a good interpreter. I've

recommended him to the Embassy for future employment. He'll have a steady job."

"Can they keep him safe?"

"Hard to say. I guess it depends on how it works out. After we left Vietnam, it didn't go very well for the South Vietnamese who had helped us. It's what happens when you lose a war. I'm not saying we lost this war—because we didn't. But it sure feels that way, doesn't it?"

In late May, King left Iraq. After five frustrating months, Aubrey's State Department contacts had agreed that the security situation made it too dangerous for the project to continue.

King decided to stop in New York on his way back to Washington, and he called his father to let him know. He took a cab to his parents' apartment on the Upper West Side. It was strange to sit down to dinner with them in the peace and quiet of a soft spring night. Julia had ordered takeout Chinese food and they ate at the dining room table. King looked around the apartment, at his father's crammed bookshelves and his mother's new kitchen, recently redecorated, and shook his head—it was so removed from his recent reality.

"Wonderful to be back," he said. "But it's a bit surreal. No gunfire or explosions in the distance."

James smiled. "No call to prayer, either."

His mother sighed. "I'm just so happy that you're here in one piece. I worried for you. The news about Iraq has been terrible. The suicide bombers. Fallujah. Abu Ghraib. The fighting."

"It's fading from the front page," James said. "Foreign news doesn't sell very well. Most of us go about our lives oblivious to what is going on in the rest of the world. It's the blessing, and curse, of being an American. And then every so often you have a Pearl Harbor and a 9/11 and suddenly we do pay attention. For a while, at least. You win the war, and it's back to business as usual."

"Except we're still in Baghdad," King said.

"And Kabul. The costs of Imperium."

Julia spoke up: "Your Uncle Beau thought Iraq was a mistake from the start."

"I'm surprised to hear that," King replied. "I thought he was a hawk."

"He used to be," his father said. "Beau believed that we had to go into Afghanistan, had to deal harshly with the Taliban for harboring Bin Laden. He thought we should hit hard and then get out. Different when it came to Iraq. What he saw during Desert Storm convinced him that it would be a mistake to invade and occupy. If we had to contain Saddam it could be done through expanding the no-fly zone and the overflights of our aircraft. Any time Iraqi radar locked on one of our jets, we could strike at their command-and-control centers. Do it often enough and you encourage the Iraqi generals to get rid of Saddam."

"The premise of the war was to eliminate Saddam's weapons of mass destruction," King said.

"So much for that," Julia said. "Just as you arrived in Iraq, Condoleezza Rice admitted it was an intelligence failure. No WMDs to be found." She paused. "I've read everything I could get my hands on about Iraq and our reasons for going to war. It was a mistake, King, for us to be there."

"At the time, it seemed to make sense," her son said. "We believed that if we removed Saddam, then we could reconstruct Iraq as a liberal democracy. It's clear now that was a delusion. I can testify to that having been there."

"How long can you stay?" Julia asked. "More than tonight?"

"I'm heading back to Washington tomorrow," he replied. "I have to find an apartment. Then, I'm going to finish my doctorate. I've decided I want to teach."

"That's wonderful," she said. "A second Professor Kincaid in the family. Your grandfather will be delighted."

"It will take some time. I have to write a thesis."

"Any ideas on a topic?" his father asked.

"A few. I'd like to explore the lessons of our occupation of Iraq, and what our foreign policy decision-makers can learn from the experience. Professor Aubrey will be my dissertation advisor, and he thinks it's time to educate a generation or two of foreign policymakers about the limits of American power."

"Will you have to go back to Iraq?" Julia asked. "For your research? Interviews, that sort of thing."

"If it turns out that I need to, I'll wait until things settle down," King said. "I'm in no rush. Trust me, it's not exactly a welcoming place at the moment."

THIRTY-NINE

HANNA

December 2005

When Rose first asked me about attending the Christmas Eve service at the Church of the Incarnation in Santa Rosa, I had hesitated. I knew Nate would disapprove of the idea. We talked about it after Rose had gone to bed.

"She's just curious," I told him. "One of her friends, Megan, told her about the service. Invited her. I'm willing to take her."

"I won't be going." His face had hardened. It was a look I wasn't used to seeing. Unwelcome. Grim.

"It's an Episcopal church," I replied. "I grew up in that church. It's very laid-back. No fire and brimstone."

He shook his head, his lips tight and pursed. "I thought we had agreed that we weren't going to have the kids ever do Sunday School. Or church services. No brainwashing."

"You're making too much of it."

"And you're making too little of it." Nate frowned. "You know how I feel about this. I hate the idea of Rose being taken in by all the lies and half-truths. The hypocrisy."

I didn't want to argue with him. I tried to explain that Megan was Rose's best friend, and Rose was eager to accept the invitation.

"You take her, then, if that's what you want. I won't be going with you. I'll look after Des here at home."

I was disappointed. I had hoped that he would agree for us to attend as a family, but I had underestimated the depths of his feelings. He was seething. It wasn't like Nate. When we argued, which wasn't very often, he was always the calm and logical one—I was the emotional one. I knew his response stemmed in large part from the legacy of his feelings about his father. They had parted on the worst of terms. Nate hadn't been very forthcoming about the details, but I knew that Pastor Nils Sorensen had been very hard on his son and the two had never reconciled. And then his father had died, which meant no resolution of the breach. No closure. A wound that had never been healed.

"The music will be lovely," I said. "And Rose is eager to go. I don't see how this one time is going to hurt her. One service, Nate. I wish you would come with us." I tried to lighten the tone. "When I was her age, I found church excruciating boring and thought my parents were mean for making me go. Des and I used to joke about our lucky friends who only turned up in church on Christmas Eve."

"I have no interest in attending," he said. "Stop pushing me, Hanna. I'm not going to change my mind." He muttered something about some unfinished paperwork, left our bedroom, firmly closing the door behind.

I wasn't going to back down. Rose and I would go to the service by ourselves. Desmond would be happy to have his Dad to himself. Des was my cheerful child. I wondered if Nate had been like that as a boy before his mother died and his father grew bitter and unforgiving.

I decided to make the best of it. I purchased a cute dark red velvet Christmas dress for Rose. She was delighted by the gift of the dress and insisted on immediately trying it on. I brushed her hair and tied it back with a red ribbon and she studied herself in the full-length mirror in the bedroom. I told her how pretty she looked and Rose smiled at me.

"Will everybody dress up for the Christmas Eve service?" she asked.

I nodded. "It's a special time. A celebration."

"I can't wait," she said, hugging me.

When December 24th arrived, Nate was grim and quiet all day. I ordered pizza for dinner because it was Desmond's favorite and I knew he would feel left out when Rose and I left without him. I gave him a kiss and a hug. Nate hung back, but I went over and kissed him on the lips.

On the drive to Santa Rosa, I explained to Rose how we would be expected to behave. "It's simple," I said. "We stand to sing, sit to listen, and kneel to pray. The minister will tell us when."

"Did you go to church when you were my age?" she asked.

"I did. And we always tried to go on Christmas Eve."

We met Megan and her parents outside the church and followed them inside. Rose turned to me with a radiant smile when we reached the nave, which had been decorated with greenery. At the end of each pew, there was a candle holder with a red ribbon affixed, and a lit white candle.

"The candles are so pretty, Mom, aren't they?"

I nodded, reminded of my childhood memories of Christmas. I realized that the last time I had set foot in church had been more than ten years ago—my mother's funeral in Princeton.

I helped Rose follow the service, switching back-and-forth between the Book of Common Prayer and the Hymnal. She moved closer to me and I put my arm around her shoulders, hugging her close.

When it came time for Holy Communion, we initially watched as the congregants, starting from the front of the church, made their way to the sanctuary and the altar rail, with the ushers silently shepherding them pew-by-pew. Rose looked over at her friend, Megan, who had risen with her mother and father to move to the aisle. "Can we go up?" she asked, whispering.

I hesitated and found myself nodding and taking her hand, walking together to the line forming to take communion. We knelt at the rail, and, without thinking, I held my hands out for the wafer, and took a sip of the wine. The minister blessed Rose and I heard her sigh softly.

We walked back to our pew, hand-in-hand.

"This was wonderful," she said. "All the candles and the music and the people looked so happy to be here. Happy to sing. I wish Dad and Desmond had come with us."

"Des wouldn't last through the service," I explained. "He's still too little."

"Maybe they can come next year?"

I knew better than to make promises that wouldn't be kept. "We'll see, Rose. I'm just happy that you enjoyed tonight."

I kissed her on her cheek and squeezed her hand, but didn't say anything more.

After the service ended, we said our goodbyes to Megan and her parents. On the drive home, Rose fell asleep, and when we arrived, Nate came to the car and carried her in his arms to her room. I watched as he kissed her forehead and tucked her into bed.

PART FIVE

FORTY

KING

There is a legend in our family that the first Kincaid in the New World, Jonathan, married an Indian princess. In fact, Jonathan Kincaid arrived in Massachusetts Bay Colony as a prisoner-of-war, having fought on the losing side in the English Civil War and been punished with a sentence of indentured servitude in the New World.

My great-aunt Priscilla—my grandfather Alexander's sister—laughed when, at the age of twelve, I asked her about our princess.

"Princess? Hannah Kincaid was no princess. She was an Indian, I'll grant you, but I'm convinced she was a common squaw, plain and simple. The only reason we know anything about her is that she turned up in the court records for her constant quarreling. She had an argument with one of the neighbors and tried to bite her ear off and got hauled before a judge."

"Then why are there stories that she was a princess?" I asked, puzzled.

"We live in a fallen world, King Teilhard Kincaid," she said, relishing the chance to say my full name out loud. Around the time of my birth, my father had been captivated by the writings of Pierre Teilhard de Chardin, this French Jesuit philosopher, hence my strange middle name. King is my mother's maiden name, and what everyone calls me. Thank God for that.

"What does that have to do with Hannah Kincaid?"

"In a fallen world, people care about the wrong things," she said. "I've no idea whether Hannah Kincaid was a good wife to Jonathan or a shrew. She certainly had a temper. But back then, for a Scotsman to marry a woman with red skin, there had to be an explanation. Why he chose her instead of a white woman. The easy explanation was to say that she was royalty."

"And that made a difference?"

"They used to claim during Jim Crow days that if you put a turban on a Negro, he would be warmly welcomed at the finest country club in Richmond, Virginia. As long as they believed he was a foreign dignitary, maybe an Arabian prince, they could overlook the dark skin."

"I don't get it," I said, shaking my head.

Aunt Priscilla grinned. "Shakespeare claimed a rose by any other name smelled as sweet, but he was obviously wrong. Even today some of your Kincaid relatives cling to the idea that Jonathan married into the native royalty. For all we know, he bought her with some beads." She peered at me. "Women were in short supply, you know. They died early, too. And Jonathan was hardly a paragon of virtue. He turned up in those court records a time or two, usually for sharp business practices."

"I don't think you should pay attention to what other people say about who you want to marry," I told her with the certainty of a twelve-year-old. "It's not their life."

"So will you marry a pretty girl who looks like Pocahontas?" she asked me, teasing. "Or will you stick with the girl next door? Blonde hair and blue eyes?"

"I don't know," I confessed. "But I'll make up my own mind."

"You have to give Jonathan some credit," Priscilla said. "He had courage. He could have just shacked up with Hannah, but he made her an honest woman." She paused, lost in thought for a moment. "That's more than we can say for some of our American so-called heroes. Thomas Jefferson fooling around with his slave, Sally Hemings. Sam Houston and his Cherokee maidens. General Douglas MacArthur with his Filipina actress girlfriend. They wanted to have their cake and eat it, too. God forbid they tell the world the truth about the woman they loved."

I liked talking with Priscilla. I might be twelve years old, but she treated me like an adult, and I could always count on her to speak her mind, a mind which stayed sharp well into her eighties.

She spent most of the year living on Martha's Vineyard with another woman, Dolores Campion, who had been a famous professional tennis player in the late 1930s. The Boston and New York papers said nothing about Priscilla when Dolores died, even though they had spent the past thirty years together, for better and for worse. Priscilla made sure that in her own obituary that the *Vineyard Gazette* described her as "the faithful life companion of Dolores Campion." She was another Kincaid who cared little for convention.

When in the tenth grade I saw the classic movie *Ivanhoe* on television, I couldn't understand why Ivanhoe, as played by Robert Taylor, would ever have consciously chosen Rowena, a pale Joan Fontaine, over the dark, mysterious, and alluring Rebecca, Elizabeth Taylor.

Rowena was polite and passive and had zero sex appeal, and Rebecca, the healer and mystic, the opposite. It was brilliant casting because if you actually read Sir Walter Scott's novel (I did), it's clear that at some level, he believed that Rebecca was the better choice for his hero, and I don't know that there's an actress in the world who could have outshone Liz Taylor in 1952 when they made the film.

As it turned out, I didn't end up with Rowena, or anyone like her.

Takara Ishikawa fascinated me from the start. The daughter of Japanese immigrants who grew up in Southern California, Takara spoke Japanese fluently, attended UCLA, loved the Beach Boys, and rooted for the Dodgers. She was an appealing mixture of the familiar and the mysterious. And I suspect I represented the same for her (although I doubt I seemed that mysterious).

I met her the summer after my sojourn in Iraq when I returned to the Johns Hopkins School of Advanced International Studies in Washington. I had been invited to a beach party by Lorena Victor, a friend from Georgetown. She and Takara were both pursuing degrees in public health at American University. I was immediately attracted to Takara. As it happened, we arrived at the party wearing baseball caps—the Dodgers for her and the Yankees for me—and we began by teasing each other about whose team was better. Both squads were having great seasons. She had a great sense of humor and a wonderful smile. I wasn't looking for romance, but Takara changed my mind. Smart, beautiful, witty, and strong-willed—I was hooked from the start.

We spent most of the afternoon talking and flirting, and I knew I wanted to see her again. But when I asked for her phone number, she shook her head.

"I'm not interested in dating or a boyfriend," she said. "With my schedule this coming semester, I don't have the time for it."

"Give me a chance to change your mind," I told her. "That's only fair."

She laughed. "Why do I have to be fair?"

"Because if you're not, you'll be responsible for breaking my heart."

She shook her head, but gave me her number. Later, Takara told me that she had felt a strong connection from the start, but wasn't sure she was ready for a serious relationship.

I spent the rest of the summer and the early fall pursuing her. She was living in an apartment in Alexandria and I spent a fair amount of time driving across the Potomac to Virginia to visit her. By Thanksgiving, we were seeing each other exclusively, and I flew out to Los Angeles for Christmas to meet her family.

In January, I invited her to Boca Grande for a long weekend and it was her turn to meet my parents. And on the beach there I went down on one knee and asked her to marry me. She said yes, and we hugged and then she laughed.

"I never expected this," she said. "You and me. I wasn't planning on getting married yet."

I told her the truth, that it was as unexpected for me as for her, but that I couldn't bear the thought of losing her if I didn't act on my feelings.

"Just so you know, King, I'm going to finish my master's before we have children," she said.

"I can wait," I said. "Although I don't really want to."

We went back to the house to tell my parents and call hers on the phone.

I never understood the stereotype about Asians and their supposed inscrutability. As we spent time together, I discovered that Takara's moods and emotions quickly flickered across her face. Today, after years together, I can read the subtle but expressive changes that signal her unhappiness or joy or tenderness.

Strangers always remark on Takara's physical beauty—and I admit it was what first drew me to her—but at some point that becomes a given, and what matters are the other aspects of your beloved. I know that beauty being only skin deep is a cliché, but I'm fortunate that Takara's loveliness has proven to be of the far deeper kind.

So where does this attraction to the Other come from?

My college buddy, Sam Espinosa, who went on to get a master's in marine biology, had his own theory. He introduced me to the concept of genetic interchange. Sam spent a year in Florida studying dolphins in Sarasota Bay and learned that the males of the species are very territorial and guard their females fiercely. Yet, despite that, when the scientists took DNA samples they found that ten percent of the dolphin newborns were fathered by dolphins from outside of Sarasota Bay.

"Interlopers," Sam explained. "Somehow, even when she's closely guarded, the female finds a way to mate with an attractive outsider. It's nature's way of upgrading the gene pool. You find it in all mammals. Genetic interchange."

"All mammals?" I asked.

Sam smirked. "Yes, including humans. That fact hits most guys where they live. Believe it or not, researchers have found in any hospital maternity ward that for about eight percent of the babies their DNA doesn't match the father named on the birth certificate."

I must have looked at him skeptically because Sam pressed on. "I know, I know, it's a very reductive theory. And it's disturbing from a male perspective in some ways. What guy likes the idea that his newborn may not share his DNA? It's the punchline from the old joke where the rabbi explains why Jewish identity is tied to the mother: 'At least we know who she is.'"

He punched me lightly on the arm. "You've told me about Jonathan Kincaid and his Indian princess and their marriage matches the theory. Opposites attract and make that gene pool a bit stronger. And you wouldn't be here if they hadn't taken a walk on the wild side, would you?"

Aunt Priscilla told me that she and her younger brother Alexander had teased each other as children, and she had regarded him as a bit of a pest when he was little. Later, she grew to appreciate him and love him. She admired him for marrying a foreigner and for producing three sons.

"He's done his bit for the Kincaid family tree," she said. "Bringing in some new blood into the line with Karin, and having boys."

"And why should that matter?" I asked. "Does the world really need more Kincaids? Or the Kincaid line?" I hoped to provoke her, to see what she would say.

"Careful what you wish for, King," she said. "Your existence is a direct result of my brother's virility. The Kincaid line stretches back to Scotland because the Kincaid men observed the Biblical injunction to be fruitful and multiply. We helped build this country, fought for it, and kept adding branches to the family tree. On the whole, a good thing."

"That's a pretty good argument," I said, smiling. "Not completely convincing."

"Don't grin at me," she said with a mock scowl. "You'll need to do your part when the time comes. Not that any red-blooded Kincaid man ever objected to that duty."

Although Aunt Priscilla did not live to see it, I think she would have appreciated my choice of Takara, and how, in a way, it represents an updating of the Jonathan Kincaid legend. It's likely that our children (Jack and Penelope) resemble the offspring of Jonathan and Hannah Kincaid—Charles, Jacob, Elijah, and Mary—a blend of European and Asian features (the people who became Native Americans migrated from Asia across the Bering land bridge after all!). If Jack or Penny were transported back in time to colonial New England and met their Kincaid ancestors, I believe that all would be amazed by the family resemblance.

FORTY-ONE

Princeton, 2006

It was a health scare for Alexander Kincaid that brought Beau back from San Diego on a red-eye flight. James met him at Newark Airport in the arrivals area and they embraced. Beau looked fit and healthy, his hair close-cut, with none of the midlife weight gain that James had battled, a campaign that in his case had not been completely successful.

James explained their father's medical situation on the drive to Princeton. "As I told you on the phone, Dad felt dizzy and out of breath and then he fainted. It's heart-related. They ran some tests and determined that his heart is failing. His doctor says it's congestive. They've got him on medication and he's resting in the hospital. He's not happy about that, wants to go home, but they're going to keep him in for another day or so."

"Can I see him?"

James nodded. "No problem. They're pretty relaxed about visiting hours. He's in a private room."

"Did Julia come with you?"

"She stayed in New York, but she'll come to Lafayette Place tomorrow."

"Dad is, what, eighty-two?"

"Eighty-three. Just turned."

Beau grunted. "I missed calling on his birthday again."

"No worries. He's not celebrating them anymore."

"Well, he's damn tough," Beau said. "I'll give him that. I thought after he lost Mom that he wouldn't last. But he did."

"I'm glad you came," his brother said. "How is Catalina? And the twins?"

"She's fine. The boys are fine."

Beau lapsed into silence, lost in his thoughts. When they reached the turn-off for Princeton, he asked to go straight to the hospital instead of stopping first at Lafayette Place. They agreed James would drop him off, park the car at Lafayette Place, and return to pick up Beau after his visit with their father.

When Beau arrived in his father's room, Alexander was sitting up in his bed, an IV in his arm, a book in his hand. He peered over his glasses at Beau and nodded a welcome.

"I came as soon as I could," Beau said.

"There was no need," his father said. "I told your brother that. I'll be out of here soon enough. Did you know I'd never spent a night in a hospital before? Don't plan to stay a minute longer than I have to."

"Jimmy says your doctor is being careful," Beau replied. "That's a good thing. They don't want to release you prematurely and have you turn up in the emergency room a day later."

"Sit down," his father said, and Beau settled into the chair facing the bed. "Lying here flat on my back has let me do some thinking.

You know that my parents died in a car crash coming back to Boston from the Vineyard. Died comparatively young. I always wondered how long my father would have made it. His eighties? Like me?" Alexander paused. "Always expected that I'd go first, before Karin. But that wasn't to be." He shrugged. "All of our days are numbered. Yours. Mine. It appears that I have fewer left now, and that's as it should be. No father should ever see his children die before he does. That's the biggest regret of my life. What happened with Desmond."

"Desmond was sick," Beau said. "You can't blame yourself for that, Dad. Something awry in his brain chemistry. The day will come when they can fix that, but not yet."

"I wish there were other things I'd done differently. With you. I was hard on you, Wilson. We always seemed to be battling, didn't we? Never saw eye-to-eye. Your mother blamed me, felt I drove you away, that I was the reason you went into the military. And then when you and Hanna both ended up in California…"

"I enlisted because I wanted to serve," Beau said. "Not to spite you. I'm living in San Diego because I like it there. Better than here. I can't speak for Hanna. She marches to the beat of her own drum. Always has. You know that."

He nodded. "I do. She has that Kincaid stubbornness. I wish that I could have been kinder dealing with her. Listened better. Criticized less. But she is stubborn." He grinned. "Takes after her father, I'm afraid."

Beau and James walked back from the hospital to Lafayette Place. On the way, James explained that he and Julia would stay in Princeton for a week or so, making arrangements for a visiting nurse and household help and making sure that Alexander was settled in at home.

"It was a punch to the stomach to see him like that," Beau said. "He's showing his age."

"He had to, eventually. He's not immortal, after all."

"Somehow I thought he would always stay the same. He was always larger-than-life in my mind. Taller than he actually was. And now, he has shrunk in size. And it hurts to see him like that."

"How was your conversation?"

"He was philosophical. Regrets parts of the past. About Desmond and Hanna and me. In some ways, I don't completely blame him for his troubles with me. I was rebellious. I know I disappointed him. I went to the wrong school, chose to become a career military officer, failed in my first marriage. You probably see him differently. He never hammered you, Jimmy."

James nodded. "True. Only when I separated from Julia. You always drew his fire so Dad and I didn't clash much. You were the first son. He had very clear expectations about you and your future. I'm not complaining—I certainly didn't want him constantly looking over my shoulder."

"So what should we do next?" Beau asked. "Should we try to persuade him to move out of Lafayette Place? I hate the idea of him living alone in the house. Maybe some sort of assisted living?"

"Julia had that discussion with him a year ago," James said. "She handled it diplomatically, but she got to the heart of the matter. She thought he might be willing to sell the house, move someplace smaller, maybe one of those retirement complexes.

He was adamantly against any of it. He wants to keep his independence."

"I'm not surprised," Beau said. "I'm sorry that this all falls on you and Julia, with me and Hanna living so far away."

James gave his brother a gentle tap on the back. "I'm the responsible Kincaid on the East Coast. It's not a problem. Not only does Julia love any excuse to come to Princeton, but she's probably the only one who Dad will listen to. Hard to swallow, but that's the truth."

James drove Beau to Newark Airport two days later. Alexander had responded well to treatment and was expected to return home by the end of the week. Julia had made the arrangements for a housekeeper who would cook and clean. A nurse would visit twice a week.

Beau shook hands with James before leaving the car. "Call me if you need me," he said.

"You know I will."

"I'm sure of one thing," Beau said. "Dad won't go gentle into the good night. He'll fight for every last minute."

James nodded. "I wouldn't expect anything else."

FORTY-TWO

Princeton, April 2008

Alexander Tarkington Kincaid's funeral was held on an exquisite spring day, a quiet Friday. He had died four days earlier on Monday, late at night, and when James Kincaid made the arrangements with the Rev. Thompson, he delayed the service so Beau and Hanna and their families could fly from California.

The air that Friday was soft and fragrant with the lingering smell of flowers and the promise of a verdant spring. In the back yard of 4 Lafayette Place, the lilac and forsythia bushes had bloomed and Julia counted several crocuses in a garden bed.

It was the sort of glorious day that made Julia regret having moved to the Upper West Side. Returning to the city had been best for her marriage and it had brought her and James closer together, but it had meant sacrificing the comforts of her hometown. Some of her high school friends couldn't wait to leave Princeton, turned off by what they saw as the town's insularity and placid smugness, the way it revolved around the academic calendar. She never felt that way.

She had asked James if they could have an early breakfast before the funeral at PJ's Pancake House on Nassau Street, their childhood hangout. Beau and Catalina had arrived the evening before—leaving their twins in San Diego—and they had slept in, as had Hanna and Nate and their children.

Julia and James found an empty booth, and the waitress brought them coffee. They both ordered scrambled eggs and pancakes. Sitting there, looking at the tabletop scarred with the carved initials of now long-gone students, the black-and-white photographs of Tiger football and basketball teams in the glory days, brought memories back for Julia.

She remembered their many meals at the restaurant and how she and the Kincaid brothers had consumed mountains of pancakes, grilled cheese sandwiches, burgers, and fries. She had felt so proud as the only girl, the focus of attention, the special one singled out by the Kincaids. They had laughed at Des playing the clown, imitating Beau and Jimmy and their friends, mimicking their voices and mannerisms.

Those memories were bittersweet, now. Julia reached across the table and touched her husband's hand. "Did you talk with Beau last night?" she asked.

"I did."

"How is he?" she asked.

"Like you would expect. He's keeping his emotions in check. He's always been the family Stoic."

"But Catalina has softened him. She's been good for him. And being a father has helped." She gave him a long, searching look. "And how are you doing, Jimmy?"

"I've been better. Near the end, Dad was drifting. His nurse told me that he would wake up and mutter about a lecture in the morning and how he needed to get to the campus. Driven by a sense of duty."

"He always was."

James nodded. "That he was."

Later that morning, the family gathered outside Trinity Church some twenty minutes before the service was set to begin. Beau and Catalina accompanied Nate, Hanna, and the Sorensen children, Rose and Desmond. James and Julia were the last to arrive; they brought King and Takara and their son Jack and they led the way into the church. The Kincaid family occupied the first three rows of pews. Jack scrambled to make sure he was sitting right next to King.

King held Takara's hand tightly. She didn't know his Uncle Beau or Aunt Hanna very well, and he regretted that her first extended time with them would come at a funeral. She was noticeably pregnant, glowing with the expectancy of new life. He looked over the rest of the family, at Uncle Beau and his wife. Catalina could have stepped out of a Velazquez painting of a lady of the Spanish court with her delicate features and lustrous, raven-colored hair.

James and Julia sat in the first pew, eyes fixed on the minister as he began the service. James helped her find the correct page in the Book of Common Prayer and focused on the page in front of them. She sighed and leaned her head against his shoulder.

Hanna had watched her husband all day, and Nate had been on edge. He had kept Rose and Desmond close, and he hadn't spent much time with her family talking. He was pleasant—Nate was always Minnesota Nice—but she knew him well enough to see that he was withdrawing into himself.

She had asked him the night before if he wanted to talk about what was bothering him and he shook his head. "Maybe later," he said.

Hanna had wondered if her father's funeral would stir up painful memories for Nate. His relationship with his father, the pastor, had been difficult. Nate had no use for church services of any kind and he was certainly no churchgoer. He had not returned to his hometown for his father's burial. Did he regret that? He had never said anything to her.

After they had settled into the pews at Trinity Church along with the other Kincaid family members, she had a moment to reflect on the tension between her and her parents. She knew she had disappointed her father, and her mother, with many of her choices. They had been disturbed by her move to San Francisco, when she had turned her back on the conventional life they wanted her to live—college degree, professional husband, children. The appropriate path for the daughter of Alexander and Karin Kincaid. She hadn't wanted that life, and she knew they didn't understand her. Only Jimmy did, and Nate.

And with her father's death, there was no judgment left. He was gone. Her mother was gone. Her eyes filled with tears.

She reached over and took Nate's hand and squeezed it. He turned to her with a smile.

"Thank you for being here," she whispered. "For me, and for the kids."

He nodded slightly. "I'm here for you, Hanna. Always will be."

There were few tears shed during the service, and James thought that was fitting considering his father's age. Alexander Kincaid had lived a long and productive life, and it wasn't as if he had been struck down in his prime. There weren't many of his contemporaries attending the service, although James could see people filled more pews than he had anticipated.

His father had always admired the plain style of the Book of Common Prayer, and he would have appreciated the economy of his own funeral. He had left instructions for the service: he was cremated so there was no casket at the front of the church; he had requested specific hymns ("Our God Our Help in Ages Past," "A Mighty Fortress Is Our God," and "Amazing Grace"), a Bach prelude, and Samuel Barber's *Adagio for Strings* for the postlude. James and Julia shared one prayer book and hymnal as the minister led the congregation through the service. One line caught James' attention: *We brought nothing into this world, and it is certain we can carry nothing out.* That might be true, he thought, but it obscured what a man like Alexander Tarkington left behind: his life's work, his children, and his grandchildren. The eulogy was brief—the Rev. Thompson didn't know Alexander very well—and James took to the pulpit to deliver a short remembrance including a few humorous episodes from their years in Princeton that Beau and Hanna had contributed.

After the service, James, Julia, Beau, and Hanna took their place in the narthex and greeted those who had attended, while Nate, Catalina, and Takara watched after the children.

Beau spotted Angela first, recognizing her almost at once, as she moved gracefully up the aisle after the service. She approached him tentatively. Angela was still stunning, even in her late forties, with her high cheekbones and smooth, tanned skin. She wore a black dress and carried a small clutch purse.

"Hello, Angela," he said, taking her hand in both of his. "Thank you for coming."

She nodded. "I'm sorry, Beau. He was an amazing man."

Beau had been surprised by Angela's appearance at the funeral service. He had told Catalina about her, about how intensely he had felt, but he had been convinced that he would never see Angela again and in the unlikely event he did, he wouldn't be moved or stirred. It had been more than thirty years since he had last seen her. But when he came face-to-face with her, he felt the attraction. It was still there.

Angela had retained much of the beauty of her youth. She was a handsome woman and she carried herself with an unchanged grace and confidence.

"Go talk to her," Catalina told him.

"Come with me?"

She shook her head. "She's here to see you, Beau."

Beau nodded and walked over to Angela, who was standing by herself. She gave him a smile.

"I'm sorry about your father," she said. "I happened to be in Princeton when I heard that he had passed." She shook her head. "I haven't been back in fifteen years. I figured it was a sign of some sort that I should come to the service."

"I'm glad you did," he said. "How have you been, Angela?"

"I've been good," she said. "Two wonderful children. Rene is a nurse in Washington and Albert is in the Navy, of all things. We live in Newport News. My husband, Ralph, just retired. We met at Howard. I think you'd like him. A grandchild is on the way." She paused. "You look like you're happy, Beau. Your wife is lovely."

"I got damn lucky on my second try," he said.

"I heard about that," she said. "The first try. I bumped into Adrienne Harris years and years ago and she told me that your marriage hadn't worked out. I'm sorry."

It was his turn to shake his head. "It was for the best. It was a mistake for both of us."

"I did want to say something to you," she said. "I came by not only to honor your father but also to say something that needs to be said. I regret how it ended between us, Beau. I know that I hurt you. I could have been kinder."

"I don't blame you," he said. "Relationships are hard enough without having to fight the world. And we were kids." He glanced over at Catalina. "It's different today, I think. Fewer barriers in the way. I won't lie to you, Angela, I've always wondered what it would have been like for us. It would have been hard. You were right about that. But we were good together."

"Your wife knows about us?" Angela asked.

"She does."

He stopped, and she didn't say anything. He kissed her on the cheek.

"Thank you for coming," he said. "It took some courage, but you've always had that."

"I wondered how it might have been, too, Beau," she said. "But I'm happy that things have worked out for you. So, no regrets?"

He smiled and shook his head. "A few, Angela."

"Yes, a few."

They gathered at Lafayette Place later that afternoon. Julia had ordered a light lunch of sandwiches, salad, and brownies, and they sat around the kitchen table. After they finished their meal, King, Takara, and Nate occupied the children while Beau, James, Julia, and Hanna closeted themselves in the study.

Alexander had named James his executor, which made sense with Beau and Hanna living in California.

James quickly explained the essential elements of the will, which his father had shared with him a year before. "He kept it simple. Equal shares for the three of us. The largest asset is Lafayette Place, and there are some scattered investments."

"Unless Jimmy and Julia want it, I say we should put the house on the market," Hanna said.

James shook his head. "We're happy in the city. It's too big for us. Couldn't afford the upkeep and taxes, anyway."

Julia nodded. "Jimmy and I talked about it, and it wouldn't work for us. Better to sell now. The late spring is a good time to put a house on the market."

"Then we should sell," Beau said.

There was a long silence. James was surprised to find his eyes misting and a sudden ache in his throat. Selling was the logical thing to do, but it somehow didn't feel right to let the house leave the family.

"I wish it weren't so," Hanna said suddenly. "I wish we could find a way to keep it, and meet here every Thanksgiving and Christmas."

James turned to her, surprised. "I didn't expect that from you, Hanna. Didn't think you'd be sentimental about the house."

"The holidays were the best times," she said. "I remember how we were all together, and I remember we were happy." She sighed. "But I know we can't live in the past."

She looked around the study. "It's strange knowing I'll never set foot inside this house again. For that matter, I'll probably never return to Princeton with my life in California, now."

"We're still family," James said.

"There's the Boca Grande house," Beau said. "The trust Dad set up for it five years ago means the house will always stay in the family. It's a place where we can get together."

"It won't be the same," Hanna said.

"Few things ever are," James said, and put his arm around his sister's shoulder. "But we can always be there for each other."

FORTY-THREE

HANNA

To: jkincaid@gmail.com
From: hannaks@gmail.com
Date: May 15, 2008
Subject: Dad

Dearest Jimmy,

We've settled back into our routines here. Taking Rose and Des out of school was fairly disruptive, but I thought it was important that they come for the funeral.

It was wonderful to see you and the rest of the family, despite the somber circumstances. I hadn't been in Trinity Church since Mom's service and I'm afraid it's become a place for sad memories.

I'm sure that all of us have been contemplating our relationship with Dad, now that he's gone.

It's hard for me to think of him as anything other than this larger-than-life figure who always had all the answers. Of course, it's clear to me now that he didn't have those answers. No one does.

And then there's the judgment thing. I always felt he was judging me, judging all of us.

I know I disappointed him. Repeatedly. He didn't understand. My classroom is the outdoors. I'm no intellectual. I just wasn't cut out for academics. And my personal life had to bother him (and Mom). While he never said anything directly to me, I can't imagine my boyfriends and romantic ups and downs were pleasing to a traditionalist like him.

Des once said something about our father that I will never forget: he clearly is a great man, but is he a good man? I'm not sure that he is, or was. You say that he had mellowed over time. I wish that were so. I do.

You don't need to respond. I just needed to get things off my chest.

love, Hanna

To: hannaks@gmail.com
From: jkincaid@gmail.com
Date: May 16, 2008
Subject: Re: Dad

I think I was better prepared for Dad's death after watching his decline over the past few years. He was a proud man and I know he hated not feeling independent and in control. In some ways, it was time for him to go.

The dynamics of my relationship with Mom and Dad and yours were different. You felt that they judged you constantly. You were the only girl, and you didn't have the same interests as your brothers.

I also know that Dad loved you. Mom loved you. They may have been incapable of expressing it in ways that you could appreciate, but they did.

I realize now that Dad's way of caring was centered on making sure that his children followed the right path, a path that he saw clearly. He thought he was building character. He thought he was preparing us for adulthood. That didn't work for Beau or for you and that meant conflict at times. It didn't mean that he didn't love you. He didn't know how to love unconditionally, but you do. Rose and Des will always feel that love from you and Nate.

Dad always was curious about what you were doing—he knew that we corresponded—and I only wish the questions he asked me about you were ones he asked you directly.

It's true that Mom wasn't the most demonstrative woman. But she glowed for days after you came to Princeton for the party celebrating her paintings. She told Julia that she hated that you were so far away, that you had built a life so removed from the East Coast and from family.

We have all missed you, sweetheart. It would be wonderful if you and Nate could bring the kids to Boca Grande this coming summer and we could meet you there.

Julia sends her love. We're planning a trip to Maryland to see King and Takara and the grandkids and I promise we'll send photos.

Love, Jimmy

To: jkincaid@gmail.com
From: hannaks@gmail.com

Date: May 18, 2008
Subject: Re: Re: Dad

Thank you, Jimmy, for what you've written about Dad and Mom and how they felt.

I don't claim I had a terrible childhood. Difficult, but not horrible. Nothing as scarring or damaging as Nate's, where his father invoked an angry God whenever he thought Nate had misbehaved.

But Dad and Mom disapproved of me through my teen years and my twenties. I was never as wild as they thought; I was just trying to find myself.

I wish I could go back. I wish I could tell them how I felt at the time. I know I can't and that's one reason I feel bitter at times.

I'm trying to forgive. I focus on the happier times when I was close to Mom, when I could sense Dad's affection for me.

You're right about me as a mother and Nate as a father. I let Rose and Des know every night when I tuck them in that I love them, will always love them. No matter what. Nate is even more intent on demonstrating that in his own quiet way. He likes to give our kids bear hugs and tousle their hair. That's his way. Less talk, more action!

What is it the Beatles said—in the end, the love you take is equal to the love you make? I agree with that.

love, your sister

FORTY-FOUR

JAMES

New York, September 2013

My favorite season is fall, and more recently I've loved escaping to Princeton with Julia for a weekend or two to enjoy the changing colors. And Manhattan is different in late September and October, the air crisper and the sunlight a light golden color as it touches the brownstone facades in our Upper West Side neighborhood.

The fall does make me think about the passage of time, and in my case, my own mortality. As I approach my sixties, I realize that, even if I live as long as my father, I'm closer to the winter of my life than the spring.

I've never been one for dwelling on the past, but the autumn does make me take stock.

I have always collected maps. In my file cabinet in my makeshift home office, I have filled two drawers with maps. They sit in folders, filed alphabetically. I've saved more than my fair share from trips, vacations, and work assignments.

Why do I keep them? I do work for a publishing company that specializes in travel guides and books, but most of my maps aren't germane to my work, and it's unlikely that I'll ever make use of them again for return trips. No, I keep them because when I pick one up, the streets and landmarks on the map bring the memories back. For Julia, photos do the same thing—her photo albums are filled with family images and snapshots from places we've been.

Of late, I've found my maps a comforting reminder of my childhood. I learned how to use a compass and map at a summer camp in Vermont that Beau and I attended one July. I found it deeply satisfying to successfully make my way through unfamiliar terrain, navigating hills and trails employing a Boy Scout compass and a topographic map.

These days when I find myself spending time with my collection, I seem to gravitate to the detailed street map of Princeton that I acquired when I was in high school. I don't think there's a street in the Borough that we didn't travel down on our bicycles. When I look at the lined boxes that represent the University buildings, I can picture them in my mind. Vividly. Despite the sounds of the New York City street outside the windows of our apartment, I find myself thinking about my childhood.

I realize now what a strange, mixed-up experience it was. On the one hand, it was very much like the upbringing of our contemporaries, but it was different because of our parents. Their expectations, spoken and unspoken, meant that we were raised in what had to be a distinctly Kincaid manner.

Julia once laughed at me when I suggested we'd had a normal childhood.

"Normal?" she asked. "There was nothing normal about it. I could see it clearly because I was an outsider. You had this glamorous moody Swedish mother and a brilliant intimidating father. You and Beau were always being challenged to excel. It made you who you are."

"I guess it was different."

"I don't think it was healthy for Des or Hanna."

"I thought they had it easy," I said.

She shook her head. "You would think that. They felt they had to follow in your and Beau's footsteps. That wasn't fair to them."

I kissed her on the cheek. "You have a different perspective on it."

"I thank God that I was on the outside," she said. "I don't mind being the normal one. Somebody has to be." She looked at me directly. "When we married, I swore to myself that it would be different with our children. And it has. I believe that King knew when he was growing up that he was loved without conditions, that he didn't have to follow a path that we chose."

I had to smile. "And now he's a professor, just like his grandfather was."

My wife returned my smile. "But he chose that path. And that makes all the difference in the world."

There is no map to one's life, no way to know the direction to follow in advance. When I think about my journey, I know at times I lost my way. I regret that I resisted having more children with Julia, that in effect I put my career before her deep yearning for family (for that is what it was, I think now). I regret that I didn't spend as much time with King when he was younger. And then there was my moment of madness, when I left Julia, when

I jeopardized my marriage and came close to making the worst mistake of my life.

One of the advantages of living some five decades is that I think I know myself better, not only my numerous flaws but also my few strengths. I'm a better husband and father for that self-knowledge. And I'm less likely to stray from the course that I should take.

FORTY-FIVE

HANNA

March 2014

I've learned that when you don't resolve a family conflict, when you sidestep it, sooner or later you'll have to confront it directly.

And sooner or later, there comes a crisis.

So it was for the unresolved issues between Rose, my wonderful daughter, and Nate, my wonderful husband. Since she was ten years old, Rose had been drawn to the community she found in church. Through her teen years, she had continued to attend services in Santa Rosa, her faith growing. While he never said anything to her directly, Nate made his disapproval crystal clear.

Rose approached me on spring break from college to talk about her plans for graduate school, divinity school, to be precise. She worried that Nate would be angry with her, but she thought she knew what she wanted for her future. She was nineteen, almost twenty, no longer a child. A spirited young woman with a mind of her own.

"I want to be a minister," she said. "I feel called to it. I've prayed about it, and I know in my heart and my mind that this is right for me."

I told her that her happiness was what mattered to me, and Nate felt the same way.

"Dad won't like it."

"You need to talk to him about it," I told her. "Explain how you feel."

Her dreams were different. I never would have imagined when she was a child that Rose would become so fascinated with philosophy and theology. Rose never left me in doubt about how she felt. And I knew her emotions were stronger, more intense, than mine or Nate's. Was she more sensitive, more easily bruised, because of her adoption? I hoped not, but she had only to look in the mirror to see that she looked nothing like me, nothing like Nate.

We never loved her any less than Desmond. Did she doubt that?

Was it a form of rebellion? Rose never went through a Boy Crazy phase as a teenager. A little experimentation with drinking, but not with drugs. Friends of ours had struggled with the horrors of addiction with their children. We'd been so lucky to not have to deal with that.

Rose had her discussion with Nate the next day. It didn't go well. Nate didn't argue or shout. He just shut down. Underneath his calm exterior, there was a deep bitterness over his childhood, an unresolved bitterness. He had been wounded and never completely healed. That Rose was thinking about following in her grandfather's footsteps and becoming a minister was troubling for Nate. Where had he gone wrong? Had she not been listening to him about the hypocrisy and shallowness of organized religion?

I could see how hurt Rose was by his silence. It introduced unwelcome tension to our family. Nate brooded, unwilling to talk about his feelings. Despite being wrapped up in playing video games and attending soccer practice, Des sensed the unrest.

So I confronted Nate, convinced that we shouldn't let Rose return to college feeling that her father was angry with her.

It was one of the hardest conversations we'd had as a couple. I didn't hold back. He was wounding Rose and she was bewildered by his hostility. She didn't understand why her gentle father was so negative, so sarcastic and cynical, about something that deeply mattered to her. I realized that he was channeling his anger with his father, but Rose didn't.

"You need to love her, Nate," I told him. "No matter what she decides to do. She'll never be like your father, can't you see that? She's drawn to the community of a church. She wants to heal, not hurt. She's our daughter, your daughter."

Nate shook his head. "I know all of that. That's logical, Hanna. What I feel inside isn't logical. I feel angry and resentful. Once, when I was ten years old and my father was whipping me for my sinfulness, I promised myself that I'd stay as far away from religion as I could. When I feel this way, I'm scared that I'm becoming my father. As narrow and harsh and unforgiving when I don't get my way. There's the irony. I'm no better than him, but instead of forcing Christian pieties down someone's throat, I'm trying to do just the opposite. It makes me sick."

"Then don't be your father," I told him. "Go to Rose. Let her know that you'll love her and support her however she wants to live her life."

"She knows I'm not going to be happy about her plans."

"Whose life is it, Nate? It's hers. And maybe she's out to repair some of the damage caused by men of the cloth like your father."

He surprised me by smiling. "Men of the cloth? Hanna, that's a turn of phrase I haven't heard since I left home. You do amaze me."

"Go talk to your daughter, and amaze me."

I hoped that he would do the right thing. I hoped that he wouldn't let his resentment toward his father, his hurt from the past, keep him from supporting Rose.

I knew that Nate had talked with Rose and that it had been a different conversation because of my daughter's smiling face the morning she was to leave us to return to college.

She took both of my hands in hers. "Thank you for talking to Daddy," she said. "He told me that I should follow my heart and if I wanted to be a minister, he'd know I would be a caring one."

I kissed her on the cheek and smiled, trying hard not to cry.

"It's not easy being a parent," I told her. "It can be very hard to let go, to let your children choose their own way. It's out of love."

Rose hugged me. "I know that, Mom. I've never doubted it. Not for a moment."

And that's when my wonderful daughter made me cry. Largely because of her wonderful father.

FORTY-SIX

KING

Boca Grande, Florida, August 2015

My father described this convergence of the Kincaids on Gasparilla Island as a gathering of the clan, but I reminded him that the only thing even remotely Scottish about us, other than the family name, was the Dewar's bottle in his liquor cabinet.

The family had gathered for my father's sixtieth birthday party, a celebration organized by my mother. To my surprise, everyone came. Choosing to hold the get-together just before Labor Day meant that school obligations didn't get in the way. It was the off-season when Florida is too hot and humid for most tourists, but as a barrier island, Gasparilla enjoys cooling Gulf breezes. And none of us were going to complain about fewer people crowding the town and the Gulf-side beach.

Takara and I and the kids flew into Fort Myers and rented a car for the drive north to Boca Grande. Jack and Penelope became increasingly excited as we neared the island; they had been to the Kincaid summer house twice before and had greatly enjoyed their vacation there.

We joined Mom and Dad in staying in the summer cottage. The rest of the family found rooms at the Gasparilla Inn. The California Kincaids turned out in full force: Uncle Beau and

Catalina and their eleven-year-old twins, Philip and Marco; Aunt Hanna and Nate, with Rose, now almost nineteen, and Desmond, fifteen years old. The Kincaid generations had become a bit scrambled with Beau and Hanna having children later in life.

I knew my father had been ambivalent about the festivities. He didn't like being the center of attention. Mom had persuaded him that it was more of a family reunion than a birthday celebration, and that had finally persuaded him. He still seemed a bit reluctant.

"Is he okay with this?" I asked her when we had a chance to talk in private.

My mother nodded. "He's grumbled about it, but I think he's secretly pleased. He loves having the family in one place. It's been quite some time since we got together."

"You two seem happy."

I knew there had been a bad stretch in their marriage when I was in college. They had separated for a time and I had worried that a divorce might follow. But they had patched things up and it seemed they had resolved whatever issues had separated them. But who knew what truly goes on between a husband and wife? Certainly Takara and I haven't always seen eye-to-eye and she has struggled with balancing her career and raising the children and has felt at times that I haven't been supportive enough of her needs.

The state of my parents' marriage wasn't something that I talked about with either of them. I could see that they were treating each other with affection, teasing each other, and that was enough to reassure me that they had put their troubles behind them.

"I am happy," my mother said. "We're in a good place. I only wish we saw more of you and Takara and my grandchildren. When is Penny's birthday party? October is just around the corner. She only turns seven once. We'll drive down for the party."

"Penny would love that," I told her and was rewarded with a hug. "And maybe you and Dad can come to one of Jack's soccer games."

My mother has always had a flair for organizing and planning events, and she had Dad's celebration well in hand. She had rented bicycles and golf carts so we could travel around the island, and had sign-up sheets for those interested in tennis, boating, and fishing.

The birthday dinner was scheduled for Friday evening. In the afternoon, we gathered for a picnic on the beach, with a group photograph of the family with the lighthouse framed over our shoulders for later in the day.

It was a warm, lazy afternoon. We had a picnic lunch of sandwiches, salad, potato chips, and brownies. There was plenty of beer for the adults and soda and lemonade for the children.

I glanced over to see my father and Beau standing shoulder-to-shoulder, the bond between them still strong. They were so different in many ways, and yet they had remained close over the years. I envied them. I had no siblings—I know it had been a lingering issue in my parent's marriage—and growing up I wished for a brother or sister. I imagine it was why I had been so eager to have children, and I was thankful that Takara had so willingly embraced motherhood.

My father left Beau and came to my side. He put his arm around my shoulder and with his free arm waved at the scene. "What do you think of all this, King?"

"You've got your gathering of the clan," I said. "Although I see you decided against wearing a kilt."

He laughed and tugged at my shoulder. I glanced over at him. He had aged well; he didn't look sixty years old. He hadn't started to gray yet, and his face remained relatively unlined.

"It's something to see all the little ones," he said. "Your two. Beau's twins. Rose and Desmond. Past, present, future…all in one place at one time."

"I guess it's a day to be philosophical," I replied.

"It is. Time passes so quickly. The hours turn into days, the days into weeks, and before you know it, you're watching your grandchildren play on the beach at your sixtieth birthday party."

I looked over to see that Rose and Takara were wading into the water with Penny, each holding one of her hands. My daughter giggled. "It's so warm," she called out to me. "Like bath water."

Further up the beach, Beau and Nate were tossing a football with Desmond and Marco. Nearby, Philip and Jack were busy building a sandcastle.

My mother joined us and linked her arm with mine. "It's so peaceful here," she said. "The photographer just arrived. Time to herd cats for the family photo."

It took twenty minutes to shepherd everyone into place and for the photographer, a stocky young woman with aviator sunglasses, to be satisfied with the arrangement—Mom had insisted that the photo include the Gasparilla Island Lighthouse framed in the background. I stood next to my parents in the front row, with Takara and the kids by my side, and we all laughed when the photographer asked us to say "cupcake" instead of "cheese."

We all crammed into a private room at the Gasparilla Inn for my father's birthday dinner that night. We ate well, with a main course of grouper, mixed vegetables, and spring potatoes. The adults polished off several bottles of wine and the noise level in the room increased as the night went on. After a dessert of ice cream and cookies, Beau rose to his feet and waited until the room quieted.

"We're all here to wish Jimmy a happy birthday," he began. "I look at my little brother and I don't see an old man of sixty. Just an old man." He paused for our laughter. My father grinned at him. "Instead, I see my comrade in arms from the golden days of our neighborhood adventures..." He looked over at my mother. "And Julia running after us, trying to keep up. She's still along for the adventure, and I know that's been a blessing for Jimmy and for all of us."

Beau raised his glass. "Happy birthday, Jimmy. Here's to another sixty more."

We all toasted him, and then my father reluctantly stood up to take Beau's place.

"Thank you all for coming," he began. "This wonderful celebration is all because of Julia, my better half." He bent over to kiss my mother on her cheek.

He turned back to address us. "If Alexander Kincaid were alive today, I know my father would be filled with pride at the sight of the next generation of Kincaids. He'd see a family that will endure. We've been blessed, generation after generation, since our ancestor Jonathan Kincaid came to this country, and we have a responsibility to give back for those blessings in whatever way we can."

It was his turn to raise his glass: "To the Kincaids!" We echoed his words as we toasted.

Mom had arranged for a disc jockey to play music, and the children quickly ended up on the small, polished dance floor, followed by most of the Kincaid adults. Penny hesitated and Rose took her by the hand and pulled her onto the floor.

My mother came over to where Takara had joined me to watch the scene on the dance floor. She linked her arm in ours and invited us to come outside.

The night sky was clear and there was a slight breeze. I could see the stars above and pointed them out to Takara.

"This has been a wonderful time," my wife said. "Thank you, Julia. I know how much planning had to go into making it run so smoothly."

"It was worth it," she said and looked over at me. "Would you like to hold your sixtieth birthday party here, King?"

"That's a long way off," I replied. "It's not exactly top of mind, to be honest."

Takara laughed. "It's just a matter of time, King."

"I'm serious," my mother said. "Please do it. Here on the island. Invite the family. Your kids and Rose and Desmond and the twins can bring their families, their children."

"If I do, I'll expect you to cut the birthday cake," I said. "And to dance with Dad."

She smiled. "Wouldn't that be lovely? We'd be well into our eighties." She squeezed my arm. "Promise me, King."

I smiled back. "It matters that much to you?"

"It does. This family matters. Even when I'm gone, even when Jimmy and Beau and Hanna are gone, I'm counting on you and Takara to keep it together. With the summer house in a trust, there will always be a place to come to for the Kincaids. And you're the oldest of the next generation. You'll be the one to pass on the Kincaid stories to the others, the history, the jokes, the memories. The need to be useful, to serve. What makes this family so special."

"That's a tall order," I said, surprised at her passion.

"It hasn't always been one big happy family," my mother said. "You know that. I want you to promise to never let that happen again, as best you can. No estrangement. No distance. No Kincaids outside the circle."

I put my arm around her shoulder. "I promise, Mom," I said. "I won't forget."

She turned to my wife, blinking away tears. "You heard him, Takara. I'm going to rely on you to remind him."

"I will," my wife said. "Count on it."

I didn't have to say anything. It was a promise I would be sure to keep in the years ahead. I was a Kincaid, after all.

ACKNOWLEDGEMENTS

While *Lafayette Park* is a work of imagination, it does touch upon historical events. In dealing with the past, I've tried to stay as true to the facts as possible.

My portrait of the Kincaid family's colonial world owes a great deal to Carol Gardner's deeply-researched *The Involuntary American: A Scottish Prisoner's Journey to the New World*. For historical context on the Reykjavik summit in 1986, I turned to Ken Adelman's *Reagan at Reykjavik: Forty-Eight Hours That Ended the Cold War*. For accounts of life in Baghdad's Green Zone in 2004, I consulted the reporting of William Langewiesche and Rajiv Chandrasekaran.

Any errors of historical fact or interpretation are mine alone.

Readers of my short story collections have encountered members of the Kincaid family before. I have borrowed liberally from my previously-published short stories "Family Tree," "Morning in America," and "Princess" for this novel.

Once again, I turned to Glenn Speer, a long-time friend and skilled editor, for his insightful criticism and eagle eye for accuracy.

And finally, I'm thankful for the support of my wife, Maisie, who never ceases to amaze with her patience and grace.

ABOUT THE AUTHOR

Jefferson Flanders has been a sportswriter, newspaper columnist, editor, and publishing executive. He is the author of ten novels and two short story collections. Flanders has lived outside of Boston with his family for more than two decades.